DEATH BY HIGH HEELS

THE KIM MURPHY PI SERIES
BOOK #1

BY VIOLET INGRAM

DEATH BY HIGH HEELS

Limitless Publishing, LLC
Kailua, HI 96734
www.limitlesspublishing.com

Formatting: Limitless Publishing

ISBN-13: 978-1-68058-662-6
ISBN-10: 1-68058-662-9

DEDICATION

I'd like to dedicate this book to my husband, children, Sarah, and Violet.

Chapter One

Sunday Evening

Cops hated it when you vomited all over their crime scene—a mistake I had no desire to repeat. Then again, the fact I'd just trampled all over this scene was probably a whole new mistake I should have avoided. I stared at the corpse and fought the urge to hurl. If only I hadn't answered the door, I'd be eating dinner instead of standing in my neighbor's apartment looking at a dead guy.

Said dead guy was just sitting there in the chair. You would think he was asleep—if not for all the blood and guts spilled onto his lap. I tore my eyes from him and asked the question I most wanted the answer to.

"What the heck did you hit him with?"

Lindsay dropped the strand of blonde hair she'd been twirling and glanced down at the floor. "My shoe."

"Huh?"

"I've already told you. Twice. I hit him with *my*

1

shoe."

"Damn it, Lindsay, you can't kill someone with a shoe!"

"*Hello*, they're *Via Spiga*."

"Ugh." I glared. There was no way in hell she had done this kind of damage with a shoe. If she had, women would soon be saying goodbye to their much-beloved accessory. Men—even NRA members—would insist on an instant ban of the deadly yet sexy weapon.

I set my hands on my hips. "Any idea how he got this giant hole in his stomach?"

"What? No, I hit him and ran." Lindsay's face paled and she leaned against the doorframe.

"Come here and see if you recognize him."

"Gross, no way. Besides, you're the detective, you figure out who he is."

Technically, I was a private investigator, a fact that had continually escaped my neighbor.

"Get over here!" I turned toward her and spotted Lakeview, Ohio's oldest beat cop standing behind her, his gun drawn. It would have been scary if only he didn't look like Santa Claus dressed as a cop for Halloween. With the beginnings of a snow white beard and a pot belly in the making.

"Ah hell," I muttered. "Hey, Duncan."

"Kim Murphy. Oh man, the chief's gonna be pissed," Officer Duncan said.

"We don't really have to tell him, do we?"

"You don't think he's gonna find out his daughter got herself mixed up with another dead guy? You didn't kill this one too, did you? Wait, don't answer that."

"I didn't kill him. Jeez."

The last time I'd been caught standing over a dead guy was because I'd shot the miserable son of a bitch. It was self-defense and besides, the guy deserved it. Thankfully there were several witnesses and the grand jury had dropped the matter. Which was why I was enjoying the comforts of my own apartment when Lindsay came banging on my door.

Duncan looked over at her. "Now who might you be, miss?"

"I'm Lindsay Pembrook."

He glanced my way. "I guess that's the dead guy. You sure he's dead?"

"Yeah, I'm sure," I said, looking away from the object of our discussion.

I stepped back and took a deep breath. I regretted it immediately. Just when I thought I'd gotten used to the smell, the nausea returned. My four brothers, all cops, claimed you could will yourself not to vomit. What a load of crap. My stomach roiled in misery.

"Stay put, both of you. I need to call this in." Duncan talked into his radio and requested a detective for the scene. Finished with his call, he walked over and stood next to me.

"Oh boy, that's a lot of blood. Somebody gutted him open like a fish."

My stomach rolled and I clapped a hand over my mouth.

"So, then, what happened here?" Duncan asked, turning his attention back to Lindsay.

Lindsay held up her hands. "I came home and found him sitting there. I took off my shoe, hit him in the back of the head, and then ran to Kim's for help."

"Did you call 9-1-1?"

"Yes, after I went next door to Kim's. I wasn't staying here with him." Lindsay pointed to the dead guy as if Officer Duncan and I wouldn't know who "him" was.

"Why'd you hang up on the dispatcher?"

"Sorry to interrupt but, uh, she's wearing evidence," I said.

We all looked down at Lindsay's feet. Sure enough, she was wearing both black, two-inch heeled shoes.

Lindsay looked annoyed. "Well, of course I am."

Duncan frowned at her. "Miss Pembrook, please remove your shoes."

"Do you have any idea how much these cost?" she asked.

"Nope. Don't care either. Take them off and leave them there." He pointed to the floor near the door.

I'd had enough. "I'm waiting outside. He smells bad."

Lindsay glanced at me. "Really? I can't smell anything."

"Lucky you," I muttered.

As we waited outside, an ambulance parked in front of the apartment building. The paramedics hopped out and rushed toward us. I gave them the bad news they were much too late to help the guy inside. Being true professionals, they didn't take my word for it and went inside anyway.

Lindsay and I sat down on a concrete bench to

stay out of the way. Unfortunately for us it was a typical June evening in Lakeview, Ohio. The mosquitoes were so bad if we stayed outside for long, we would look like the idiots, I mean, contestants, on *Survivor*.

All the commotion brought the neighbors outside. Eager to keep the situation contained, Duncan told everyone to return to their apartments. The neighbors across the street continued to stand in their front yard and gawk.

"Are those colored contacts?" Lindsay asked.

"What? No."

"Are you sure? I mean, I've never seen someone with eyes that green naturally."

"I don't wear contacts." No way was I going to tell her the thought of sticking something in my eye made me woozy. I could barely stand eye drops after a long night.

"Please, next you'll tell me that's your natural hair color."

"It is."

"Whatever. So, the fat cop said you killed someone?" Lindsay whispered, her eyes wide as she stared at me.

"Yeah, but you're the one with a dead guy in your apartment."

"I didn't kill him!"

"Well, somebody did."

Her expression crumpled. "I swear it wasn't me. I don't understand why this is happening." She covered her face with her hands and began to cry.

Swell. Contrary to popular belief, just because I happened to have a uterus didn't mean I could handle other women crying. Though I figured I was better equipped than men, I had just never been a touchy-feely kind of person.

"Lindsay, the police will find the person who did this," I said, feeling awkward as I patted her on the shoulder. I dropped my hand and Lindsay turned her face toward me. Just freaking great, she was one of those beautiful criers. I really hated women like that. When I cried, my face turned red and blotchy. Not an attractive look.

"You're sure?" she asked, her expression hopeful, a little wistful.

"Of course, it's what they do."

"Oh yes, you're right. Thanks, Kim."

I couldn't believe this woman had managed to alienate all of the neighbors and yet here I was comforting her. It was pouring rain the day Lindsay moved in and parked in my spot. Thanks to the movers and her friends, they'd managed to take all the other spots. I'd had to park on the street, half a block away. With arms filled with grocery bags, an umbrella hadn't been an option. I'd come down sick the next day.

From our places on the bench we heard Officer Duncan explaining the situation to the new arrivals. The paramedics turned and left. We were still sitting on the bench, swatting at mosquitoes, when the city's silver-haired medical examiner, Ralph Gardner, arrived. Unfortunately, so did the newest homicide detective, Grant Tompkins.

I wasn't sure if it was anger or lust that caused my face to flush and my heart to race. I had a sneaky suspicion it was both. The first time I'd met

Grant I'd been standing over a dead body. He had taken one look at me and branded me a murderer. If he wasn't so hot I'd have remembered to ask for my lawyer, Zachary Wellington. Which, considering our numerous sexcapades, Zach's being there would have made the whole awkward, drooling over the cop arresting me even more humiliating, though I wasn't sure if that was even possible.

Grant strode up the sidewalk. His head turned. Spotting me, he scowled before stepping inside.

"Kimberly, how are you? I haven't seen you in a bit." Doctor Gardner smiled, revealing a set of perfect white teeth that seemed out of place in the wrinkled face.

"I'm fine, doc. How about you?"

"Good, except my knee hurts like the devil every time it rains."

"Sorry to hear that."

"Well, I'd rather be alive and complaining than dead with no complaints at all."

I smiled, not sure what to say.

"So, where's my dead body?"

I made a face. "Ugh, inside."

"One of yours, is it?"

"Jeez, shoot a couple people and everyone thinks it's your new hobby."

He laughed. "Well, you've not been keepin' me that busy, but that's okay. Those two losers got just what they deserved. Kidnapping, drugs, murder. Lordy, what is this world comin' to?"

"Too bad it's not filled with more people like you," I replied.

"Oh, I'm not so sure the world could handle

more than one of me."

Detective Tompkins walked over and stood glaring at me. "Doc, maybe you should go inside."

"Always in a rush. It's not like the dead are goin' anywhere, my boy." He winked at me before heading toward the apartment.

"Charming as always, Grant," I said.

He sighed and shook his head. "Kim, what are you doing here?"

"I live here, remember?"

Grant cleared his throat. "Well, you can go now and let the professionals handle this."

"Ooh, that's gonna be a problem, detective. Kim and Miss Pembrook here were inside with the body when I got here."

"Of course," Grant muttered. "All right, Kim, go on back to your place. When I'm done here, I'll come get your statement."

I knew a dismissal when I heard one. "Fine." I stood up and walked toward my apartment. Glancing back, I watched as Lindsay flashed a one-hundred-watt smile at Grant. I couldn't hear what she was saying, but whatever it was required her to talk with her hands, which kept coming into contact with Grant's muscular biceps. I wasn't about to think about why that bothered me.

It seemed Lindsay had one hell of a fast recovery. I almost felt sorry for Grant. He might be a royal pain in the ass, but I wasn't sure if he deserved my airhead neighbor sinking her claws into him. He had been so quick to assume my guilt after I killed the son of a bitch who kidnapped me.

Oh well. Grant was a big boy and could take care

of himself. He was armed after all.

The news vans arrived. Oh goody, my apartment building would be on the evening news. It wouldn't take long for the nosy reporters to make a connection to me. They were persistent, and it would take a bit of effort to dodge them and their questions. I stepped back inside my apartment and headed for the kitchen. I had been about to heat up leftovers when Lindsay banged on the door. Unfortunately, the spaghetti no longer held any appeal, resembling a little too closely what was in that poor guy's lap. I made a turkey sandwich instead and grabbed a Diet Pepsi out of the fridge. I was just finishing up when the phone rang.

"Hello."

"I just heard. I'll be there in ten minutes," my dad said in way of a greeting.

"Dad, I'm fine. This has nothing to do with me."

"You *shot* someone! What do you mean it doesn't have anything to do with you?"

Even my dad had assumed I was guilty. This was really getting old.

"No, Dad. My neighbor came home and found a man in her apartment. She came over and asked for my help."

"So you killed him to protect her? That's fine as long as she corroborates your story."

"Dad, I didn't kill him. He was already dead when I got there."

"Oh, good." I could hear the relief in his voice. "All right, then, if you're sure you don't need me, I'll get going to the city council meeting. I need to explain the budget increase."

For a moment, I considered telling him I needed him here. After everything he did for me the least I could do was rescue him from such a horrible meeting. Sensing he wouldn't appreciate the rescue, I told him everything was fine and I'd call him later.

Bored, anxious, and frustrated, I flipped on the TV, hoping a comedy would distract me. It didn't. An hour later the doorbell rang.

When I opened the door I barely refrained from rolling my eyes. "Lindsay, I'm honored, twice in one day."

My neighbor twisted her hands in front of her. "I'll be staying at the Lakeview Inn for the next couple of days. I wanted you to know how to reach me if anything comes up," she said, ignoring my sarcasm.

"Okay, great. Try to get some rest," I said.

"Thanks."

After Lindsay left, I sat back down on the couch. Half an hour later the doorbell rang again. I opened the door and let Grant inside. My heart began to race. If anyone asked, I'd lie and say it was from the upcoming interrogation, not the rush of lust I felt whenever the pain in the ass was around. He sat down in a chair across from me while I curled up on the couch. It only seemed fair that I should be comfortable while being grilled by one of Lakeview's finest and hottest detectives.

"Start from the beginning," Grant said, not wasting time on little things like pleasantries or manners.

"There's not a lot to tell. Someone started banging on my door. The second I opened it,

Lindsay started screaming that she thought she killed some guy in her apartment."

His gray eyes narrowed. "Wait a minute, she confessed to killing him?"

"No. She told me that when she got home some guy was sitting in the chair. Supposedly, she took off her shoe, hit him in the back of the head, put her shoe back on, and then ran over to my place."

"Then what happened?"

"I went inside her apartment, she stayed by the door. I was looking at the body when Officer Duncan arrived."

"What time did she knock on your door?"

"About six thirty."

We spent the next few minutes going over everything again. Finally, I filled out the statement and signed my name.

"I'm sorry you had to see that," Grant said.

I thought I had managed to hide my revulsion rather well. I should have known better than to try to hide something from a homicide detective.

"Thanks," I whispered as I handed him the paperwork.

Grant placed his hand over mine. I closed my eyes and had to remind myself to breathe.

"Oh, hell."

I opened my eyes in time to see Grant toss the papers onto the coffee table. He leaned down and brushed his lips against mine. The simple taste wasn't enough. Grant must have felt the same as he took full possession of my mouth with his. For months I'd wondered what he tasted like and now I had my answer, coffee and chocolate. How lucky for me those were two of my very favorite things.

I slid my hands up his arms, feeling the tightened muscles through his clothes. Grant groaned and pulled me against him. I tore my lips from his to whisper, "Upstairs."

Grant opened his eyes and suddenly stopped his delectable assault on my mouth. His hands dropped to his sides and he sighed as he stepped away from me.

"Damn! You make me forget where I'm at."

"Thanks."

"That wasn't a compliment."

What the hell did that mean?

"I've got to go or the chief will have my head."

My dad was a tough but fair man. However, if he discovered one of his detectives was too busy pawing his daughter to get his work done, there was no telling what punishment my dad would dole out.

"Well, I'll be in touch if I need you for anything else."

A sigh escaped my lips. "You know where to find me."

"Yeah, I do." He lifted his hand toward me and dropped it back at his side. "Good night." He closed the door behind him.

I curled up on the couch and grabbed the remote. Half a dozen channels later I settled on a *Last Cake Standing* marathon. A knock on the door made for the fourth rude interruption of the day. Worse, I was going to miss the teams moving their cakes to the judging area. At the door, I peeked through the peephole. With the front porch light on I recognized the local news station's reporter, Mr. Abraham, who, along with several others, had been relentless six months ago. I had never been especially fond of reporters, sticking their microphones in peoples' faces and asking them how they felt. There had to be a more useless job somewhere in the world but I just had no earthly idea where or what that would be. I did know the next one who got in my face was going to get a lot worse than a few nasty words flung their way. Careful not to make any sound, I crept back to the couch. On the show, one team was applying butter cream frosting—one of man's greatest inventions. Now that should be on an episode of *Modern Marvels*. There was one more round of knocking and then silence. A few minutes later the phone began to ring.

Choosing to ignore the phone, I went back to watching TV. The downside was these kinds of shows always made me hungry. I suffered for an hour before going into the kitchen in search of a chocolate fix. Several minutes of frantic searching and I came to the horrible conclusion that there wasn't even a crumb of chocolate. This was a crisis, not of biblical proportions, but more like it was the week before my period and there was no chocolate. This was so not good for someone who carried a gun.

After the day I'd had, the smart thing would have been to go to bed. My need for chocolate would almost always win over the need for sleep. I grabbed my purse and headed out before I came to my senses. Fat chance that would happen.

There was street parking in the front, but most of us preferred our assigned spots in the lot behind the building. Each apartment received one assigned space. Carports were available for an additional sixty bucks a month. I lived on a budget and it so wasn't worth the money. Besides, the snow still managed to get inside and cover the cars anyway.

I got into my 2010 black BMW. The car had been a tight squeeze with my income but it had been a necessary expense. My job took me to some fancy neighborhoods. I needed a car that would blend in. Housekeepers would report a suspicious vehicle if I parked on the street in a twelve-year-old Honda Accord, my previous vehicle.

My apartment was only three minutes away from a pharmacy open twenty-four hours. Once inside, I grabbed a basket and went straight for the candy aisle. For some reason I always found it necessary to scope out every item even though I always bought my favorites: Reese's Cups, Hershey's Bars, and 3 Musketeers. After dumping a couple of each into my basket, I made my way to the book and magazine aisle where I added a *People* magazine and three *Harlequin Blaze* romance books.

The pimply twenty-something boy behind the register asked if I needed anything else. I was tempted to ask for a pack of Capri Menthol cigarettes. Instead, I paid for my purchases then glared at him when he was dumb enough to ask if I needed a bag. No, I thought I'd juggle the stuff back to my car. With a sigh, he stuffed my items into a plastic bag and muttered for me to have a good day.

Back home, I parked in my space and started to cross the parking lot. Everything looked normal, lights on and doors closed, until I glanced at the back of Lindsay's apartment. A sliver of light peaked through the sliding doors. I veered toward her apartment. As I got closer I could see the light was escaping the open door.

"Teenagers," I muttered.

Our apartment building backed up to one of the city's many parks. There was a playground, a soccer field, and a baseball diamond. Police patrolled the area looking for teenagers determined to get into all sorts of mischief. My guest bedroom had a view of the picnic tables and the bathrooms.

I used the bag to slide the door open several inches and gasped. Couch cushions were sliced open and an end table lay on its side. Paintings had been taken off the wall and ripped from their frames. It was hard to believe how just a few hours earlier the place had been spotless, well, except for the chair with the dead guy in it. The police certainly hadn't done this and I didn't believe teenagers had either.

I reached into my purse for my cell phone and cried out at a sharp pain to the back of my head.

CHAPTER TWO

After several attempts, I finally managed to get my eyes open. At least I thought I had. It was so dark, who could tell. I moved around and regretted it immediately. I could have sworn some teenager was using the back of my head as a set of drums.

I sat up slowly and checked the rest of my body for injuries. Finding none, I sighed in relief at the realization I was fully clothed. I stood up and waited. Nothing bad happened so I started my search for a wall and a light switch. I took five steps and promptly fell forward, landing with a thud.

"Ouch!" Where the heck was I? The palms of my hands burned from what I assumed were about a billion tiny shards of glass. Okay, it was probably closer to a hundred, but dang it hurt.

Crawling, trying to avoid more obstacles, my hand brushed against what I sincerely hoped was my purse. I reached inside, searching for my cell phone. What I found was a flashlight. I flipped it on and looked around. Evidently, whoever attacked me had dragged me into Lindsay's apartment. Swell, I had just inadvertently gotten my DNA all over Grant's crime scene.

Using the flashlight, I looked in my purse for my cell phone. Of course I had to get past a can of mace, a hairbrush, and my checkbook before my hands closed around my phone.

The blood made dialing difficult but I finally managed to make my call.

"Hello," a sleepy voice answered.

"Grant, it's Kim."

"Look, Kim, if you remembered something or wanted to confess, you could have waited until the morning to call."

"I thought you'd want to know your crime scene's been tampered with, but if you're not interested…good night."

"Wait a minute. What the hell are you talking about?" Grant shouted into the phone.

"Lindsay's back door was open and the tape was off." For my own safety I didn't mention the destruction inside or the damage I'd done. He was a smart guy, he'd figure it out for himself.

"Did you call this in to the station?"

"No, I thought you'd want to know first."

"Fine," he said before hanging up on me.

"You're welcome," I muttered.

Deciding I'd done enough damage, I tried to stay as still as possible while I waited for Grant.

"Freeze, hands up!"

I didn't recognize the patrol officer who showed up a few minutes later. "Really, do I look like I'm moving?"

"Oh jeez, you're bleeding."

17

Wow, the guy was a genius. I was going to have to talk to my dad about the hiring requirements. He grabbed his radio and mumbled into it. Lucky me, he was probably inviting more people to the party.

"What the hell is going on here?" Grant demanded.

I couldn't believe he showed up dressed in a suit and had even managed to put on a tie. The guy must sleep in his clothes. Actually, a guy like Grant probably slept naked. I looked him up and down and stifled a groan. I was positive that under the suit and tie was a rock hard body I'd love to get my hands on. Now was not the time to be considering Grant's sleeping habits, or any other kind of habits, as I tore my eyes from his crotch.

"It's nice to see you too," I said.

"Detective, she was sitting there on the floor."

"Go outside and secure the perimeter. I don't want any reporters getting their cameras in here."

"Yes, sir." The poor guy practically ran out of the apartment. I guessed getting yelled at by a detective wasn't his idea of a fun evening. It was a shame I couldn't make the same fast exit.

"What are you doing in here?"

"Your concern for my well-being is somewhat lacking. Don't you think?"

"Sorry. Don't move. I'll be right back."

"Could you hurry up? I have plans."

He didn't need to know my plans involved reading a romance novel and consuming more chocolate in one sitting than a human should in a week.

Grant returned with a camera in one hand and a

towel in the other. He gently wrapped the towel around my hands. I sat in the middle of the carnage while he snapped away, getting every angle he could. These pictures would definitely not be making it into the family photo album.

Flash, flash, flash. "Kim, hold still."

"Sorry. I'm just glad my being attacked hasn't interfered with you doing your job."

Flash. "Attacked? What do you mean attacked?" he asked, the camera down at his side.

"As in someone assaulted me. Didn't they teach you about that before you made detective?"

"Shit! Kim, I'm sorry. I thought…"

"What? Go on say it."

"Look, it's not my fault. You've been at too many crime scenes lately. I thought you were at it again."

"At what again?" I asked.

"Snooping."

"Snooping? You are such an—"

"Ass, yeah, I know." Grant tossed the camera strap over his neck then leaned down. He grabbed my arms and pulled me gently to my feet. We stood mere inches apart.

"I'm sorry. I should have known you wouldn't—"

"Detective, what the devil is going on here?"

Grant dropped his hands and stepped back.

"Chief, I was just helping her up."

"Kimberly, what happened to you?"

"Dad, I'm fine, really, just some cuts and a bump on the head."

For a moment, Sean Murphy stopped acting like

19

the tough but fair police chief and became the worried, loving father that was his other job.

I walked over to where he stood just inside the doorway. Concern etched lines in his strong, weathered face. A face I had always been able to depend on. The last thing I wanted to see was disappointment. "Dad, I swear I didn't do this."

He looked around the room. "Of course you didn't. Your mother and I raised you better than that." He turned toward Grant. "Get the paramedics here now."

"Yes, sir." Grant walked past us and stepped outside.

"Dad, I'll be fine."

"Yes, you will, because you're going to the hospital," he said in a voice I knew from past experience would not tolerate any argument.

"Okay."

"Good. While we wait, can you tell me what happened here?"

"I came home from running an errand and noticed one side of the police tape wasn't attached. I could also see light coming through the door. I figured it was kids, but when I got closer I realized the sliding door was open."

"Then what?"

"I got hit in the back of the head. When I woke up I was on the floor. I got up to find a way out and tripped over the mess on the floor."

"That's how you got the cuts on your hands?"

"Yes."

"Damn," Grant muttered.

I glanced over and saw him standing in the

doorway.

My father sighed. "Is there any way I can talk you into quitting this job, getting married, and giving me grandchildren to spoil?"

There it was. What he wanted for all of his children, but most especially for his daughters. My sister, Brenna, was doing her part to populate the Earth, so why wasn't I? He probably wondered where he and my mother had gone wrong.

"Dad, this had nothing to do with my job."

"Well, I suppose..."

Grant cleared his throat. "Chief, the paramedics are here."

"About time," my dad muttered.

I was forced into the back of the ambulance. Grant's frowning face was the last thing I saw before the doors were closed and I was whisked away to Lakeview Hospital North. I'd always found the name choice odd since there wasn't a Lakeview Hospital South, East, or West.

After several shots to numb the pain, a cute doctor with a wedding band plucked every piece of glass out of my skin. Only a few were deep enough to require stitches. Luckily, the bump on my head didn't require any. My parents and brothers arrived just in time to hear the news that I had suffered a mild concussion. My mother looked ready to nurture. If my dad hadn't been holding her hand, she probably would have tossed the hospital staff out of my room so she could take over my care.

I became less thrilled with the doctor's medical expertise when he announced I'd be spending the night for observation. A female officer arrived and stayed in the room while I removed my clothes. She placed the bloody mess into a bag and sealed it shut. Instead of being stuck in a hospital gown, I was able to change into clothes my mom brought with her.

Over the next hour, half the female staff must have come in to check my vitals, see if I had enough pillows, or to make sure I was warm enough. It would have been appreciated if their motive had been dedication to their patient instead of lusting over my twin brothers, Justin and Jason, who had both arrived at the hospital in their SWAT uniforms.

It was nice having so much of my family there, but when my mom finally kicked everyone out, I was grateful for the quiet. After watching her dispose of the hot and bothered nursing staff, I was pretty confident my mom could get a job as a bouncer at even the roughest bar in Dayton.

My dad left promising to return in the morning. My mom made herself comfortable in the empty bed next to mine. I closed my eyes and tried to keep the tossing and turning to a minimum so as not to disturb her.

I must have drifted off because I awoke to something moving across my forehead. As I suffered from an acute fear of anything creepy, crawly, or slithery, I jerked up and barely missed bashing my head into Grant's face. "What the hell!"

"Quiet. You'll wake up your mom."

I glanced over and she was on her side, facing me with her eyes closed.

"What are you doing here?" I whispered.

"I wanted to see for myself that you were all

22

right."

"Thanks, but I'd feel better if I were at home in my own bed."

Grant cleared his throat and looked away.

"What?" I asked, placing my hand on top of his.

"Just thinking something I shouldn't."

"Well, now you have to tell me."

Grant leaned down and whispered in my ear, "Taking you home to bed. You're smart. I'm sure you can figure out just exactly what I'd like to do to you."

A groan escaped my lips. Grant placed his hand on the side of my face and turned me toward him.

"Sir, visiting hours are over."

We turned and found one of the horny nurses from earlier standing in the doorway, her hand on her hip.

Grant sighed. "I was just leaving." He placed a chaste kiss on my cheek then walked quietly past the rude intruder and out of my room.

"Lord, you have more handsome men visiting you than a girl has a right to."

"Just family and friends."

"Uh-huh. That man was looking at you like you were on the menu."

I sighed.

"No more visitors tonight. You need your sleep."

CHAPTER THREE

Monday

It was still dark when I was released from the hospital. Back home, thanks to a lift from my dad, I stripped out of my clothes then crawled under the covers. It was one o'clock the next time my eyes opened. A growling stomach led me down the stairs and into the kitchen. I started a pot of coffee then stepped outside to retrieve the newspaper. On my way back to the kitchen I noticed the flashing number four on the answering machine.

"Stupid reporters."

Each message turned out to be from the jerk from last night. I took immense pleasure deleting each and every one before heading into the kitchen in search of something to eat. I had a tough decision to make—breakfast or lunch? Out of cereal and only one egg left, I settled on a bologna sandwich, a dill pickle, and a handful of potato chips. I sat in the kitchen and ate my lunch with several cups of coffee.

With lunch over, the idea of crawling back under the covers held great appeal. Sadly, that option didn't get the bills paid. I ran upstairs; I took a quick shower, got dressed, and headed out. My office, like all the others on the south side of Wilmington Way, was a former ranch house converted into office spaces. On the other side of the street sat a grocery store, a gas station, a strip mall, and several fast food restaurants. A used bookstore and a library finished out the block. All the things a woman, well, this woman anyway, could want conveniently located.

When most people imagined a private investigator's office, it was safe to assume, my office didn't come to mind with its pink flowered wallpaper from the eighties and the mint green carpet. It reminded me of my grandparents' old house. It was ugly as sin but the rent was cheap and the utilities were included.

By the front door was a reception area just big enough for a small desk and chair. Since my income was only enough to support me, barely, it sat empty. I walked through the building, flipping on lights as I went. More out of habit than need, I made a pot of coffee.

Sitting at my desk, I had absolutely no interest in getting anything accomplished. Tempted to call my friends, I looked at the clock. They were either busy at work or, in Melissa Richie's case, still in bed sleeping. Melissa was a romance writer and she claimed her muse worked the night shift. Any of her friends suffering a crisis better be considerate enough to schedule it for early evening.

I had just lifted my mug when someone began banging on the front door.

"Crap. Just what I needed, a coffee stain on my favorite t-shirt."

I stepped out of my office, hung a left, and walked past the empty reception desk. Before opening the door, I plastered on a half-assed smile. Lindsay stood face flushed, bags under her eyes, and strands of hair escaping her ponytail holder. She had her hand raised and was about to knock on my forehead. In the short time she had been my neighbor I'd never seen her with as much as a hair out of place. She had even unloaded moving boxes in full makeup and a pair of two-inch heels.

"Oh, thank God you're here," Lindsay said, brushing past me.

"Sure, Lindsay, come on in," I muttered.

"Oh, Kim, you have no idea what I've been through."

Probably not, but I had the uneasy feeling I was about to hear all about it.

"I can't even stay in my apartment. Not that I'd want to after that horrible ordeal. Luckily I got that room at the Lakeview Inn."

Yup, I was right. I was about to hear how tough her evening had been. "Let's go in my office." I turned and led the way.

"I would love some coffee," she said, glancing down at the mug still in my hand.

Swell, she planned on staying long enough to drink a cup. I wasn't sure I could spend that much time with her without killing one of us, preferably her. Since I was already a suspect in one murder it didn't seem wise to push my luck. I should have known better than to complain about being bored. This was just the universe's way of getting even.

"Cream or sugar?"

"Oh, black, please. Do you know how many calories are in cream and sugar?"

I had no freaking idea, but I wasn't about to give up either one.

"Have a seat. I'll be right back."

I filled the mugs and resisted the temptation to dump some of the evil calorie-filled sugar into hers. Back in my office, I placed the mugs on the desk and parked myself in my chair.

"So, how can I help you?"

"That awful Detective Tompkins actually believes *I* killed that man."

Good. Maybe that meant I was off the hook. It also felt awesome he hadn't fallen for her little helpless act. Yay.

"Well, *someone* killed him and he was in *your* apartment," I said.

"I didn't do it. I swear," she said, then burst into tears.

I sipped my coffee and waited for the waterworks to end. When she noticed her tears were having no effect on me, she wiped her face with a tissue and demanded I help her.

"This is a murder investigation. Let the cops handle it."

"Look, Kim, I'm in trouble. I expect you to help me."

"Excuse me?"

"Technically, the police found you with the

27

body. I'd say you have about as much to lose as I do." She looked around my office. "Well, maybe not as much, but I'm sure you don't want to spend time in jail. So, I think you owe me this. I am willing to pay you."

I really hated people who thought the world revolved around them.

"I'm sorry, but I can't. The police department won't like my nosing around one of their cases."

"Your dad's the chief of police. What can they do to you? It's not like they would arrest you or anything."

"It doesn't work that way. I get caught, I get locked up the same as everybody else."

"Then don't get caught. Here's a check for three thousand dollars. I assume that's enough to get started."

She was obviously used to getting her way by throwing money at a problem.

"Lindsay, that's double my normal deposit."

"I don't care. I need you to find who killed that man, and I'm willing to pay whatever it takes. I'm not letting my freedom rest in the hands of the police department."

If I turned her down, I'd never get rid of her. She wasn't the type to take no for an answer. The fastest way to get her out of my office was to agree to take her case, a mistake I'd probably live to regret. I should have handed her back the check and kicked her out.

A few minutes later, Lindsay left my office with a signed contract and a smug smile on her face that I could have done without. She drove me nuts, and it wasn't her blonde hair and blue eyes. I was quite happy having inherited my father's auburn hair and green eyes. Of the six kids, I was the only one to resemble our Irish father. My siblings had inherited our mother's black hair and brown eyes. I wouldn't have minded having their darker skin instead of the milky white I insisted on tanning, or rather burning, each summer.

I couldn't believe after all the trouble Lindsay had caused, here I was helping her. She'd barely been there a week when she'd called the landlord to complain about the old guy in the apartment on the other end of the building. He was old and losing his hearing, so his television was turned up loud each evening while he watched the news. Instead of taking him to the doctor for a new pair of hearing aids, his kids had moved his television to the other side of the apartment, so as not to bother Lindsay.

Then a few weeks later she had called animal control about a stray cat and her kittens. They were too wild to let anyone touch them, but my neighbor, Mrs. Benson, always left bowls of food and water on her patio for them. She had been heartbroken when they were taken away. Needless to say, Lindsay had not endeared herself to any of us.

Sticking it to her checkbook was one reason I was helping her after all of that. The other, larger reason was I was nosy as hell and wanted to know how the dead guy ended up in her apartment. The thought that Lindsay was responsible flitted briefly through my mind. I couldn't imagine the blonde neat freak killing someone and leaving such a mess.

After locking up my office, I drove to the bank

and deposited the check. Normally my first step would have been to try to get information out of the detective in charge of the case. Grant was in charge and not exactly in a sharing mood, at least not about the case. I was going to have to figure out another way to get the information I needed. I'd also have to do this while avoiding my dad and half a dozen other family members.

There was only one person, not related to me, who could give me enough information to get me started. Back in my car, I followed Main Street south for several miles before turning onto Third Street. I drove past the brand new police station and fire station. A mile down the road, I turned into an empty parking lot, barely avoiding several large pot holes. In several places the brown paint had peeled off the front of the building. A small section of the gutter, above the door, was missing.

Inside, I made my way over to the front desk, where a gray-haired woman dressed in Pepto-Bismol pink sat reading a newspaper.

"How can I help you?"

"I, um, was wondering if Doc Gardner's available."

"That depends. What's your name, sweetie?"

"Kim Murphy."

"Well, you just hang on a sec."

After a whispered conversation, she hung up and told me to take the elevator behind her to the basement.

Well, shoot, I hadn't thought this through. How bad did I really want his help? Maybe I could return Lindsay's money and go home. Yeah, right, like that was going to happen. My heart was racing. I hated elevators and yet there I was about to take one to the last place on Earth I wanted to be. I took a deep breath and stepped inside. Just as the doors closed I lurched forward, but it was too late. When the doors opened a few minutes later I found myself only a few feet away from the inside of the Lakeview city morgue.

I stood there, not moving, for so long the elevator doors started to close. I rushed forward and came face to face with Dr. Gardner.

"Kimberly, it is so good to see you again. Come in, come in."

It was too bad I wasn't as excited as he seemed to be. Wanting to avoid appearing like the coward I truly was, I stepped inside. The room was cold and filled with the scent of chemicals and God only knew what else. All but one of the tables was empty. Fortunately, it was the furthest one from the door.

"So, I bet you're here about the gentleman from yesterday."

"Yeah, I was hoping you could give me some information."

"Well now, I just sent Detective Tompkins a copy of my preliminary report."

"Anything in it you could share with me?" I asked.

"Afraid I can't help. As you can see, I have a young gentleman waiting for me, but if you'd like to have a seat at my desk, I'm sure you could find some fascinating reading material." He winked and turned around. Walking over to the back table, he began to hum.

Desperate to avoid watching him work, I sat down, grabbed the file, and began to read. After finishing, I grabbed a pen and jotted down notes on a scrap piece of paper.

The victim was identified as Brian Lewis. Time of death was between one and three p.m. yesterday. The toxicology report wouldn't be available for several days. Not that it mattered. Drugs hadn't killed this guy. The cause of death was listed as exsanguination. Brian had bled to death. The wounds had been caused by a serrated knife. There were no defensive wounds. It was as if the guy just sat there and let someone carve him up like a Thanksgiving turkey. I placed the file back on the desk and stood up.

"Thanks for the help. I should get going," I said, avoiding looking in his direction.

"I trust you found it helpful."

"You bet. I'll show myself out. Thanks again."

"No problem. Come back and visit anytime."

As nice as Dr. Gardner was, I had no intention of ever going back inside there again—ever.

In my rush to escape the building, I plowed into Grant.

"Slow down there next time," he said, stepping back, a smile on his face until he realized who I was. "Kim, what are you doing here?"

Under most circumstances, my ability to lie on the spot was second only to my skill of making a pan of fresh baked brownies disappear. Too bad my mind was a complete blank. I didn't know if it was just bad luck or karma but my brain locked up and refused to reboot.

"Grant! What are you doing here?" I sputtered.

"I just asked you that. I'm doing my job. What about you?"

"I'm…uh…just, well, I was just visiting a friend."

"A friend? I didn't realize you were friends with the victim."

Oh crud. I was busted. The inability to lie to him was beginning to make my life extremely complicated. "I was just curious, that's all."

"You are nosy as hell and one day it's going to get you into trouble you can't get yourself out of." His eyes glared down at me.

"I can take care of myself!"

"Yeah, but when you need help, you're too stubborn to ask for it!" he shouted.

"Look," I said, trying to calm down. "I found the guy and—"

"Which is why you need to stay the hell away from this case," Grant snapped.

"I don't take orders from you."

"You'd better, because if I catch you interfering in this case, I'll lock you up."

I had never understood what genetic defect was responsible, but whenever someone told me I couldn't do something I became hell-bent on doing it. "You wouldn't dare."

"Don't tempt me. Go back to following cheating spouses and stay the hell away from my case."

"Screw you."

Grant moved so fast, I didn't have a chance to get away. His hands grabbed my upper arms and pulled me to him. I was suddenly pressed up against a very angry and very hot body. What the hell was wrong with me that I was noticing his body while angry at him?

"Kim, this guy was butchered. Don't think for a second the person responsible would hesitate to do the same to you. Stay out of this, because if I have to, I will lock you up, and I don't care what the chief thinks."

"My safety is none of your business."

"I've decided it is since you don't seem to be able to take care of yourself."

Jerking out of his arms, I stomped over to my car. Twenty minutes later I was back in my office and still hadn't calmed down.

Just who the hell did he think he was giving me orders? Oh yeah, he was a homicide detective, that's who. I was sure Grant figured because he had shut me down I'd have no choice but to drop the case. Well, I'd be oh so happy to disappoint him. I had my own sources in the police station. The one most likely to help me was Jackie Agostino, who was married to my cousin, Anthony, on my mother's side. For the past ten years, Jackie had worked at the police station right along with a majority of my family. She had access to anything and everything. I used her as a source when I had no other options. Unfortunately, this was one of those times.

I loved Jackie to pieces. She was family after all. The problem was what she would expect in return for her help. I would spend an entire day shopping, having lunch, getting a manicure, and watching a chick flick, which, on second thought, didn't seem like all that bad of an idea. Before I could second guess myself, I picked up the phone and dialed.

"Lakeview Police Department, Jackie speaking."

"Jackie, hey, it's Kim."

"Hey, girl, what's up?"

"Not much. How are Anthony and the kids?"

Those were the last words I spoke for the next ten minutes. We had talked just last week, so I was truly amazed at how much she had to say.

"Oh, yeah, I heard all about you finding that body last night."

At last, I was making progress. She was the first one who hadn't accused me of killing the guy. "Yeah, well, I need everything Detective Tompkins has on the guy."

"Ooh, so is it the file or Detective Tasty you want to get your hands on?" She laughed.

The truth would have been both, though, at the moment, if I got my hands on Grant, I wasn't sure if I'd strangle him or drag him off somewhere to put an end to my sexual dry spell. Since it would have been unwise to let her know this, I kept my mouth shut. Otherwise, the second we got off the phone she'd inform the entire family I had it bad for Grant. So I lied and claimed my only interest was the file.

"Too bad. Every available female here has flirted with that man. So far he hasn't taken any up on their very raunchy offers."

"Really?" I said, trying to sound uninterested.

"Oh yeah. Rumor has it he's not as single as he claims."

What the hell did that mean? He didn't wear a

wedding band. So did that mean he had a girlfriend, or worse, a fiancée? The thought made me nauseous, especially since he'd had his tongue in my mouth. If we hadn't been interrupted, I'd have probably dragged him to my bedroom. The jerk.

"So, is there any way you can get me that file?"

"I'm going to forgive you for doubting me, 'cause we're family."

"Thank you."

"You're welcome. Besides, everybody here was so relieved you weren't responsible for that guy being dead."

"I'm sure they were."

"Yeah, Anthony said you weren't dumb enough to get caught standing over the body. Tommy figured you were smart enough not to leave any witnesses."

"It's nice to know my family has so much confidence in me," I snapped.

"Look, it's getting busy in here. Your dead guy has a record. Give me ten minutes and I'll email you everything we've got."

"Thanks, Jackie, I owe you one."

"You bet your ass you do."

While I waited for her email I opened the desk drawer in a desperate search for something to eat. Luckily, I found a multigrain bar and a Hershey's Chocolate Bar. The temptation was almost too much, but somehow I found my willpower and grabbed the candy bar. When the chocolate was gone, I opened Jackie's email. Deciding to avoid eye strain, I printed out the file and began to read.

Included in the file was contact information for

Brian's mother and sister. Conveniently, both had local addresses. The name of Brian's parole officer and a list of his known associates were also included.

Grant had been a very busy detective, while I had been very busy doing not much of anything. Next up I read Lindsay's statement. It wasn't a big surprise it provided no helpful information. According to Grant's notes, he had yet to find a connection between Lindsay and the dead guy in her apartment.

Without a better place to start, I decided to begin questioning the people on Grant's list. It may not have seemed productive but I had found that many times I could get more from someone than the police could. Not everyone was eager to talk to the cops. I called and set up an appointment with Brian's parole officer for Thursday morning. I was shocked but pleased he had agreed to see me.

Deciding to speak with the victim's family, I locked up the office and headed for the south end of Lakeview and Brian's mother's home. I parked and made my way up a set of stairs that creaked with each step I took. I rang the doorbell and waited. The door was opened by a woman in her twenties wearing Garfield scrubs. This must be Sara Lewis, Brian's sister. Her eyes were bloodshot and her blonde hair needed a few swipes with a brush. She also seemed vaguely familiar.

"My name is Kim Murphy. I'm a private investigator. I was looking for a Debbie Lewis."

"What do you want with my mom?"

"Actually, I was hoping to speak with both of

you about your brother."

"No."

"I understand this is a bad time—"

"You're right, it's a bad time. My brother's dead," she interrupted.

A woman, an older version of Sara, walked up and stood behind her daughter. Both women had blonde hair and brown eyes. There was no resemblance between them and the young man lying on a slab in the county morgue.

"Yes, I know. I'm very sorry for your loss."

"Sure ya are. You don't know us. We're busy, so just get outta here."

"Sara, the last time I checked, this was still my house and I'll decide who stays and who goes."

"You wanna talk to her, fine, but don't think I got anything to say." With that, Sara Lewis turned and walked away.

"I'm sorry, Mrs. Lewis."

"So what does a private investigator want to talk to me about?" she asked.

"I'm looking into your son's murder and I had a few questions I was hoping you could answer."

"Well, then, come on inside. There's no sense you standing out there in the heat."

"Thanks. I promise not to take too much of your time."

I followed her through the house, past a dining room barely big enough for the table and six chairs. We ended up in a family room that felt just as hot as it had outside. Mrs. Lewis sat on the couch and gestured for me to have a seat across from her. Sara came in and stood next to the couch without saying a word.

"So, go ahead, ask your questions."

"Aren't you gonna ask her why she's doin' this? She ain't a cop," Sara said.

"Hush, Sara. Please excuse my daughter. This has been hard on us. Brian was such a good boy."

"Yeah, good at getting caught," Sara muttered.

Feeling like I owed Mrs. Lewis and even Sara some sort of explanation, I admitted to finding the body.

Mrs. Lewis gasped. "You found him? How? Where?"

Since either one of them could turn on the news and get most of this information I saw no reason to lie. "I found him inside a neighbor's apartment. The police arrived and took over."

"That detective told me Brian died real quick," she said, staring at me.

God bless him. Grant may make my eye twitch, along with a few other body parts, but I was so glad he'd spared her any additional grief. So, I looked her in the eye and lied without an ounce of guilt. No way in hell was I going to enlighten a grieving mother about the last few excruciating minutes of her son's life. Determined not to drag this out, I started firing away with questions. "Had Brian had an argument with anyone recently? Did he have any enemies?"

"No. Everyone liked Brian. He was such a good boy. He helped Mrs. Stephens with her trash cans every week."

"What about an angry girlfriend?"

"He hadn't dated anyone regular for a while."

39

"Yeah, that's 'cause they didn't stick around after they figured out he was broke and had moved back in with his mom," Sara said.

"Stop talkin' about your brother like that."

"What about his friends? Any of them have a reason to hurt your son?"

"No way, those boys grew up together."

"I don't know why you're askin' about those guys. None of them guys would've cut Brian up like that," Sara said.

"According to his file, he did time with a few of them."

"The boys got mixed up with a couple of creeps at that bar on County Line 32."

There was only one bar on that stretch of road, The Spitting Parrot. It was only slightly better than a rundown hellhole. Bar fights were viewed as nightly entertainment.

Mrs. Lewis's hand trembled as she pulled a tissue from her pocket. I glanced at Sara and was rewarded with a glare before she turned back to her mother.

"I guess that's all I need for now," I said, standing up.

"Miss Murphy, please find out who did this to my son," she said as tears streamed down her face.

"I'll do what I can." I stood up and handed her a business card before making my way to the front door, Sara following close behind.

"Don't come back here again!"

"I'm sorry. I'm only trying to help," I said just as the door was slammed in my face.

"That didn't go well. Did it?"

"Wow, my favorite reporter. What are you doing here?"

"Same as you, I suppose, visiting the victim's family. I can do that later if you have a few minutes so we could talk."

"Gee, let me think about that. Uh, no."

"You can't ignore me forever. Besides, the public has a right to know the truth. Wouldn't you like to be the one to tell them?"

"I don't owe you or the public a damn thing." With that I brushed past him and got in my car without looking back.

Ten minutes later I parked in front of a duplex with green siding and brown doors. The grass should have been mowed several weeks ago. An old Ford pickup, with more rust than paint, was parked in the driveway.

I made my way up to the front of the duplex, being sure to stay on the walkway for fear of what could be lurking in the tall grass. I rang the bell and knocked several times before the door was finally opened by a young man whose unkempt appearance resembled the yard.

"Yeah?"

I stepped back a couple of feet, trying to get away from the obnoxious fumes emanating from inside. After taking a breath of fresh air, I asked to speak with an Adam Mullen.

"I'm Adam."

"My name is Kim Murphy. I'm a private investigator and I'm looking into the death of Brian Lewis."

"Look, I ain't got nothin' to say to you. I already

talked to the cops," he said before slamming the door in my face.

Undeterred, I knocked on the door again. He yanked it open and shouted, "Look, lady, you better leave or I'm callin' the cops!"

"Go right ahead. I'll wait right here. I can't wait to hear how you explain the smell."

He muttered something under his breath before inviting me in. "You got five minutes, then you get out of here."

"No problem."

Stupid, that's what I was. I should have insisted on talking with him outside. With each breath I feared I was inhaling enough pot fumes to be high for a week. My only personal experience with the stuff had been in an ex-boyfriend's dorm room our freshman year of college. I needed to ask my questions and get the hell out while I could still think straight.

I sat on the edge of the only chair not littered with food-encrusted Styrofoam containers. The surface of the coffee table was covered with empty beer bottles and two overflowing ashtrays. Fighting the urge to shower in hand sanitizer, I got down to questioning Adam. Unfortunately, he was about as useful as an umbrella in a tornado.

"How did you know Brian?"

"We've been friends since the third grade."

"When was the last time you saw him?"

"Last week," Adam said, staring down at the floor.

"What did you guys do?"

"We drank beer and watched baseball."

"Where at?"

"Here."

"Was anything bothering him?"

"No, he was cool," Adam replied, scooping up his lighter, then flicking it on and off.

"Was Brian having any trouble with anyone?"

"Nope, everybody liked him."

"Well, evidently not everyone."

"He was my best friend. Don't you think I'd have told the cops if I knew anything?" he asked, slamming his fist onto the edge of the coffee table, sending one of the ashtrays flying. I reached down and put it back on the table.

"I would hope so," I replied as I watched him swipe at the tears in his eyes. I found my own eyes watering, but not from grief. Deciding I had spent long enough in Adam's apartment, I tossed a business card down on the coffee table and suggested he call me if he thought of anything useful. I figured I'd get a call from Adam the day I forgave my ex-husband for continuing to live. The least he could have done was move far away to a place with lots of predators, like Alaska.

Outside in the fresh air, I took several deep breathes, trying to clear my lungs and any brain cells effected by my short stay in Marijuanaville. In the car, I looked up the address before driving to David Jenson's place with the windows down and the air conditioner on full blast.

David's apartment was a converted two-story house on a corner lot, just south of the downtown historic district. I was lucky and found a parking space on the side street. I walked up the stairs and knocked on the door to his apartment.

A man wearing a yellowed white t-shirt and faded jeans opened the door, a can of Budweiser in his hand. He looked me up and down, staring just a bit too long at my chest.

"Yeah?" he asked, then gulped his beer.

"Hi, I'm looking for a David Jenson."

"You found him."

"Great. My name's Kim Murphy. I'd like to talk with you about your friend, Brian Lewis."

"He's dead."

"Yes, I know. I'd like to find out how he got that way."

"He was stabbed."

"Sorry, I should have been clearer. I'm trying to find his killer."

"Lady, I don't know nothin' about it."

"Maybe you know something that doesn't seem important."

"I know you've got some nice tits," he said, glancing down once again at my chest. "You wanna come in and party?"

"No, thanks."

"Fine, then get outta here," he growled, and slammed the door in my face.

"Asshole," I muttered.

I stomped down the stairs. As I stepped outside, my phone rang. "Hello."

"Kimberly, I'm so glad you answered. I was hoping you could come over."

"Sorry, Mom, I'm kind of in the middle of something."

"Oh, okay. I just thought you'd like to have

dinner with us. I guess I could send the extra lasagna home with Michael."

My mother was up to something. I felt it much like Luke Skywalker sensed a disturbance in the Force. Despite this knowledge, I was about to willingly walk into whatever trap my mom had set. There wasn't much I wouldn't do for her lasagna and she knew it. "I'm on my way."

A few minutes later I opened the front door and followed the scents of garlic, fresh baked bread, and coffee into my parents' kitchen.

"Hi, sweetie. Can you help me set the table? Everything will be ready in a few minutes."

"Sure, Mom. Not that I'm complaining, but what's up with the impromptu dinner?"

"Kimberly, there's nothing impromptu about dinner. I just thought it would be lovely if we had a nice meal together. With everyone's crazy schedules we just don't get together as often as we should."

My mom had taken out only four place settings. There was still hope. The trap could very well be for one of my brothers. It sure as heck wasn't for my sister, Miss Baby Factory. She had married right out of college and started a family immediately after saying "I do." My older brothers were also married and had provided my parents with several grandkids to spoil. That left my single brothers, Michael and Brandon, and me, the divorced daughter. This had better not be a setup or I was out of here, which would be a shame if I missed out on my mom's amazing cooking, but with all the fast food restaurants, I wouldn't starve.

"Where's everybody else?" I asked.

"Brenna's at home. She was a bit tired. Justin and Jason are both working. Your father is having dinner with your Uncle Charlie."

Charles Wellington wasn't really my uncle; he was my dad's best friend. Over the years I had dated his son, Zach, on and off, keeping it hidden from our families. Zach and my brother, Michael, were best friends and that would not have gone over well with Michael.

Brandon and Michael walked into the kitchen from the mud room.

"You're late," my mom chided. They slid into their chairs and began to shovel food onto their plates.

"Sorry, Mom," Brandon said.

"God, who smells like pot?" Michael asked, glaring at me.

"I don't want to talk about it!" I grabbed my own plate and filled it with food.

After grace, we dug into our food.

"So, Kim, I heard this time you stabbed a guy. Nice going," Brandon said.

"Don't be stupid. Knife wounds are too bloody for Kim. She prefers to shoot her victims from far enough away she doesn't get any blood spatter on her," Michael said.

"You're both so damn funny."

"Kimberly, language, and, boys, don't tease your sister," Mom said, using the voice that took no sass from any of us.

"Yes, ma'am," we muttered.

"Since we're discussing this unfortunate

incident, Michael, the least you could do is help your sister."

"Help her with what?"

"She has a client who needs help."

"Wait, how do you know that?" I asked.

Instead of answering, she looked at me and smiled. The only answer I could think of was that Jackie must have spilled her guts.

"Mom, you know I can't. It's an open case and it's not even mine."

"So you're going to sit in my house, eat my food, and refuse to help your baby sister? I can't believe it. I thought I raised you better than that."

Guilt was a weapon my mom rarely used, but when she did, it was a beautiful sight, as long as it wasn't pointed at me. It also became clear why my dad wasn't present for dinner. No way was he going to get involved in the middle of this mess. At least not until he had to, and, oh God, did I hope it didn't get bad enough that I needed his help.

"Mom, you know he can't help her," Brandon said.

My mom turned her stare on him. "Eat your dinner," she ordered.

For several minutes the only sound was the grandfather clock chiming to let us know it was five o'clock. Finally, Michael began to tell me what he knew, which was mostly information I had already learned. He wrapped up, suggesting I look into Brian's ex-girlfriend.

"Do you know her name?"

"No, but she's a waitress at The Spitting Parrot."

"Oh man, you've gotta mean Angie. The rest of

the waitresses are either married or gay," Brandon said.

"Does Angie have a last name?" I asked.

"I'm sure she does, I just don't remember what it is," Brandon replied.

"Ha, ha, ha."

"If I were you, I'd avoid Tompkins. Man, was he pissed when he got back from the morgue."

"Michael, language."

"Sorry, Mom."

We finished dinner and my brothers took off for work. I helped clean up and put the dishes in the dishwasher.

"Thanks," I said.

"You're welcome for dinner anytime, dear."

"Yeah, well, for that and for getting Michael to discuss the case."

"You didn't kill that young man, and since you've agreed to look into it, the least your brothers could do is help you."

"How did you know I was working this case?"

"Kimberly, dear, you're not the only one with informants," she said, winking at me.

"Mom, you're the best." I laughed and hugged her goodbye.

CHAPTER FOUR

I grabbed the list of names and addresses off of the passenger seat. I made notes next to the names of the people I had already spoken with. Figuring my luck was due to run out, I picked up my phone and called the next person on my list. He answered and was willing to talk to me if I got there soon. He delivered pizzas and was due at work in an hour.

I parked on the street in front of his apartment building and rang the doorbell. A man in his early twenties opened the door wearing a Domino's Pizza shirt. He was six feet tall, with blond hair and gorgeous blue eyes. He looked like he should be on the cover of a men's health magazine. "Hi, I'm looking for Kevin Alberts?"

"I'm Kevin."

"Great. I'm Kim. I just spoke to you on the phone. I wanted to talk to you about Brian."

"Sure, you must also be the woman David mentioned."

"He mentioned me to you?"

"Yup, he said some hot lady was asking stupid

49

questions about Brian."

"He wasn't exactly very helpful."

"Sorry about that. David's a good guy. It's just that Brian's death hit him hard."

"How long did you know Brian?" I asked, keeping my opinion of David to myself.

"Since high school. We hung out together, well, until recently anyway."

He invited me inside, but I declined. After spending time in Adam's apartment, I wasn't eager to go inside Kevin's.

"Can you think of any reason someone would want to murder him?" I asked.

"Murder? I guess I assumed it was suicide," he replied.

"Why'd you think it was a suicide?"

"He had been a bit depressed the last couple of months. It had gotten a bit worse lately. He didn't even want to hang out anymore."

"Do you know why?"

"He'd lost his job, his girlfriend, and his apartment. That'd be enough to make anyone depressed."

I looked up from the notebook I'd brought with me to jot down notes in. "Wow. Do you know why he lost his job?"

"The company claimed it was making cuts but Brian figured it was because money was missing from the petty cash. They must have figured it had to be the ex-con."

"Four of you did time together," I said.

"We were young, stupid, and on drugs. We all got clean, did our time, and moved on."

"What about his ex-girlfriend?"

"Angie Davis."

"Why'd they break up?"

"Angie was using drugs. Brian wanted her to quit and they argued. He flushed her drugs down the toilet and she freaked out."

"What kinds of drugs?"

"She had some pot, Vicodin, and some crack."

"Wow, that's seems like a lot for one person."

Kevin looked down and began to pick at imaginary lint on his shirt.

"So, maybe she was using and selling?" I asked.

"Maybe," he said, looking back up at me.

"Did you tell Detective Tompkins?"

"No. I didn't want to get her jammed up with the cops."

"I understand."

"Look, I've got to get to work."

"Yeah, thanks for your help."

"No prob." He chuckled.

"What?"

"I didn't think your questions were dumb, but David was right about one thing."

"What's that?" I asked.

"You're definitely hot." He winked.

Only a few years separated us, but since men matured at a much slower rate, I had kind of made a rule against dating younger men. Plus this one was part of my investigation. It didn't matter in the least that this yummy-looking guy thought I was hot. It sure felt good though.

I gave him my card and asked him to call me if he thought of anything else. On the walk back to my car I couldn't help but smile. My ego had gotten a much needed boost.

It was still too early to try Angie at the bar, so I drove home and spent a few hours channel surfing. I didn't bother changing clothes. Dressed in jeans, a t-shirt, and gym shoes, I'd fit right in. I moved my Glock from its regular spot on my belt to inside my purse. There was no need for me to announce I was armed. Not that I'd be the only one. Ever since Ohio passed the concealed carry law, even soccer moms were heavily armed. Though the law allowed people to carry a concealed gun inside a bar, the person was not allowed to drink. So what were they doing in a bar if they weren't there to drink? The law made little sense to me, but then the lawmakers didn't ask for my opinion.

The Spitting Parrot earned its name twenty years ago from the original owner. Otis Barnes kept his parrot, Spike, in the bar. Spike had the disgusting habit of spitting seeds at people as they entered the bar. Eventually a health inspector threatened to shut the place down if the parrot wasn't ousted. Otis shut down the bar for several weeks. When he re-opened the bar, he renamed it The Spitting Parrot. Sometime during those weeks the inspector disappeared. Everybody figured Otis was involved but there was never any proof. Spike and Otis lived the rest of their lives in a double-wide trailer behind the bar. They died a few days apart. Rumor was that just before the funeral, Otis's sons hid the bird in their dad's coffin.

To this day the place was still run by his two sons. Since they took over, the place was cleaner, but the clientele had gotten worse. If you were looking for a nice guy or girl to meet the parents, go someplace else. If, on the other hand, your type was the ex-con, then this was the place for you.

By the time I arrived there were only a few empty seats. I grabbed the lone empty stool at the bar. The bartender's arms, covered in tattoos, looked like an ad for one of the local gangs. When he made his way to me, I swapped a five dollar bill for a bottle of Coors Lite.

I picked up the bottle and looked around the room. It soon became clear I was in the minority. There was more ink showing in there than on all three of the bookcases I had in my living room. I did technically fit in, but my little tattoo was small and in a spot usually covered by clothes. Besides, the people in this bar would laugh their butts off if I tried boasting about mine. There was nothing scary about a butterfly and a book with the words *'Let your dreams take flight.'*

To celebrate my eighteenth birthday, my best friend, Melissa, got her hands on an assortment of alcohol. Of course we had felt it necessary not to let any of it go to waste. She and her mom lived over a tattoo parlor. Her mom was working the night shift at the hospital. To get our first tattoos we only had to stumble down a flight of stairs and hand over some cash. That weekend had started out great but went straight into the toilet, which was where I spent Saturday, Sunday, and most of Monday. It was the hangover to end all hangovers. My parents thought it was the flu, or at least pretended it was. I swore to God if I survived, I'd never get that drunk again. Ten years later and I'd kept that promise. Sort of, well, I'd tried to anyway.

Man, just being in this place had me reaching for a pack of Capri Menthol cigarettes. I quit six months ago thanks to my mother's nagging, I mean, heartfelt concern for my well-being. I especially wanted one while driving, after eating, and after sex. Not that I'd had a whole lot of that last one lately. It had been so long even some of these guys were kind of looking good.

Fortunately, before my libido could take over, I spotted a red-haired waitress in a too tight t-shirt, a black skirt that barely covered her butt, and two-inch spike-heeled shoes. The small nametag identified her as Angie. I watched as she effortlessly moved from table to table, taking orders, delivering drinks, and ignoring the occasional ass grab. These guys didn't realize how lucky they were. If I'd been their waitress, they'd have ended up with a pitcher of beer dumped in their laps.

Two hours and lite beers later, Angie walked out the front door. A minute later I stepped outside and found her a few feet from the door smoking a cigarette and fending off the rather crude advances of yet another admirer. I really didn't think her meager hourly tips and wages were worth that kind of harassment, but what did I know. One thing was for sure, the waitresses at this place had better be escorted to their cars each night. The jerk finally got the message and went back inside the bar. I could smell the alcohol from several feet away. This guy was a DUI waiting to happen.

"God, what a jerk," I said with what I hoped was

a sympathetic smile.

Angie smirked. "He's not as bad as most of these guys."

"Swell, that's good news."

"Are you applying for the waitress job?"

"Ugh, I was thinking about it," I lied.

"Don't let that scare you off. It's not a bad place to work and the tips are okay."

"How long have you worked here?"

"Almost five years."

"Wow, that's a long time to work in those shoes every night."

Angie glanced down at her shoes and back up at me before answering. "At first my feet hurt like hell, but then I got used to it."

The breeze sent the smoke from her cigarette into my face. I sucked it in like a drunk downing their first drink of the day. Angie noticed and offered me a cigarette.

"Thanks, no, I'm trying to quit," I said, a frown on my face.

"I hope you have better luck than I've had."

"Thanks." This totally sucked. She seemed so nice. The few drug dealers I'd had the misfortune to be around were total bastards. It was time to get this over with and go home. "Angie, I have a confession to make, I'm not here about the job."

"Oh, look, you're great and all, but I don't date women."

Oh my God, she actually thought I was hitting on her. How the hell did I get myself into these things?

"No, I'm a private investigator. I wanted to talk to you about your ex-boyfriend, Brian."

"Oh jeez. Look, I heard about what happened but that's it."

"Why did you break up?"

"We just did, no reason," she said, tossing her cigarette butt on the ground.

"That's funny, because I've dumped and been dumped and there's always a reason."

"There wasn't."

"Really? I heard it was because of your drug problem."

"Drugs? Are you kidding me? I don't do drugs. I'm clean."

"So you're not using, but what about selling?"

"No way, I'm done with that stuff and selling is too dangerous."

"So then what happened?"

"Oh hell, I guess it doesn't matter now. He was hanging out with a bunch of losers. I warned him to stay away from them, but he wouldn't listen to me."

Before I could ask who the losers were, the door slammed open. There in the doorway stood the bartender, glaring at us. "The girls are swamped. You here to work or what?"

"I'm coming, jeez," Angie replied.

"Wait, I just need another minute."

"Sorry, I gotta go."

"Can we talk again, soon?"

"Yeah, I guess."

"Here's my card. How about breakfast tomorrow? I'll buy."

"I guess, one o'clock at Max's Diner on Main."

"Perfect," I replied, avoiding making eye contact with the irritated, very muscular bartender.

I got in my car and pulled out of the parking lot. Ten seconds later flashing lights appeared behind me.

"No freaking way." I pulled over to the curb and rolled down my window.

"License and registration please."

I looked up and found myself staring into a bright light. "Brandon, turn off the flashlight."

"So, ma'am, have you been drinking tonight?"

"Call me ma'am one more time, and I'm gonna kick your butt."

I could have sworn I heard him chuckle before ordering me to step out of my vehicle. "You've gotta be kidding."

"I'm just doing my job, sis. Step out of the car."

"Shit," I said, opening the car door and stepping out onto the street.

"Nice language."

"Do you honestly think I'd drive drunk?" I asked, no longer sure he was just giving me a hard time.

"No, but I had to make it look good. So, did you talk to Angie?"

"I'm sorry, but weren't you the one who said we couldn't discuss this case?"

"Oh, come on, Kim, you know I had to say that or Michael would have reamed me a new one."

"I guess."

"So, what'd Angie say?"

While I was quick to get myself entangled in one mess after another, I wasn't eager to get my brother mixed up in another of my messes. "She didn't say much."

"God, you really suck at lying."

"Shut up."

"Kim, you need my help."

"No, I don't. Besides, if you got caught helping me, there isn't a police department anywhere that would hire you, not even Dad's."

"That's my business, not yours."

"Fine, and *this* is *my* business, so butt out. If we're done, I'm outta here."

"Include me or…"

"Or what?"

"I'll tell Detective Tompkins you're interfering in his case?"

"Go right ahead, he already knows."

"Fine."

"Fine," I said, feeling like I'd had this argument before.

Brandon called my bluff and reached into his pocket and pulled out his phone. Like every member of the Murphy family, Brandon had the Lakeview Police Department on speed dial. His finger hovered over the button, taunting me. I grabbed for the phone and missed.

"Ah, too slow. So what's it gonna be?"

"All right, you can help, but I'm in charge, not you."

"Fine," he said.

"Oh, and you can't tell anyone."

"That's too bad because I'd planned on them putting it on the morning news."

"Funny," I said. "Max's Diner at one o'clock."

"Cool, I'll be there."

"So, can I go now, or are you going to give me a

58

field sobriety test?"

"Go. I know you're not dumb enough to drive drunk."

"You're a good cop," I said.

"I know. Be safe."

"You too."

Glad to escape, I drove home, careful to pay attention to all of the traffic laws, even the posted speed limits, which I normally tended to think of more as suggestions than actual laws.

CHAPTER FIVE

Tuesday

I was being chased by a giant cigarette when an incessant buzzing penetrated my subconscious. According to the alarm clock it was only six o'clock in the morning. No sane person would visit at that ungodly hour of the day. Fearing a family emergency, I got out of bed and rushed down the stairs. The buzzing began again.

"All right, already, jeez."

I looked through the peephole and grimaced. What the hell was he doing here? For a moment, the idea of going back upstairs and crawling under the covers was oh so tempting. It was just too bad Grant was a cop and had probably already spotted my car parked in the back lot. A sudden banging on the door confirmed my suspicion. He'd never leave. There was only one way to make this problem go away, so I opened the door. Without a word, Grant stormed past me.

"Come on in," I muttered.

"You just couldn't stay the hell away from this case!"

"There better be a good reason you're yelling at me at six o'clock in the morning."

"Oh there is. Your fingerprints are all over my crime scene."

"We already had this conversation. You know the only thing I touched was the lamp I tripped over."

"I'm not talking about *that* crime scene. I'm talking about the one I just left."

"What the hell are you talking about?"

"Where were you between ten last night and four this morning?"

"Wait a minute. What's going on?"

"Answer the question."

"Not until you tell me what happened."

"Kim, where were you?"

"Jeez, fine. I was at a bar for a couple of hours then I came home and went to bed," I answered, trying to be as vague as possible. There was no way I was bringing Brandon into whatever the hell was going on.

"Alone?"

"Yes, alone," I snapped.

"Too bad, at least you could have had an alibi."

"An alibi for what?"

Not bothering to answer my question, Grant pulled a pen and small notebook from his suit pocket.

"I need times, places, and names of witnesses. If you have any."

This was bad. Very bad. He still hadn't told me

what happened. The image of an orange jumpsuit and a bunkmate named Big Bertha caused my heart to race. I took several slow, deep breaths. I opened my eyes, with no memory of having closed them. "What happened?"

"Adam Mullen was found dead this morning."

Grant said dead, but what he meant was murdered. This also meant I was a prime suspect—again. Otherwise, he sure as heck wouldn't be here wasting his time yelling at me. Crap.

"How?" I finally managed to ask.

"You're not in a position to ask questions. How did your fingerprints end up in Mr. Mullen's home?"

"He was a friend of Brian Lewis's, the dead guy in Lindsay's apartment."

"I know that."

"Well, I went over to Adam's to ask him about Brian's murder."

"Did he give you anything helpful?"

"Not a thing. Didn't you talk to him?"

"No one answered the door when I went. After seeing the place, I can understand why he didn't want to let a cop inside."

"Yeah, I was only there a short time and I was afraid I'd get a buzz by just being in the same room."

"I'd have paid to see that." Grant smirked.

"Grant, he was fine when I left."

"You had means and opportunity."

"Fine, but what about a motive? I just met the guy. You can't believe I killed him."

"Kim, if I thought for a second you murdered

him, we'd be having this conversation in an interrogation room instead of your apartment."

He believed me. Tears streamed down my face. The last time, he hadn't believed me, but this time was different. He wasn't demanding a DNA test, an airtight alibi, and my fingerprints. Though, actually, he already had those, what with them being on file thanks to our previous encounter and my subsequent arrest.

I wasn't sure why his belief in me was so important. I'd have to think about that later, but for now there was another dead body and a killer out there somewhere.

Grant left and returned with a handful of tissues. "Here, wipe your face."

Just great, as if things weren't bad enough, Grant got to have a front row seat to my crying fit. My eyes would undoubtedly be red and puffy.

"Thanks." I used the tissues to wipe away the tears. It was just too bad they couldn't make the burning in my eyes and the pounding in my head disappear.

"I'm still going to need that list of names."

Unfortunately, it was a short list: the bartender and Angie. Though odds were the bartender wouldn't remember me, I put him down anyway, just in case. This so didn't look good for me but I refused to put Brandon's name down. I got myself into this mess and I'd have to get myself out.

"That's it?"

"Yeah. So how did Adam die?"

"We'll have to wait for official word from the doc, but it looks like blunt force trauma to the back of the head."

"Yuck."

"Do you smoke?"

"Not anymore. Why?"

Grant's cell phone rang before I could ask about the weapon. He glanced at the display.

"Shit, I've got to go, but we're not done." His look locked onto mine and for a moment I completely forgot how to breathe.

"Are you okay?" he asked.

"Sure, fine," I choked out between coughs.

"All right, I'll get in touch later."

He left me there, embarrassed, confused, and preoccupied with inappropriate thoughts about the whole getting in touch comment. Crap.

Working out held no appeal, so I went upstairs and crawled under the covers. The next time I opened my eyes it was nine o'clock. With my priorities set, I started a pot of coffee and started for the stairs and a much needed shower, when the doorbell rang. Assuming it was Grant back for round two, I yanked the door open. Unfortunately, Lindsay stood on my doorstep looking perfectly groomed and pissed off.

"I paid you good money to find the monster that has ruined my life and instead you spend the day in bed."

"Lindsay, I didn't get to bed until after four this morning and I've already had a conversation with the police about your case today."

"Good, you have been working. So what have you found out?"

"Right now I need a shower, some coffee, and a

jelly donut."

"All of that can wait. Well, maybe not the shower." She sniffed. "But I need to know what you've learned."

"I haven't had breakfast, but, more importantly, I've had little sleep and no caffeine. Also, I've been interrogated by the police more times in the last few days than you can imagine. So maybe you can give me a break and I'll be happy to fill you in later."

"Fine. I didn't feel like going into the office today, so you can reach me at the hotel."

"Great, I'll call you."

Glad to have Lindsay and her overbearing perfume gone, I went into the kitchen and started a pot of coffee. Nothing else was going to get accomplished until I sucked down some much needed caffeine.

Finished with my breakfast, I walked into the bathroom and groaned. Smeared lipstick, black smudges under bloodshot eyes, and hair sticking out in half a dozen directions was the scary sight in the mirror. I was impressed Grant hadn't run away screaming when he saw me. Though, considering the icky, disgusting things he saw on the job, my face wasn't so bad in comparison.

I couldn't believe Grant had seen me like this. Just great. I stripped and stepped into the shower. I considered stuffing my hands into sandwich bags again but decided against it. I was willing to risk infection rather than fight to rinse the conditioner out of my hair. All too soon the water turned cool. Feeling human again, I toweled off and got dressed. To compensate for my earlier appearance I spent extra time applying my makeup. This meant I actually put on more than just lipstick and mascara.

Over my favorite Victoria's Secret bra and matching panties, I pulled on a purple v-neck t-shirt and skinny jeans. With socks and shoes on I was ready to go. I grabbed my purse and headed out the door.

Two cups of coffee had been a good start but I was starving and needed something more. Desperate, I pulled into the McDonald's drive-thru and ordered an Egg McMuffin, a hash brown, and a large orange juice. At my office I sat at my desk and gobbled down my breakfast. I tossed the empty wrappers into the trash and checked the machine for messages.

The first was from Lindsay, left shortly after her morning visit. The second was from Brandon reminding me of our one o'clock appointment. Like I could forget. Okay, I could have, but I hadn't.

The third was from a woman who hired me to see if her *loving husband* was really a *lying, cheating bastard*. Evidently her hubby had called to say he was hanging out with a couple of his buddies after work. I would need to be at his office by five thirty in time to follow him.

Since following suspected cheaters around was how I made most of my income, it paid to always have a camera at the ready. A few times I had even hired someone to come on to the suspected cheater. This method had proven successful but cut into my profits. It didn't appear the *bait* method would be necessary for this one.

I turned on the computer and deleted a bunch of

junk emails offering to either enlarge or harden my nonexistent penis. The last one was from someone claiming to be from the FBI wanting to warn me there was a million dollars waiting for me in an account in Belgium but I needed to hurry before the account was closed. Yeah, right.

I began searching the websites of the local news stations. It seemed my luck was holding. So far only the one reporter had made a connection between Brian, Lindsay, and me. Unfortunately, I knew it was only a matter of time before the others made the connection and began hassling me, especially now after Adam's murder.

Several months ago, when I'd been involved in a shooting, I was front page news for weeks. The press had seemed to take immense pleasure in pointing out I was the police chief's daughter. Some business savvy people suggested I should consider it as free advertising for my agency. The reality was it had been a giant pain. I was not a fan of hunting, but if the government had open season on reporters, I would have seriously considered getting a hunting license.

The incentives to wrap this case up were increasing daily. The problem was I didn't know what my next step should be. Though the causes of death were different in both cases, odds were they were connected. It was unusual for a killer to use more than one method to kill his or her victims but not completely out of the realm of possibilities.

Lindsay had hired me to solve one murder and now there had been another. I wondered if she'd be willing to pay extra for the new case. Probably not.

Like I did with Brian, I went online and found out whatever I could about Adam Mullen. According to his grandmother's obituary, Adam was raised by a single mother until she died when he was thirteen. From then on he lived with his grandmother in the duplex he still lived in today. Adam's grandmother, Jocelyn Mullen, died last year after a long battle with breast cancer. I wondered if her illness was why he had turned the empty side of the duplex into a marijuana grow facility. Doubtful. From what Grant had said, there were enough plants in there to give a third of the town a buzz.

Besides three arrests for drugs—big surprise— Adam had a lead foot, five speeding tickets in the past year. His last arrest had been with Brian, David, and Kevin. One would assume he'd been clean since then unless they'd had the misfortune, as I had, to spend time in his home shortly after he'd lit up.

Jeez, this kid had had a tough time. He was only six years younger but it seemed like a much bigger age gap separated us. Since I was already snooping, or rather searching, court records, I began looking into his friends' records and Angie's as well.

Though there were a few little surprises, nothing stood out that shouted, *Look at me. I'm going to kill a bunch of people.* David's arrests included petty theft, drug possession, assault during a bar fight, and drunk driving. His license was under suspension for the drunk driving offense.

Angie had two arrests for marijuana possession. The most recent was two years old. She also had received two speeding tickets three months apart last year. Other than that she was clean.

Kevin seemed to have gotten his life turned around. He only had the one arrest and zero traffic tickets. Good for him. Heck, even I couldn't say that. I was a member of the lead foot society.

From the bits of information I had learned about the people in Brian's and Adam's lives, I wasn't any closer to finding who killed them. I didn't even have a possible motive for their deaths.

We were fast approaching the forty-eight hour mark on Brian's murder and no suspects in sight. Personally, I wouldn't mind if David turned out to be the killer. I had no real reason to believe he had anything to do with his friends' murders. I just didn't like the guy. It was probably a good thing I didn't have the power to arrest people I didn't like. The jails were overcrowded as it was.

Lost in thought, I jumped when the phone rang. "Murphy Detective Agency."

"Hello, sweetie. How are you doing today?"

"Fine."

"Kimberly, you know you can't lie to your mother."

I laughed. She was right. Even on the phone I couldn't hide things from her. The ability to lie was an important part of a private investigator's job. As an adult I had managed to become quite good at it. I'd spent a great amount of my teen years in my room thanks to my inability to lie successfully to my parents. That had totally sucked.

"You don't sound fine, sweetie."

"Really, I'm fine. This case is just driving me nuts. I'm no closer to solving it than when I started.

If it's possible, I've actually gone backward instead of forward."

"From what I overheard of your father's conversation, that nice, young Detective Tompkins isn't having much luck either."

My initial reaction was joy to know Grant was also struggling, but there was also a part of me that wished he'd wrapped up both cases and I could get Lindsay out of my hair. Unlike unwanted strands of gray, there wasn't a bottle to wash her out. Not that at my age I'd know anything about that, yet, but if there was such a wonderful product, I'd buy it whatever the cost.

"Detective Tompkins seemed convinced the cases were connected and he was looking into the friends and families of those poor young men," she said, jarring me from my thoughts.

The knowledge Grant and I were on the same path to finding the killer or killers held little comfort. "If the same person killed them both, he used two different murder weapons."

"I just don't understand why that first young man just sat there and let someone stab him. That is rather scary."

I'd been wondering about that myself. According to the autopsy, Brian's body showed no signs of defensive wounds. "Don't worry, Mom. I'm sure Grant will have this all wrapped up soon. He's a good cop."

"Well, of course he is, dear, or your father wouldn't have hired him."

My mother's faith in her family, even when we didn't deserve it, was one of her finest qualities.

After assuring her we'd talk soon, I hung up the phone.

I couldn't let go of the thought Brian had probably known and even trusted his killer. It kind of made me want to reevaluate the people in my life. Not that I thought any of my loved ones would come after me with a sharp object. They'd be much more likely to torture me with embarrassing stories from my childhood. Like the time my brothers convinced me there were piranhas in the neighbor's pond just before they tossed me in. My screams could be heard for miles, as could the sounds of my brothers' laughter.

Things weren't looking good for Lindsay, but they weren't looking so great for any of Brian's friends either. What were the odds that, with the exception of Lindsay, all the suspects had been home alone? Without witnesses to corroborate their stories, any one of them could have killed Brian.

What was Brian doing in Lindsay's apartment? Who called 911? Presumably, it was the killer, but why? Why was Lindsay's apartment ransacked after the police seal? It would have been too late to worry about cleaning up evidence.

I had plenty of questions but none of the answers I needed. It was like being back in school at exam time. Only this time if I didn't come up with the answers, an innocent woman, namely me, could go to jail, and so could Lindsay.

I didn't gamble. I worked too hard to just give away my money, but I'd bet serious cash that this hadn't been a robbery gone bad. Nothing had been stolen from Lindsay's apartment. What kind of robbers broke in and forgot to take anything?

Just great, another question.

The killer was pretty gutsy. He or she broke into an apartment in the middle of the afternoon, killed a guy, and then broke in again after the cops were done.

As hard as it was to believe this kind of violence happened in my hometown, it was even harder to wrap my brain around the fact it happened in my quiet little apartment complex. I moved in three weeks after walking in on my now ex-husband giving our slutty neighbor a breast exam with his tongue. If he had claimed he had been using his penis to give her a pap smear, I swore I would have shot them both.

After cussing them out and tossing a few breakables in their general direction, I fled to my parents' home where I was fussed over and fed the best Italian food outside of Palermo.

It took exactly twelve days of my parents' smothering, er, comforting, and a nightmare of me in my forties and still living with my parents before I combed through the want ads searching for an apartment I could afford on my own. Two movers over six feet tall arrived on the big day and made quick work of getting my stuff safely packed and loaded onto their truck. They were hard workers and cool enough to ignore when Michael *accidently* dropped my *loving* husband's beloved flat screen TV.

Until Lindsay moved in less than a month ago, I was the newest resident in the building. The other residents had been there for ten years or more.

Ninety-two-year-old Irene Kanisky was the former resident of Lindsay's apartment. Irene had been independent until the last couple of months. That was when she'd had to have a home care nurse. She died on a Monday morning and her son emptied her things out by Wednesday evening. Two weeks later, Lindsay moved in.

All this thinking was giving me a headache. I was never far from a bottle of Tylenol. Thanks to Ohio weather, sinus headaches were one of the constants in my life. I took two with the last of the coffee in my mug. I laid my head down on my desk and waited for the Tylenol to kick in. When it did I picked up the phone and called the real cause of my headache. I needed to talk to Lindsay in person. She agreed to meet me at her hotel in twenty minutes.

I gathered up the mug shots of Brian and his friends. Just because Grant and I hadn't found a connection between Lindsay and Brian didn't mean there wasn't one. I was determined to find out what the connection was. Before leaving I took a Hershey's Bar from my top desk drawer and tossed it into my purse. Conversations with Lindsay were draining.

Stepping outside, the heat smacked me in the face like a two-by-four. I put on a pair of sunglasses before getting into my car. Not wanting all the work I had done on my hair going out the open windows, I flipped on the air conditioner. I seriously could have done without the blast of hot air, though it was probably exactly what I was going to get during my conversation with Lindsay.

The Lakeview Inn was next door to the

Lakeview Mall. Convenient, I guessed, if you shopped so much you couldn't make it home. After parking in the half-empty lot, I walked inside the lobby and past the front desk. An older gentleman with gray hair smiled and nodded his head. Having been raised by an Irish father and Italian mother, it had been drilled into me about respecting our elders. I smiled and waved at the old guy, then pressed the button for the elevator.

When I was a kid my family took a vacation to Canada. The hotel we stayed in had these cool glass elevators on the outside of the building. One evening, my siblings and I spent an hour going up to the twentieth floor, where a restaurant was located, and all the way back down to the lobby. Even better, the hotel had been built on top of a hill overseeing the small town. We were too young to appreciate the amazing view of the city lit up at night. We were, however, just the right ages to pretend we were on a grand adventure. Though I was sure the guests who had the misfortune to join us on one of our trips probably hadn't seen it quite the same way, especially on our last trip when Justin and Jason pressed the buttons for every floor.

The elevator doors opened and I hesitated. Sucking in a breath, I stepped inside and pressed the button for the fourth floor. It was my bad luck that elevators no longer invoked the feelings of excitement and adventure. Now when stepping inside I had the urge to jump back out and run away as fast as I could. For a brief moment I had considered taking the stairs but it just didn't seem worth the effort. I tried to think of it as a way to make up for my skipping my morning workout but decided it was okay to skip one day. I'd work out an extra hour tomorrow, I lied to myself.

Relieved when the doors opened, I rushed out, almost knocking into a young couple. I mumbled an apology before making my way down the hall. Before I could come to my senses and leave, I pounded on the door. Lindsay opened the door, a fake smile firmly in place, and invited me inside. She was still wearing the same clothes she had been wearing during her early morning visit. The only difference was she had removed her two-inch Jimmy Choo Faith Lace Peep Toe Pumps. The only reason I knew what they were was my best friend had the same exact pair. They had set Melissa back nine hundred bucks. With that amount of money, I could pay the rent on my apartment for two months and have enough left over for a very nice dinner for me and a guest of my choice. Okay, dinner for me anyway.

We sat in matching hunter green side chairs. I noticed a man's tie on the floor beneath her chair. Not big on small talk, Lindsay wanted to know what I had learned since this morning. Instead of answering her question I handed her the mug shots and asked if she recognized any of them.

"What kind of person do you think I am that I would associate with these kinds of people?"

"Just look at the pictures," I snapped.

"Fine."

As she flipped through the pictures, I watched her face for any sign of recognition.

"Sorry, I don't know any of them. Who are they

and what do they have to do with me?"

"This one," I said, picking up the picture of Brian, "is the young guy who ended up dead in your apartment."

Lindsay looked down at her lap and brushed at imaginary lint before talking. "Oh, yes, of course. I didn't recognize him."

Truth was, she probably didn't. Lindsay seemed to have an infuriating habit of dismissing anyone or anything not important to her. Not in the mood to lecture her, I picked up the rest of the pictures. "This one is…was Adam Mullen. He was a friend of Brian's. The police found him dead last night," I said, not bothering to mention I was suspect number one in his murder.

"Good."

"Why is it good?" I asked

"Well, obviously these men's deaths are related, and since I don't know either of them the police will have to clear my name. This ordeal has been absolutely trying on me. I want to get my life back."

I was sure Brian and Adam, wherever they were, would like theirs back also. "Detective Tompkins and I are both doing everything we can."

"Oh, well, if he has any more questions, I'll be sure to be available."

I'd bet. "I'm sure he knows your number. So, are you sure you don't recognize these other two?"

"Kim, don't you think I'd have told you if I'd seen them before?"

At this point there wasn't much I was sure of. "Look, I don't believe you had anything to do with the murders, but somehow you are involved in all of this."

"I did not hire you so you could turn around and blame this on me. You have no idea how stressful this whole ordeal has been for me."

It would be pointless to tell her I knew exactly how she felt since I myself had been a murder suspect a time or two. Considering my lovely early morning chat with Grant, it was more than likely I was about to live through that experience again.

Since Lindsay didn't seem the type to be interested in anyone's problems but her own, I turned the conversation back around to a possible connection. "Your apartment was broken into and searched. Nothing was stolen, but they left a dead guy."

"I already know all this."

"Just be quiet. I'm trying to work something out."

"Fine."

"Okay, so, when Brian and his friends were arrested, all four used the same defense attorney, Evan Hardin."

How had Brian and group been able to afford the services of the Hardin Law Firm? It wasn't the most prestigious firm but it sure as heck wasn't the public defender's office. There it was, the thing that had been bugging me. "The Hardin Law Firm is in the same office building as your office."

"Okay, but what does that have to do with any of this?" she asked, clasping her hands in her lap. Lindsay's face was flushed and her eyes looked anywhere but at me.

"You know Evan Hardin."

"I met him a few months ago."

"I'm gonna need a bit more than that."

Lindsay whispered something, but since I didn't have ears like an elephant, I had no idea what the heck she said. Leaning forward, I asked her to repeat herself.

"I said Mr. Hardin is my attorney."

"Your attorney?"

"Yes, I needed help with my grandfather's estate."

"I'm confused. Why did you go to a defense attorney instead of a probate lawyer?"

"I met Evan about six months ago. We were both working on a Saturday afternoon. I went to the restaurant downstairs for lunch. I sat at the table next to him and we got to talking. I told him about my grandfather and he offered to help."

"Just like that?"

"Yes. He sent me to a probate lawyer in his firm."

"Did you pay for the services?"

"Of course I did. What kind of question is that?"

I ignored her and asked another question of my own. "How did you pay?"

"With a check. What does any of this have to do with clearing my name?" Lindsay asked, her face flushed and her hands trembled.

"I honestly don't know yet, but I've got to see where it goes." I stood up to leave, expecting Lindsay to walk me to the door, but instead she remained in the chair.

"What's wrong?" I asked.

"I'd prefer it if you didn't talk with Evan."

"Relax, he's not going to tell me anything confidential."

"Please, Kim, I just think it would be better if you didn't discuss this with him."

"You've been telling me from the beginning how much you want your life back to normal. I finally find a connection, granted a small one, and you don't want me to follow up on it. Why?"

"He isn't involved in this. I'm sure."

"Lindsay, nobody cares that you slept with Mr. Hardin."

She gasped. "How do you know?"

I was tempted to tell her I had a brain but I thought she wouldn't like that much. "It's my job to figure things out. Just like I figure he's married."

"We didn't mean for it to happen."

"I get it. You accidently slept with a married man."

"His wife doesn't understand him. He's staying for the kids. The youngest one will graduate high school next year and then we can be together."

"How nice for the two of you."

"See, that's why I didn't want to tell you. I knew you'd judge me."

"You're my client. I work for you. It doesn't matter what I think of you. You're not paying me to be the morality police."

"Good, I'm glad we got that straightened out. I'll let Evan know you need to talk to him."

"So, has he been giving you any legal advice through all this?"

"Of course, but he had another lawyer in the firm go with me to the station when I was being questioned."

"That's good. I'm glad you had someone with you."

"Yes, thank you for your concern."

Familiar with the interrogation process, from both sides, I knew just how stressful the experience was. It didn't matter if you were innocent or not. It sucked having a police officer look at you like you were lying. In my case, the detective had chosen not to be so sarcastic or overbearing. I was sure knowing the chief was on the other side of the glass watching his every move had a bit to do with his attitude.

This was as close to bonding with Lindsay as I wanted to get. I got up to leave and she stopped me.

"Here, this is the card for the company the police recommended for cleaning up. Call them and make an appointment. They'll be releasing my apartment on Saturday. Oh, and here's the key."

I took the card and the key, then walked out, wondering just when the hell I became her assistant. The trip down in the elevator wasn't quite as bad as the trip up had been. It helped that a hot guy in a business suit made the trip down with me. Embarrassing myself in front of strangers was so not an option.

Back at my car, I slammed the door and cranked up the air conditioning. Lindsay's sleeping with a married man was just one more example of how different the two of us were. I had never understood cheaters. If they weren't happy, why the hell did they stay with their significant other? My ex had tried to claim some bull about a sex addiction. I told him he was just a lying, cheating asshole.

My phone chose that unfortunate instant to ring. "Hello."

"What are you doing talking to Lindsay?" Grant asked.

"Are you following me?" I looked around as if I could spot him. "Answer the question."

"No."

"No, you're not following me, or no, you're not answering my question?"

He sighed. "I'm not following you. Your turn."

"I'm trying to find a connection between Lindsay, Brian, and Adam."

"Any luck?"

"Not yet. What about you?"

"Sorry, I can't discuss an ongoing investigation with you. You should know better."

"Hey, Grant."

"What?"

"Bite me."

He laughed. "Maybe later. Right now I'm still on the clock."

I had an image of Grant's lips working their way down my neck while his hands did glorious things to my southern region.

I gasped.

Grant laughed.

For that he must pay.

"I just thought you should know I'm sitting in my office all alone and, well, I was running late this morning and didn't bother to put any underwear on," I lied.

His laughter stopped. "What?"

"You heard me. No panties. No bra. Boy, it's getting really hot in here. I just might have to take off my jeans and t-shirt."

Silence.

"Are you still there?" I asked.

"Shit, Kim. How do you expect me to get any work done after that?"

"Enjoying the image?"

"Oh God, yes," he rasped.

"Good." I laughed before hanging up.

After my saucy conversation with Grant and the desert-like temperatures in my car I was regretting my decision to buy a dark colored vehicle. Outside it was hot enough to melt off my liquid foundation. Inside the car it could melt the acrylic on my nails. At least my mascara was waterproof, otherwise I'd look like a member of the raccoon family that lived behind the garages at my apartment complex.

I heard the wicked witch from *The Wizard of Oz*. Despite knowing who was on the other end of the phone, I answered it anyway. "Hello, Brenna."

"Have you bought Mom's present yet? You know her birthday is on Sunday."

Brenna was only thirteen months older than me but acted like she was the more mature one responsible for her younger, clueless sister.

"Brenna, I haven't forgotten Mom's birthday since I was eight years old."

"Of course you haven't, because I always remind you."

"Thanks for the friendly reminder. Why don't you call our brothers and remind them. I'm sure they would love your help."

"I already talked with them earlier today."

"Lucky them," I muttered.

"What?"

"Nothing, thanks for the unnecessary reminder, but if that's all, I'll see you on Sunday."

"Tomorrow evening I'll pick you up and help you pick out Mom's gift."

With three kids under seven she shouldn't have any time to spend bothering me. The last thing I wanted was to go shopping with Brenna. She would insist on dragging me to the mall and into the most expensive stores. My sister was under the illusion that everyone could spend two hundred dollars for a piece of art.

I loved Brenna but I could only handle her in brief bouts of time before the urge to strangle her overwhelmed me.

"Kim?"

"Oh, thanks anyway, but I've already got an idea for Mom's present. Oops, gotta go, bye."

I hung up before she could argue me to death. Yeah, sure it was not an official cause of death, but it could happen.

After finding the paper with the Hardin Law Firm's phone number, I called and set an appointment for tomorrow afternoon. I wasn't due at Max's Diner for an hour, plenty of time to find a gift.

Following Spring Valley back toward my office, I turned right onto Franklin Street before a quick left on Maple Avenue. My friend Charmaine Boudreaux's shop was on the right. I parked and went inside. The jingle of four small bells

83

announced my arrival. Near the front of the store, I could see Charmaine helping a customer with what looked like a pair of dinosaur statues. Charmaine looked over and gave a little wave. Charmaine was five feet two when spotted in her two-inch heels. She had dark brown eyes, black hair, and skin like Halle Berry.

I waved back and began my search. It didn't take long to find a dozen things my mom would love. Since Charmaine's store was in the historic district of downtown Lakeview, her customers were typically from the extra rich side of town. Luckily for me I got the BFF discount, which was much better than what she charged certain members of her own family.

A glass shelving unit held a collection of music boxes. Before I could reach out, a slender hand with French tips and a diamond big enough to play baseball with snatched the one I had been staring at. I turned toward the body attached to the sneaky hand and cringed. The hand belonged to none other than Maria Gonzalez-Feldman.

In high school, Maria had been on the cheerleading squad with my sister. She had spent absolutely way too much time at our house. In front of my family she always pretended to be so sweet, when, actually, she was a slutty bitch. She tried to make my life hell and in return I did the same to her. Instead of maturing as we'd gotten older, Maria managed to get even bitchier. If it wasn't usually aimed in my direction, I would have been impressed.

"Kimberly, it's so good to see you."

What a load of crap. Maria's mother used to brag of naming her after a saint. I'm sure her namesake has looked down and wished Maria's parents had named her Satan instead.

"Maria, what a surprise. It's been too long," I lied.

"Yes, it has," she lied right back. "What are you doing here in the middle of the day? I hope you're not looking for a job." She smirked.

"No, just doing some shopping, same as you. The beauty of being your own boss is you can pick your own hours."

"Oh, that's right, you have that little detective agency."

She made my work sound like a hobby. Man, I really wanted to hit her.

"So, how's the family?" I asked, trying to be polite since she was one of Brenna's friends. More importantly, Charmaine would kill me if I beat the crap out of one of her customers.

"The family is great. My husband just got a promotion and the kids keep me so busy with all their activities."

"Wow, a promotion. He must have worked hard for that." I smirked. "Don't his parents own the company?"

"Yes, but that had nothing to do with it. He earned that promotion." Her eyes narrowed.

"I'm sure."

"Ladies, welcome. Maria, I see you've picked one of my favorite new pieces," Charmaine said, a smile plastered on her face.

"Actually, it doesn't really fit my taste." Maria

sniffed and placed the music box back on the shelf.

"She's right," I said, looking at Charmaine. "It's classy and elegant and you—"

"Maria, why don't you try the counter next to the register? We have some lovely new pieces of jewelry," Charmaine interrupted, glaring at me, daring me to say something else.

We watched Maria turn and walk away. "So, Kim, I assume you're not here to chase away my wealthy customers," she said after Maria was out of earshot.

"She's a bitch. How can you stand being nice to her?"

Charmaine smirked, hooked her arm in mine, and led me toward the back of the store. "You're right, she is a bitch, a rich one, and a lot of her rich friends shop here because she does."

"Sorry."

"Also, I charge her full price and make a killing on every item she buys."

We looked at each other and laughed.

"So, am I forgiven?"

"If you buy something."

"Good, because I need something for my mom's birthday."

"Of course you do, and I have the perfect gift for her. Let's go in the back."

The stockroom was currently filled with boxes. A desk in the corner held a computer, stacks of papers, and two empty coffee mugs. I sat at the desk while Charmaine went on a search.

"Close your eyes," Charmaine said.

"What?"

"Just do it."

"Fine." I sighed.

"Open up."

I did as ordered and gasped. "Oh my God, it's perfect."

"Of course it is," she preened.

In her hands she held a foot-tall glass carousel horse. It would be a wonderful addition to my mother's collection. I couldn't wait for her to see it, and if I was honest, seeing the look on Brenna's face would be good too.

Brenna always spent way more on us than we spent on her. It wasn't her fault the rest of us weren't in the same tax bracket as she was. After graduating college she had married her college sweetheart, who had started his own successful accounting firm. Personally I couldn't think of many jobs duller.

"How much?" I asked.

"Thirty."

"Charmaine…"

"What?"

"It's worth at least three times that much," I protested.

"Actually, it's worth five times that, but it's my store so I decide what the prices are. You want it, fine. You don't, maybe I'll go out front and see if Miss Bitchy wants it." She smirked.

I gasped. "You wouldn't."

"Nah, but boy was it great to see the look on your face."

"You're evil."

"Back at ya."

"I'll take it before you change your mind."

Charmaine laughed. "I figured that out before you even saw it."

"So, how was your date last night?"

"It was okay."

"Just okay?"

"We went to dinner. It was nice."

"So what was the problem?"

"Nothing, let's just drop it."

"Oh, you know I can't drop it. Spill."

"Fine, he spent half an hour telling me about his stuffed animal collection."

"His what?"

"Don't you dare laugh," she ordered.

"I'm not." I bit my lower lip to prevent the giggles from escaping.

"Tell me what man in his right mind collects stuffed animals and dresses them up in clothes."

"He dresses them up? Oh jeez." I tried but couldn't fight the giggles. I kept my purse close in case I had to toss it at Charmaine in an attempt to escape. In high school she'd taken martial arts classes and there was no way I was going to stand around while she used some freaky moves on me. I was rather partial to my face just the way it was.

"Damn it, Kim!"

"Sorry," I said before Charmaine burst out laughing. It wasn't long before tears streamed down our faces.

"Ah hell, I haven't laughed that hard in weeks," Charmaine said, wiping away the tears.

"Me either," I admitted.

"That dude was crazy. He names them. I got

outta there so fast I left half my food on the plate and didn't even get a doggie bag."

"The next time you meet a guy at the gas station, maybe you'll find out a bit more about him before you give him your phone number."

"Relax, it's not like he was a gang banger or something."

"Okay, but I just think you need to be a bit more selective next time."

"Maybe I should just hire you to do a background check on every guy I go out with."

"Then when would I have time to take on any other clients?" I laughed.

"That's true. Besides, you're probably too busy lookin' for who killed that dude in your apartment."

"It wasn't in my apartment!"

"Okay, sorry. You don't have to bite my head off."

"No, I'm sorry. It's just getting old. Why does everyone keep assuming I'm guilty?"

"Kim, nobody's assumin' anything."

"Ha!"

"Okay, you're right, they are, but you gotta admit it makes sense."

"Yeah, I guess."

"That don't mean you gotta like it."

I laughed. "Well, I don't."

"So what are you gonna do about it?"

"Nothing for now." I glanced at a grandfather clock in the corner. "Ooh, I've gotta go. I've got a meeting."

"Meetings suck."

I couldn't argue with that. We went up front, and

thankfully Maria was gone. Charmaine wrapped the gift while I paid the cashier. I left, promising to call her if I needed to talk.

CHAPTER SIX

I drove south until I reached Willowhurst. A busy intersection unless it was the middle of the night, I waited through three turns at the light before making a left.

At the diner, I parked in the lot and headed inside. Brandon had claimed a table with a window overlooking the parking lot and his precious Ford pickup truck. I slid into the booth across from him. Max's Diner was the place everyone went for comfort food. If you liked your food cooked in grease and covered in gravy, Max's was for you. The décor left something to be desired, but just one bite of the food and you wouldn't care if you were sitting in your pajamas on the roof. The white Formica tables had paper placemats and paper napkins. The booths and chairs were a black vinyl while the floor was black-and-white checked linoleum. He motioned for a waitress. When she arrived at the table she flashed her pearly whites at him.

"Could we get another coffee?" Brandon asked.

"Sure thing." She glanced at me, the smile replaced with a frown. She left and returned a minute later, plopping the mug down in front of me.

"Just let me know when you want something." She winked at Brandon and walked away, swinging her hips as she went.

"Switch cups."

"What?"

"You heard me. Switch."

"You're crazy." He laughed.

"The little blonde was into you. She wanted me gone."

"So?" he asked.

"She probably spit in that one." I dumped sugar and cream into the cup I snatched from him before he could ask for it back. All the men in the Murphy family never drank their coffee any other way than extra strong and black.

"That's disgusting and illegal."

"Like that's ever stopped anyone."

He stared down at the mug then pushed it aside. "So, did Brenna track you down?"

"Oh yes, we had a lovely chat."

Brandon raised his brows.

"Why does she always have to treat me like I don't have a brain?"

"She's just trying to be helpful."

"I know, and I love her, but sometimes it drives me crazy."

"At least it's a short drive to Crazyville for you." He smirked.

"Ha, ha, ha."

Brandon chuckled. "So, would it be rude if we

went ahead and ordered? I'm starving."

"Yeah, it's rude, but I'm hungry too. Let's order and maybe she'll show up by the time our food gets here."

He waved his hand again and our waitress bustled over.

"Hi, we're ready to order. I'd like the Big Platter with the eggs sunny side up and my sister'll have…"

"Banana pancakes, please. Oh, and could you get him a new cup of coffee? Mine tasted funny and he was sweet enough to give me his," I said, pointing to the aforementioned mug.

She looked down at the mug and back up at me. "Uh, yes, sure." She grabbed the cup and headed for the back.

"So, do you think my food will be safe?" I asked.

"It better be!"

I laughed. My brothers had always been protective of Brenna and me, unless of course they were the ones harassing us.

"So, have you talked to Dad?" Brandon asked.

"Not since the other night. Why?"

"Man, is he pissed off."

"At me?" I asked, worried I had pushed my dad too far this time.

"No, he's ticked you were there and had to see all that. He's also frustrated you're involved in another mess."

"Great."

"Don't feel too bad. He's also not happy with Tompkins's progress, or rather the lack of progress."

"I'm sure Grant is doing everything he can."

"Grant, is it?" He smirked. He stared at me, his right eyebrow lifting so high I feared it would detach from his face and fly away.

"What? That's his name."

"Uh-huh. So, learned who the killer is yet?" Brandon asked.

"Sure, but I figured I'd wait to tell Grant until after I had breakfast. Jeez."

"Come on, you've been working on this for two whole days. I bet you've got something."

"It's been a day and a half. So far I've talked with some of the victim's friends and family. I didn't get much out of them. Although, one friend figured it had something to do with drugs and Angie," I said.

"Drugs? Buying or selling?"

"Not sure. The tox screen won't be ready for another week," I replied.

"What else?"

"Cause of death was exsanguination. Doc figured it took several minutes for him to bleed out. Can you imagine just sitting there with several feet of intestines in your lap?"

I took the mug shots from my purse and placed them on the table for Brandon to see.

"What a bunch of losers," he said, pointing to Brian and Adam.

I felt the same way but I had an urge to goad him. "Wow, how enlightened for a police officer."

"Sorry, but I'm being honest."

"I was just messing with you. Most of them are. Only this guy seems to have turned his life around."

I pointed to Kevin's picture. "He's got a steady job, an apartment, and he's been clean since his arrest.

"Or he just hasn't been caught."

"Cynical much?"

"Yup. That's what keeps me sharp at work."

I couldn't blame him. I'd never forget the night he'd ended up with a scar across his shoulder from a particularly nasty domestic disturbance call. Brandon had stopped the woman's husband from stabbing her with a kitchen knife. She repaid my brother by smashing a punch bowl into his shoulder because he was arresting her knife-toting husband. The violent couple got matching handcuffs and carted off to jail.

"Some people change."

"You're right, Kim. Some do, but most of them don't."

I picked up Brian's picture and wondered what he could have possibly done to deserve something so awful.

Crash. The steady hum of the filled restaurant stopped. Everyone turned to stare. Deep in conversation, neither Brandon nor I had noticed the waitress had arrived with our food. Food that now covered the floor.

"I'm so sorry. I'll clean this up and get you new plates."

"No problem. No one was hurt. That's what matters." He smiled.

Ever the gentleman, he helped our red-faced waitress clean up the mess. She muttered her thanks and rushed off. While we waited for our food, the other customers returned to their own conversations.

"What the heck was that about?" I asked.

"Don't know. Maybe she was intimidated by me. I'm hot."

"Oh, gross. Please don't say that again. Ever."

He chuckled, then glanced at his watch. "Angie's not coming."

"She's just late."

"Bet ya twenty she's a no-show."

"She said she'd be here."

"She'll show all right, when the Reds win the series."

"Don't start."

Before he could make another snarky remark, a different waitress arrived with our order. We thanked her before diving into our food. Fifteen minutes later our plates were empty, our bellies full, and Angie was indeed a no-show. Well, hell.

"So, Kim, what's next?"

"I'm not sure. I do know I need to talk to Angie."

"Good luck with that. It doesn't look like she wants to talk to you." Brandon stood up and grabbed the bill, placing five dollars on the table.

"Hey, this was a business meeting. I can put it on my bill for expenses."

"My treat. Call me later and let me know what you find out."

I stayed in the booth for a few minutes longer, hoping Angie would walk in. Finally, I got up and left. In my car I flipped through my notes. According to Mapquest, Angie lived only a few blocks from The Spitting Parrot. How convenient. I cranked the volume, blasting a Kelly Clarkson CD, and drove toward the bar. When I got close, I turned down the volume and followed the directions to Angie's. I pulled up in front of a two-story home built in the fifties. Somewhere along the way someone had converted the large building into apartments. On the front porch, an older woman sat in a rocking chair. Wearing a pale blue nightgown, her gray hair in curlers, she watched me climb the crumbling stairs to the front porch.

"Hello, I'm looking for my friend, Angie."

"Upstairs on the left."

"Thanks."

I opened the door and gagged. The smell of sauerkraut slapped me in the face. Jeez, I hated sauerkraut. My paternal grandmother made it once a week when I was growing up. I tried everything I could to avoid going to her house. One time my grandfather told me I couldn't leave the table until I'd eaten every bite of the snot-looking goo. When my grandparents weren't looking, my dad scooped the stuff up in a napkin and slipped it into his pocket. Now that was a hero.

I took the stairs two at a time. Upstairs, the smell no longer set off my gag reflex. I knocked on the door and waited. Nothing happened so I tried again, hoping for a different result, but not surprised when, again, there was nothing. I did a quick look around to be sure I wasn't being watched, then placed my ear to Angie's door. I could have heard a mouse, it was so quiet. Either Angie wasn't home or she wasn't moving. I shivered even though it must have been eighty degrees in the hall.

This was stupid. I'd been hanging around too many dead bodies lately. She probably bailed on the meeting and left, figuring when she was a no-show I'd pay her a visit. I grabbed a pen and a business card from my purse. On the back of the card I scribbled a note, then slid it under the door. I turned to leave but stopped, unable to get the image out of my head of Angie, lifeless in her apartment.

"What the hell?" I grabbed the doorknob and turned it. "Oh, this is so not good," I muttered when the door opened. This was wrong, very wrong, but maybe it was a sign. No one left their door open. Maybe this was a sign I was meant to go inside and snoop around. Before I could chicken out, I hurried in, closing the door behind me.

Angie's apartment was small, which for searching purposes was convenient. There was a small eat-in kitchen, a living room, a bedroom, and one bathroom. The place was spotless. Angie took good care of her tiny living space. It was way too neat for a junkie. Most of them were too busy getting money for their next fix. Not knowing how long it would be before she returned, I made a quick search of the place. In a shoebox under the bed I found an empty prescription bottle with part of the label torn off and a crumpled up picture. The label was from Mr. Prescription and I could only make out the first three letters of the name, Ire. Not helpful at all, plus what odd things for someone to keep together in a box.

A car horn startled me, a reminder I had to get out before someone spotted me. I slipped the pill bottle and picture into my purse then locked

Angie's front door behind me. Going down the stairs, I held my breath until I made it outside.

"Angie ain't home." The old lady rocked back and forth.

Boy, would that have been some helpful information a minute ago. "Oh, did she say where she was going?"

"Nope."

"Was she with anyone?"

"Not as far as I could tell."

"Okay, well, thanks."

"I did see some feller tear outta here when she took off."

It could be a coincidence. It could also explain why Angie never showed up at the restaurant. "Did you see what kind of car he had?"

"Yup."

"Well?" I asked.

"What?"

I sighed. "What kind of car was the guy driving?"

"White."

Oh my God, this was actually painful. "Great, it was white. Do you know what *kind* it was?"

"It was one of them SVUs."

"You mean an SUV?"

"Yup, that's it, SUV," she replied.

"Okay, so do you remember anything else about the car?"

"You mean like stickers or a license plate?"

"Yes. Did you see any of that?"

"Nope."

My head began to throb. "Well, okay, thanks."

I gave her my card and asked her to call me if she thought of anything else.

Out of ideas and with nothing else planned, I drove past The Spitting Parrot. None of the half dozen or so cars in the lot matched the description of Angie's car. The only SUV was navy blue with Michigan plates.

With a couple of hours to kill before I was due to follow a client's husband, I drove back to the office. Lucky me, I had one message on the machine. Maybe it was the killer calling to confess. Wouldn't that be nice? I pressed play and cringed at the voice on the machine—Lindsay. Evidently she had spoken with her boyfriend and I could meet with him tomorrow afternoon.

Something besides the adultery bugged me about the all too helpful lawyer. I just couldn't figure out what it was. I Googled his name and up popped dozens of articles about him, his successful law firm, and his donations to local charities. Several of the articles included pictures of him and his wife, dressed to the hilt for some fancy function or another. His wife appeared to be close to his age— late forties. She was attractive and took good care of herself. I was impressed with the flat stomach after she'd had three kids.

I could call Uncle Charles; as a lawyer he could help, but then he'd want to know what was going on and I'd have to lie. There was also Charmaine's sister—an ADA in the Dayton District Attorney's Office. I could call her, but the last thing I wanted was to drag a friend into my mess. It was bad enough I'd gotten my brother involved. Although

Brandon had actually involved himself, so that wasn't technically my fault.

That annoying little voice in my head reminded me I had another option, a very sexy and single option. That voice needed to shut up. No way was I calling Zachary Wellington. Though I wasn't dating anyone now, keeping my distance seemed like the prudent thing to do.

Having made a mature decision, I feared it wouldn't be long before I was hiring an accountant and talking about things like annuities, stocks, and bonds. Oh, the horror. A shiver went up and down my spine.

Confused, I laid my head on my desk and closed my eyes.

VIOLET INGRAM

CHAPTER SEVEN

I lifted my head and an envelope was stuck to the right side of my face. I tossed the electric bill onto the desk and stretched, catching a glimpse at the clock. Just great. While I'd been sleeping, the rest of the world continued on without me for two whole hours. Now I only had ten minutes before I needed to leave to follow my client's husband. After a quick trip to the bathroom, I grabbed my purse and locked up the office.

On the drive over, I tried not to think about the scary reflection in the mirror. It didn't really matter. I'd be spending the evening in my car. In the dark. Alone. I was parked in the lot with a clear view of the back door and the possible cheater's car. Ten minutes later, the unsuspecting hubby stepped outside the building and headed straight for his car. I'd been following him for two weeks and was mildly surprised when instead of taking a left toward the pub he hung out at with his buddies, he took a right. Surprise turned to shock and disbelief when he parked in the United Friendship Baptist

102

Church parking lot.

That sure was an odd place to meet the woman you're having an affair with, but what the heck did I know. He got out of his car and walked toward the back of the church. When he got to the end of the walkway, I got out of my car and casually walked the same path. Around the corner there was a set of stairs leading to a basement entrance.

Swell, I could go back to my car and wait, or go down the stairs and see what the heck he was doing. The decision was made for me when an older man in what must be his eighties, from the wrinkles, stooped shoulders, and walking cane, put his hand on my arm.

"Don't be shy, young lady, we don't bite."

"I don't think—"

"You made it this far. It's just a few more steps. Get it? A few more steps." He pointed to the stairs, chuckling at his own joke.

"I guess…"

"It gets easier each time. You'll see." The stairs were wide enough that we took them side by side. "My name's Gus, by the way."

"Oh, I'm Kim." We had made it down the stairs and Gus grabbed the handle, holding the door open for me.

Whatever I was expecting, this wasn't it. Against the back wall was a table with an assortment of casseroles, chips, pretzels, and drinks. A large punch bowl filled with an orange liquid was on a separate table.

In the center of the room chairs were set up in a large circle. A dozen men and women, ranging from teenager to Gus's age, stood mingling. The man I had followed here was sitting in a chair, balancing a plate on his lap. A woman in her fifties sat on one side and a young boy who didn't look old enough to have a driver's license sat on the other.

Oh jeez, if this was a meeting for converting to the Baptist church, I was going to have to get out fast before ten generations of my family all rolled over in their graves. A few of them might deem my being here a betrayal so severe a haunting visit would be necessary. I shivered. Turning to leave, I spotted a gentleman closing the door behind him while everyone else rushed to their seats. Just great.

"Good evening, everyone."

"Good evening," everyone, including me, replied.

There were a couple of empty seats so I grabbed the closest one, not wanting to draw too much attention my way.

"It looks like we have a full house. That's great," the black gentleman said as he took one of the remaining empty chairs.

I glanced around the room, careful to avoid making eye contact with anyone, especially my target.

"So, who would like to start?"

After a moment of silence, the teenage boy stood up. "I guess I'll go first, Pastor."

"Go right ahead. Take your time."

The young man's face turned red but it didn't stop him from speaking up. "As most of you all know, I've been comin' to these meetings for the past three months. Ever since my family moved here from Tennessee."

Every head in the room, except mine, nodded in response.

"Well, last week, I finally told my family I'm gay."

"How did they react?" the pastor asked.

"My mom said she already knew. My dad was surprised but he was a lot more supportive than I thought he'd be."

"That's terrific, Ethan."

Everyone, including me, clapped. He smiled and sat down. When the room was silent the pastor asked who would like to go next. It suddenly dawned on me why my client's hubby was here. While I was pleasantly surprised with the pastor's support of a lifestyle that many religions, sadly my own included, frowned upon, this was going to be extremely difficult for my client. Hopefully, there was another support group here for family members.

"I tried to tell my wife over the weekend but I just couldn't do it. I knew she'd leave me if I told her," said my client's husband.

"We've talked about this before. When you are ready to be honest with yourself, you'll be able to tell your wife the truth. You cannot control her response. You can only control your own actions. You must be ready to listen to her. Anger, denial, sadness, these are all feelings she'll likely be dealing with," the pastor said.

"I know. It's just, I love her so much. I can't imagine my life without her."

Huh?

"We understand." The pastor waved his arm around. "We also know you can't continue to hide this part of yourself from her. It's possible she'll be able to accept your cross-dressing and continue to be the loving, supportive wife she always has been."

Cross-dressing? Heck, that wasn't so bad. I could think of a hundred things a wife didn't want to hear and this didn't even crack the top ten. I was pretty sure this was something my client could live with.

I glanced at the door, judging the distance. It was too far for me to leave without drawing unwanted attention. Just great, I was going to be stuck here until the meeting was over. While I was an extremely nosy person, I didn't think I should be in the room with these people while they poured out their darkest secrets. It made me feel guilty, like I was going to Hell for my intrusion. I spent the rest of the time praying no one would call on me, kind of like how I'd spent my time in high school. Hopefully, they would all be able to work out their problems and keep their loved ones in their lives. I hadn't heard anything at the meeting that couldn't be worked through but I was rather grateful when the pastor thanked everyone for coming.

I stood up and rushed out the door, ignoring several people's attempts to get my attention. The drive home must have been on auto pilot because I parked in the lot with no memory of the trip. Inside, I collapsed on the couch. My client had convinced herself her husband was cheating on her. After sitting there listening to all their stories, I felt for them. They were each going through a difficult time. Hopefully, they'd all be able to work out their problems.

My stomach growled, reminding me I had skipped dinner. Missing meals wasn't a common occurrence for me. Not in the mood to cook or go out, I kicked off my shoes and grabbed the phone. For delivery there were two choices, pizza or Chinese.

I picked up the phone and ordered enough Chinese food to feed all four of my brothers. Twenty minutes later the doorbell rang. Finally, the food was here. I grabbed some cash out of my purse and rushed to open the door.

"If you're trying to bribe me, you're gonna need a lot more than that," Grant said, staring at the money in my hand, a smile tugging at his lips.

"Funny. I thought you were my dinner, but I'll be sure to let my dad know you have a price," I said, returning his smile while trying to ignore the sudden jump in my pulse.

"Ha, ha, ha."

"Well, what are you doing here?"

"I thought for sure you'd want to know what we found out about your attack, but if you're not interested…"

"Oh my God, of course I want to know."

Grant stepped inside, his arm brushing against mine. I looked up and found myself staring into gray eyes. I opened my mouth but no sound came out. Uncertainty, lust, I wasn't sure which, flashed in Grant's eyes and then was gone.

I sat down on the couch while Grant sat down in an accent chair across from me.

"Unfortunately, we didn't learn anything helpful from the crime scene or your clothes."

"Well, that was a waste." I sighed. "Wait a minute. You could have told me that over the phone."

Grant squirmed in his seat, avoiding my eyes.

"I just wanted you to know whoever attacked you is still out there."

"You mean you'd actually care if something happened to me?"

"Of course."

I'd have to think about why that felt so good later on. For now, there was something else on Grant's mind. I couldn't believe he'd admitted to caring about me. Ever since we met six months ago, over another dead body, there had been an attraction I hadn't believed was one-sided.

"So let's get this over with," I said.

"Get this over with?"

"You did come here to yell at me, didn't you?"

"I've come to the realization yelling and threatening doesn't work with you. So I'm trying a new approach."

"What kind of new approach?"

"I'm going to ask you nicely to stay away from this case. It's dangerous for you to be snooping around."

"I'm not snooping. Lindsay hired me to find the real killer."

"Lord, Kim, did you ever think maybe she did it?"

"Yeah, for about a minute. You and I both know she didn't do it."

"Oh, we do, do we? Why don't you fill me in?" Grant asked.

Before I could answer, the doorbell rang. I jumped up off of the couch and made my way to the door. I flung it open and smiled at the teenage boy standing in front of me, holding a large brown bag with my dinner inside.

"Hey, Miss Murphy," Jason said. "What's up?"

"Not much."

"I was wondering when you'd call again. It's been a few weeks." He flashed a smile that quickly turned into a frown as I felt Grant step up behind me and place his arm around my shoulders.

"How much?" Grant asked.

Jason glanced down at the receipt. "Twenty-four sixty," Jason said.

"Here you go. Keep the change," Grant said, handing over two twenties and taking the bag from Jason.

"Uh, thanks," Jason said just before Grant closed the door in his face.

"This smells great. I haven't eaten anything since breakfast. This is the first break I've had all day."

"What the hell was that all about?"

"What? Oh, that." He laughed.

"I'm waiting."

"He's a teenager and he obviously has a crush on you."

"It was harmless and he's a nice kid."

"Kid being the operative word. I'm just saving him some trouble. Believe me, I did the kid a favor. He needs to focus on girls his own age, not a woman old enough to—"

"Watch it," I snapped.

He laughed. "I was going to say old enough to know better."

"Oh. Jason's a good kid and he always remembers the chopsticks."

"I'd do a lot more than that if you were aiming those big green eyes at me."

My pulse raced, despite my irritation at his Neanderthal behavior. The man raised the pulse of women by just stepping into a room. Expensive suits, polished shoes, every strand of hair in place, just begging a woman to run her hands through it.

"Kim."

"Ah, what?" I asked, embarrassed at having been caught staring.

He laughed. "Why don't you get some plates and drinks while I set this stuff out on the table?"

"Oh, yeah, sure." I spun around and rushed into the kitchen. My face burned and my heart continued its dangerous rate. I took several slow, steadying breaths and felt my heart slowing down back to a steady beat.

Back in the dining room, Grant and I filled our plates. He looked at the two bottles of beer and raised his right eyebrow.

"There's Diet Pepsi in the fridge."

Grant stood up and strode toward the kitchen, muttering something that sounded an awful lot like *stupid diet pop*. The giggle escaped despite my best effort. He returned with a glass of water.

I was impressed when Grant shoved food into his mouth with precision that most of the guys I knew couldn't do with chopsticks. Each time I raised the bottle of beer to my mouth I watched his eyes follow the motion.

"Oh hell, just drink the beer."

"I'm working."

"Technically, you're eating."

"Kim…"

"Fine, I'll drink it. Mine's empty and I'm not about to let one go to waste," I said, grabbing the bottle. Grant's hands closed over mine. Once again I found myself staring at gray eyes that resembled storm clouds.

"God, you're stubborn."

Not exactly the words I'd been expecting. I guessed I was the only one fighting the urge to rush upstairs, tear off our clothes, and have mind-blowing sex. Jeez, it had been six long freaking months. I was beginning to fear the parts wouldn't work with a partner anymore.

"Kim?"

"Huh? Oh, sorry, I must've zoned out there. What'd you say?"

"Never mind, it's getting late." He let go of my hand and stood up. I followed him to the door.

"Well, thanks for dinner."

"You paid. I should thank you."

"Next time we'll have to try Italian."

"Next time?

"When this case is over, I'd like to have a conversation that doesn't include dead bodies."

"What makes you think there'll be a next time?"

Grant grabbed my arms and pulled me close.

"You know there'll be a next time." He leaned down, his mouth mere inches from mine, and his stupid phone rang.

"Ugh." He grabbed his phone and barked into it. "Tompkins." He listened for a minute before finally telling the voice on the phone he'd be there soon.

"Work, huh?" I asked.

"Lock up behind me. Uniforms will be running extra patrols through here for the next few days." With that, he turned and left without saying anything about the almost kiss.

I'd been so angry with him for the past few months, yet whenever I was close to him, anger usually took a back seat to lust.

Getting involved with him would be a mistake. First of all, he never even apologized for arresting me. Second, he always acted so superior, bossing me around. Third, there was the tiny little detail about my dad being his boss. I also couldn't forget what Jackie had said about the possibility he wasn't single. It was driving me crazy. He didn't wear a wedding ring and he sure as heck didn't act married, not that it meant anything.

I yawned. The day had been a long one and I was ready for it to be over. I stuck the leftovers in the fridge and stuck the dishes in the sink. I'd deal with them and a bunch of other things tomorrow. Remembering Grant's warning, I checked that the doors were locked before heading upstairs. In my room, I stripped out of my clothes and tossed on a tank top and a pair of boxer-short pajama bottoms. A quick stop in the bathroom and I was ready for bed.

***

Some idiot was leaning on my doorbell. That was the only explanation I had as to why it wouldn't stop. Prying my eyes open, I glanced at the clock. I'd only been asleep for a few hours. I so did not like middle of the night visitors. I was debating what to do when my phone rang. What the hell was going on? My heart began to race. Bad things happened in the middle of the night. You never got good news past eight at night.

My hands shook as I grabbed the phone and answered.

"Hey, Kim, it's Darlene."

I couldn't figure out why the police dispatcher was calling me but she had my attention. "What's wrong?"

"Well, I've got an officer who's been ringing your doorbell for the past five minutes. The guy was about to bust your door down. He was afraid something happened to you on his watch. I told him to keep his boxers on and I'd try calling you. Hang on a second and let me tell him you're okay."

There was a click and Darlene was gone. A few seconds and another click later and she was back.

"Not that I wouldn't love to chat with you, Darlene, but what's wrong?" I asked again, not sure I wanted the answer.

"On his sweep through he noticed you had a flat tire. Trouble is it had a knife stickin' out of it. I told him to meet you at your back door."

"Oh, he doesn't have to do that. I'll deal with it in the morning."

"Sweetie, he has to so a report can be filed. This is official police business. Make sure it's Stevens

113

before you open that door. Do you want me to stay on the phone with you?"

"No, that's okay. Thanks, Darlene."

"Anytime, sweetie, bye-bye."

I flipped on the light and searched for my keys. It never failed, whenever I was in a rush I managed to misplace things. Dumping my purse on the bed, I found them and raced down the stairs. I peeked through the blinds and sure enough, Officer Stevens was waiting for me.

"Evening, Miss Murphy. Sorry to bother you."

"Hey, it's not your fault. Thanks for spotting it."

"No problem. The tech guys'll be here any minute. They're gonna dust for prints and they'll take the damaged tire as evidence."

"Okay, well, I guess I'll go inside and call AAA. There's no telling how long it'll take them to get here."

"You don't have to worry about that. You have a spare, right?"

"Yeah, in the trunk."

"Good. We'll make sure to put the spare on for you before we leave."

"Oh jeez, you don't have to do that."

"It's no problem. Heck, we'll have the car up to take off the damaged one, we might as well finish it up."

"Well, thanks."

"It didn't look like whoever did this got inside your car, but I thought we should check just in case."

"Oh, sure."

We walked over to my car, careful not to touch

anything. Officer Stevens turned his flashlight on and we both peered inside.

"You're right," I said. "The inside is fine."

"That's a relief. One less headache for ya anyway."

I smiled.

"So, any idea who'd want to do this?"

"The list is long," I joked.

He laughed. "Any names stand out more than the others?"

"Honestly, other than my ex, I haven't managed to piss off too many people lately."

"Your ex, huh? What's his name?" he asked, a notebook in one hand and a pen in the other.

As much as I'd love to have my ex questioned by the police, I'd never give him the opportunity to claim police harassment. "No, I was just kidding about him."

"Now you know if you're being hassled, we can help."

"Really, I was joking. Besides, do you think someone would really be stupid enough to bother me knowing about my dad and brothers? That would be suicidal."

"I guess you're right."

Luckily for me, the lab techs arrived before my mouth could get me into any more trouble. Twenty minutes later, the techs had taken pictures and removed the tire with the knife as evidence. Since there weren't any all-night tire stores, and if there were, I wasn't going, they put the spare on and I assured them I'd get a new one on in the morning.

The driver's side of my car looked dirty thanks

to all the powder they used to check for fingerprints. There was the awkward moment when they requested to take mine to rule them out and I had to remind them I was already in the system.

I thanked everyone and signed the report. Before I could make it back inside, Grant tore into the parking lot, lights flashing. At that point I was just grateful he'd had the good sense not to use the siren. With all the activity, we had already caused enough of a spectacle.

The car had barely come to a complete stop when Grant got out and raced over to me.

"Are you all right?" he asked.

"I'm fine. Just a little ticked off."

"Ticked off? Why aren't you on your way to the hospital?"

"I'll pass, thanks. I've spent enough time there lately," I replied.

"Wait a minute. Weren't you stabbed with a knife?"

"I wasn't, but my tire sure as heck was."

"Hey, detective, we're done here. So, I think you've got this," Officer Stevens said.

"Before you go, call in a request for extra patrols through here."

"Already done." He turned toward me. "Good night, Miss Murphy."

"Good night, and thanks again."

Grant waited until we were alone to speak.

"What am I going to do with you?"

I had a few suggestions, but I was pretty sure he wasn't talking about sex. At least not right now.

"Oh jeez, you're shivering. Let's get you inside."

116

The poor man was being a gentleman, assuming I was cold when all I really wanted to do was get him naked and take care of my sexual drought. I let him lead me inside my apartment. He locked the door behind us. Oh my, maybe he did get it. I walked toward the stairs and stopped when I realized he wasn't behind me.

"What are you doing?"

"I'm going to sleep on the couch in case you get any more unwanted visitors."

Seriously? The man was so hot I'd seen women walk into street signs while staring at him. There was also the lady who tripped over a chair, though that one was kind of funny. Yet here he was in my apartment, and instead of ripping my clothes off, he was planning to sleep on the couch. Swell. It wasn't like one more sex-free night was going to return my virginity or anything, but damn.

"I'm sure the idiot is done for the night."

"I'm staying."

"Suit yourself."

I stomped up the stairs, stripped out of my clothes, and crawled under the covers. I spent the next few hours tossing and turning. I was just about to call it quits and go downstairs in search of chocolate when my bedroom door opened. For a second I wondered if I could reach my gun, but then I realized just who it was walking toward me. He was the reason for my tossing and turning and my sexual frustration.

"Kim?"

"What's wrong? You need another blanket?"

Instead of answering me, Grant walked over to

the bed and crawled under the covers. I rolled over toward him. "Did you get lonely down there?" I asked.

"I couldn't sleep. How about you?"

"No."

"Maybe we should do something about that?"

My heart was pounding so loud I was surprised he didn't have to shout over it. The mere thought of what I wanted him to do to me had my panties wet. "Oh God, yes."

CHAPTER EIGHT

Wednesday

I hit the snooze button a dozen times before dragging myself out of bed. Just as things were getting hot and heavy last night, Grant had called a halt to our activity. He had claimed some bull about not wanting to take advantage of me. I was so horny it had taken everything I had not to beg him for it, protecting what little pride I had left.

Half a pot of coffee later I made it to Lakeview Gym and began my daily torture session. Twenty minutes into my workout I had to call it quits, thanks to my liquid motivation. I hopped off the treadmill and pretended not to notice the snarky look of the woman next to me. Since I planned on returning to the gym, I didn't give in to my juvenile urge to flip the bird. My mom would be so proud.

I rushed off to the bathroom. I was washing my hands when I heard the door open. Looking up in the mirror, I spotted Maria walking toward me, followed closely behind by her hangers on. It had been a whole twelve hours since someone had driven me crazy, so yeah, I guessed I was due.

Alone, I could take her. She'd fight dirty, but so could I. With her little posse eager to please her I'd be lucky to get out in one piece. There was only one exit and queen bitch stood between it and me. Ignoring her wouldn't be an option. Picking a fight wasn't one either. Plastering on my best fake smile, I turned toward her, eager to avoid a scene. "Maria, twice in one week, I can't believe it."

"Kim, what a surprise." She looked me up and down. "I never would have expected to see you here." Her clones giggled at their leader's wit.

"Yes, it's so much easier to work out regularly than to spend my vacation recovering from liposuction." It was my turn to smirk while the trio gasped.

There was no way Maria would let me go without peeling a layer of skin off for my act of betrayal. Maria had shared with everyone unfortunate enough to be in her presence all about her *vacation* to the Caribbean, but she had let it slip to Brenna that she had really gone to California to get some work done—like a boob job and a butt lift. I bit the inside of my cheek to stop from laughing. It was my dumb luck Maria was quick to recover. The shocked expression on her face was replaced by a smile that revealed the bleached teeth in her mouth. This was going to be bad.

"Yes, you know how it is having a career and being a wife and mother. Not to mention all the charities I volunteer for. Oh, that's right. You don't know. You don't have kids and, well, you're divorced."

Her cohorts smiled, providing her all the encouragement she needed. "It must be so difficult not being able to keep your man satisfied. How many women did he sleep with while he was married to you? Next time you might want to hurry up and get pregnant. Maybe that way you can hang on to him." Maria turned to bask in the glow of her royal subjects.

"Yes, my ex did have a thing for bleach blonde sluts. Were you number twelve or thirteen?" I brushed past the trio of bitches, careful not to touch them.

I made it to the door, freedom was a mere step away, but I couldn't resist one last dig. "Oh, by the way, your roots are showing." I hurried out, but just before the door closed I heard her shout, "Bitch."

No longer interested in working out I headed toward the parking lot. Jeez, this sucked. If she-bitch was a member, I would have to seriously consider changing gyms. I'd only been going to this one for a few months but I liked it, as much as I could like a place that contained evil machines that made you sweat and hate every moment you were there.

I'd never be able to focus knowing there was a possibility Maria was lurking somewhere. Maybe I could fix it so she got kicked out. I had no idea how I'd do it, but she had to go. I couldn't afford to change gyms, but she could. It seemed fair to me.

Back home, I took a shower and got dressed in my standard work uniform of jeans and a t-shirt; today's color choice was red. After drying my hair and adding some makeup, it was time to consider my breakfast options. A quick scan revealed my choices were nonexistent since someone, me, had forgotten to go grocery shopping. Well, it seemed I'd have to fit in a trip to the grocery store soon. Just great. Where was a fairy godmother when you really needed one? Huh, so much for fairy tales and happily ever after. For now, my stomach was empty and needed food. I grabbed my purse, got in my car, and headed straight for the nearest McDonald's drive-thru.

Once inside my office, I sat at my desk and started in on my breakfast of an Egg McMuffin, a hash brown, and a large coffee. A couple of bites in, the front door opened and closed. Just great, a client showed up and I was stuffing my face. What a way to instill confidence. Before I could get up and welcome my visitor, Grant stomped into my office.

"What are you doing here? If you're checking on my virtue, it's a little late."

"Why do you have a cell phone if you're not going to answer it?" Grant asked, ignoring my witty repartee.

"What are you talking about?" I pulled my phone from my purse and looked at the screen. Naturally, the battery was deader than my niece's goldfish, Bubbles. She was currently on Bubbles number four, or was it five? I'd lost count. Every time one went belly up, my sister would dispose of the body and run to the pet store for a new Bubbles.

"Kim, are you listening?"

"Sorry," I muttered, tossing the useless phone into my purse. "What's up?"

"Angie Davis. When was the last time you saw her?"

"What?"

"Answer the question," he growled.

"The other night at The Spitting Parrot. Why?"

"What was she doing with your business card?"

"I gave her one. What's the big deal?"

"Did you write on the back of it?"

"No. What's going on?" I asked, nausea threatening to empty my stomach of what little I had eaten.

"Did you agree to meet her again?"

I remained silent. Whatever was going on was bad and I had to be very careful how I answered.

"Kim!"

"Okay, okay, jeez. Yeah, she couldn't talk at work, so we agreed to meet yesterday for lunch. She was a no-show."

"So then you went to her apartment looking for her?" he asked, though it was obvious he already knew the answer.

"Yeah, so?"

"Last night one of our patrols found her car behind the abandoned movie theater out on Route 48."

I swallowed down the bile that threatened to escape. "Was…was she in it?"

"No. All we found were her keys in the ignition and your business card in the cup holder." Grant leaned on the back of a chair, his face covered by his hands.

There was something he wasn't telling me. Homicide didn't investigate missing persons unless there was enough evidence to suggest the missing person was dead. I had to know what happened.

Grant stood back up and sighed. "Kim Murphy, where were you yesterday between two p.m. and eight p.m.?"

I gave him the rundown of my day from waiting at the restaurant for Angie up until he arrived at my place last night, omitting the part about Brandon's involvement.

"Can anyone corroborate your whereabouts?"

I hesitated. Mentioning the waitress would send Grant running off to talk to her. While it was possible she'd remember me, she most certainly would remember I hadn't been alone.

"I...don't know. Sorry. So do you think Angie met up with someone and took off or what?"

"Leaving her keys in the car wasn't smart."

"Maybe she thought she'd be right back."

"Not likely," he muttered.

"What aren't you telling me?"

Grant ignored my question. "You might want to get an attorney." He turned to leave.

I jumped up and ran around the desk, blocking his exit. "What the hell are you talking about? Why do I need a lawyer?"

"Kim, you know I can't discuss an ongoing investigation with you."

"Maybe you should have thought about that before you told me Angie was missing."

Grant grabbed my arms, his eyes narrowed, his face flushed. After all this time I should have known better than to anger him, but I could not seem to stop myself.

"You are so frustrating."

"Looked in a mirror lately?"

My skin tingled under his grip. This was so not the time to notice his lips were mere inches from mine. Eyes that resembled storm clouds would so not appreciate where my thoughts had traveled. Realizing this was not a good idea, I stepped back and took a deep breath, hoping the distance would clear my head.

Grant shook his head as if to clear his own thoughts. "Stay away from this case. All your interfering is doing is causing more work for the professionals."

"I am a professional," I snapped.

"Yeah, one step up from a night guard at an empty lot."

"Funny. Is that the best the big bad homicide detective can come up with?"

If this had been a cartoon, steam would have poured from Grant's ears while his head whistled like a teapot. I would have giggled at the image but knew if I did, Grant would have me in handcuffs before I could move.

"Have you ever thought that maybe your meddling could be endangering peoples' lives?"

"What are you talking about?"

"Maybe you're asking people questions that are making the real killer nervous and he or she is getting rid of anyone who might know something."

"Then I'm doing the right thing."

"Are you out of your mind?"

"No, are you?"

"You should be locked up! You're not only a

danger to yourself, you're a danger to the public."

"Screw you!"

"Not now, I've got work to do, but if you keep offering, I might just have to take you up on it."

"Ugh, get out!"

"Gladly!" He stomped past me and slammed the door on his way out.

God, he could be so smug and arrogant. Then, other times, he could be sweet and funny a little voice in my head reminded. There really should be a mute button for that dang voice. I sat down at my desk and spotted my forgotten breakfast. Now cold. I tossed it in the trash. Desperate for caffeine, I took the cup into the kitchen and nuked the coffee in the microwave. As I waited for the ding, I wondered what could have happened to Angie. Jeez, I hoped she was okay. Was Grant right? Was my investigation causing more harm than good? I wasn't sure, but I had to press on, not only for Lindsay, or me, but for Brian's family. They deserved to know who killed him. The only way they would get closure was to see the person or persons responsible in jail. Though Ohio had the death penalty, it was rarely used. Being Catholic, I was supposed to be against it, but there were some monsters on Earth walking around as human beings that really did need to be exterminated.

Six months ago I had, in a sense, administered the death penalty when I had pulled the trigger. It was difficult knowing I had ended a life, no matter how much of an evil monster he was.

My large, loving family had surrounded me with love and support, almost smothering me with their kindness. It was my mom who had suggested I talk with Father Steve. I had balked at first, but eventually agreed, thanks to her pushing.

I hadn't been to confession for some time—like, before I got married. I thought it would be a little weird. I was wrong. It was very freaking weird. I mean, I was admitting to killing someone. It didn't matter that the guy kidnapped me and framed me for a murder he committed all before trying to kill me. There was this whole *Thou Shalt Not Kill* thing. That was pretty straight forward. There was no other way to interpret that.

After what seemed like forever for the both of us, Father Steve finally tried to convince me God loved me and had forgiven me. I still was not sure about that, but at least the half dozen times I'd attended Mass since then I hadn't been struck down or heard God telling me to get out, so it seemed Father Steve knew what he was talking about. I guessed. I'd know for sure when it was my time. Not that I was in any rush, especially if the good Father was wrong. Eternity in a place that required an SPF of one billion didn't really seem like my kind of place.

It took two cups of coffee before I had worked up the nerve to call Jackie. As usual she had the inside information and was willing to share—for a price. Today she was in an extremely good mood. She didn't even attempt to blackmail me into babysitting duties or anything else. I filled her in on what little I knew before asking for details.

"Well, you already know almost everything, except that they found blood in the lady's car."

"Blood?"

"Yup, not a lot. So, if she bled out, it wasn't in the car."

"Oh God."

"Sorry I don't have better news."

"Not your fault."

"No, but sometimes it sucks being the messenger."

I laughed. "It sure does, but I'm pretty fond of this messenger."

"Thanks, back at ya. Oops, gotta go, my other line's ringin'. See ya Saturday."

I hoped Angie was okay. I felt responsible for her. If my questioning her had drawn the killer's attention, I didn't know how to live with that. Now I had to find a killer, but more importantly I had to find Angie, hopefully in one piece.

How the heck did I think I could do either of these things? So far all my efforts had turned up nothing but dead ends. That stupid voice in my head was back. Why the heck did it always sound like old Mr. Bicknell? He lived next door to us when I was growing up. He was a nice man, quick to smile, until his wife got sick. She died of cancer shortly after she was diagnosed. He died a year later from heart failure.

His adult sons, expecting to receive the bulk of their father's estate, had been horrified to discover all they got was a hundred dollars each. When they found out their father left me a thousand dollars for taking in his trash cans each week, they became nasty. The rest of Mr. Bicknell's estate, approximately two hundred thousand dollars, went to cancer research in memory of his late wife. According to my parents, the sons spent thousands of dollars they didn't have on lawyers and lost. Mr. Bicknell would have been happy.

I had a couple of hours before my meeting with Brian's parole officer so it was as good a time as any to get a new tire. There was a place down the street that was fast and inexpensive. Of course when I got there the man behind the counter tried to talk me into buying two tires because of balancing or something. I assured him the other tires were fine and I only needed the one. After a few back and forths the guy finally figured out I wasn't shelling out the bucks for anything more than the basics. He told me to have a seat in the waiting area and they'd call my name when my car was ready. I sat on one of the plastic chairs furthest from the window then grabbed one of the books I'd gotten at the pharmacy from my purse. A guy in his thirties, blond hair with blue eyes, sat across from me, smirked at the book cover, and nudged his buddy in the arm. The two had a whispered conversation and chuckled. Men could be such jerks.

"You know if real men were as good as the men in these books, we wouldn't need the books."

"Maybe you haven't found the right one. Give me a ride, you won't be sorry."

"Yeah, that'll happen. Not." I stuck my face in the book and forgot about the drooling idiots. I had just gotten to the part where the heroine realized she was in love with the jerk with a kind heart when someone called out my name. I sighed, stuck a piece of paper in the book to mark my page, and went over to the counter. I considered myself lucky to get out of the shop for under two hundred bucks. I drove next door to the car wash and had the fingerprint residue removed.

It was time to leave for my meeting with Brian's parole officer. I didn't think he'd have much information to give me but maybe he could tell me if Brian had been acting shady lately. Since Brian was already dead it couldn't hurt. Not in the mood for music, I shut off the radio and made the drive in silence. I parked and went inside the gray brick building, where I gave my name to the man behind the bulletproof glass. A few minutes later I sat across from Mr. Coleman. I tried not to stare but it was hard to imagine this young man was responsible for keeping criminals in line. He looked better suited at the geek table, losing his lunch money to the school bully. Freckles covered the bridge of his nose and the apples of his cheeks. His brown eyes hid behind a pair of Harry Potter-like glasses.

"So, Miss Murphy, how can I help you today?" His voice squeaked like a teenage boy during puberty.

"I'm a private investigator, and I've been hired to look into Brian Lewis's murder."

"It was a shame to hear about Brian. I really thought he'd turned his life around."

"So, you don't believe he'd gotten involved in something illegal?" I asked.

"He was taking steps to get out of that lifestyle and to remove those in his life who were bad influences."

"What kind of steps? Which people?"

"I'm afraid I can't say."

"Can't or won't?"

He remained silent.

"Did he say anything about someone bothering him or any trouble he was in?" I tried again.

"If he did, I couldn't discuss that with you."

"I'm trying to help his family find closure. If you know something that could help, please tell me."

"Look, Miss Murphy, the only reason I agreed to meet with you was because I respect your father. I can assure you I've spoken with Detective Tompkins and told him everything I know."

"And that would be?"

He smiled. "Nice try. Now if you'll excuse me, I have another meeting."

I stood up, frustrated. "Thanks for your time." I opened the door. "You've been so helpful." I turned to leave and came face to face with David Jenson. Swell.

David was once again staring at my chest. His eyes traveled up to my face and registered recognition. The leering on his face was replaced with a look of disgust. The feeling was mutual.

"Well, if it ain't Miss Nosy."

"Mr. Jenson, what an unpleasant surprise."

"Don't you have somethin' better to do than hassling people?" he asked.

"I haven't hassled anyone, yet." With that I walked down the hall without looking back.

In the car, I leaned back against the headrest and closed my eyes. Where was Angie? Was she okay, or would hers be the next body the police found? I slammed my fist into the steering wheel, blasting the horn.

The third day on the case and all I had to show for it was a friend of Brian's had been murdered and now his ex-girlfriend was missing. There was something else missing—clues. I had two hours before my meeting with Lindsay's lawyer, Mr. Hardin. Needing to take a break from the case, I decided to be productive. I went grocery shopping at Wal-Mart, something that should never be done on an empty stomach. Half an hour and a full cart later, I checked out and began my least favorite part of shopping, putting the groceries in the car. I had just picked up two bags when an idiot wearing a t-shirt, shorts, and a ski mask grabbed my purse and turned to run, only to be yanked back, banging his leg on the cart.

What the idiot hadn't realized was I always strapped my purse into the child restraint. Thank God it worked. I dropped the bag in my hands and grabbed for his shirt. He yanked out of my grip and took off running.

A young woman with a baby on her hip and toddler at her leg rushed over.

"Oh my gosh, are you all right? I called 9-1-1 and the police are on the way."

Swell, just what I needed. Another woman, mid-thirties, hurried over. "I got the whole thing on my iPhone."

Oh no, this was gonna end up on YouTube. Worse, my family and the entire police department were going to see this. Just freaking great, let the embarrassment begin. A patrol car pulled up, lights flashing, drawing the attention of everyone in the parking lot. Wonderful, even more people to witness my mortification.

As if I hadn't spent enough time with Officer Duncan lately, he was the lucky officer to arrive. I was just pleasantly surprised when he didn't bring up the dead guy in Lindsay's apartment or ask me if I'd found another dead body. He took one look at me and whispered into his radio before making his way over to me. I filled out yet another police report while the two women filled out reports of their own. The one with the video of the incident agreed to go to the police station so they could make a copy of it. Not that it would help. I wouldn't recognize my own brothers in that outfit.

"You really can't stay out of trouble, can you?"

I turned toward the voice. "Grant, what the heck are you doing here? There aren't any dead bodies."

"Not yet."

"Ha, ha, ha. Volunteering for the role of corpse?"

"I guess you'd be volunteering as the suspect."

"You never answered my question."

"I heard you were involved so I came by to see if you, I mean, if everything was okay."

"Huh, wonder what little birdie whispered in your ear." I watched Duncan and the helpful women go back to their cars and leave. "You must not be too busy if you have time to stop by and check on me or things."

"I was off duty, and I wrapped up three cases this week."

"Brian and Adam?" I asked.

"No. Those are the only ones still on my desk."

"It sounds like you've been having as much luck as I have."

"We can't discuss this."

"You know we should compare notes. It could be the only way to solve these cases."

"You want me to compare notes with a possible suspect?" He smirked.

"Funny. You know I had nothing to do with their murders."

"Yeah, I know."

"Good, it's about time you stopped looking at me like I was a suspect."

"I don't see you as a suspect."

"Oh really, then what do you see me as?"

Grant looked me up and down and I felt a familiar sensation in my female regions. I stepped back, not wanting to embarrass myself by pouncing on him, and stepped on one of the bags I had dropped and forgotten. I picked it up and looked inside.

"Gross."

Grant walked over and peered inside. "Well, you can make scrambled eggs."

"Yeah, but I'd rather they not be pre-scrambled."

He chuckled. "That is pretty disgusting-looking."

"So, do you want to follow me back to my place?"

Grant's eyes locked on mine.

"I…I mean, I meant we could talk while I put what's left of my groceries away," I stammered.

"Are you sure that's what you meant?"

"Huh, yes, of course."

"Too bad. Well, I have things to do before

heading into the office so try to stay out of trouble."
He turned and strode back to his car.

God, I was a horny idiot. At home I put the
groceries away then had a turkey sandwich and a
Diet Pepsi. With lunch over I got in my car and
headed north on Main Street. Twenty minutes later I
found an elusive empty parking space within
walking distance to the Chase Bank building in
downtown Dayton. Inside the elevator, I pressed the
button for the eighth floor. The elevator began to
move and my heart began to pound. Maybe I should
have asked Mr. Hardin to meet me downstairs in the
same restaurant where he met Lindsay. Oh well, it
was too late now. I closed my eyes but that only
made it worse.

Finally the doors opened on Mr. Hardin's floor
and I hurried into the hall. Glass doors led to a
black-and-white marble floor reception area. Behind
a large wood desk sat a young woman in her early
twenties, with black hair and enough black eyeliner
to be seen from the International Space Station.

I told her my name and was told to have a seat in
one of the red and chrome chairs. A few minutes
later, I followed Mr. Hardin's assistant, a woman in
her fifties, her blonde hair graying at the temples,
down a hallway with purple walls and carpet. At the
end of the hall she ushered me into her boss's office
and left without another word.

"Good afternoon, Miss Murphy. Please have a
seat."

Mr. Hardin resembled the few pictures I found of
him on the web. He was six feet tall, bald, with
brown eyes. Not exactly the type I would have

expected Lindsay to supposedly be in love with. Everyone knew Barbie belonged with Ken, not Dr. Phil.

"Thank you, Mr. Hardin, for seeing me on short notice."

"Of course, any friend of Lindsay's so to speak."

Friends? Was he kidding? Evidently not. "Actually, I'm here to discuss the cases I'm working on."

"Yes, well, as I'm sure you know, I can't discuss my clients. Also, anything we discuss here I expect to be covered under a confidentiality agreement between us."

With that he slid two documents and a pen across the desk at me.

"Take your time. If you have any questions, don't hesitate to ask."

Boy, he wasn't joking. "Before I sign this I need you to understand two things. First, the only thing I'm interested in is clearing Lindsay's name. Second, if I find out anything the police need to know, I will take it straight to them."

"Good, then we're on the same page."

"Okay, so let's get to it." I pulled a notebook and pen from my purse. "I need to know where you were Tuesday from the time you got up until five o'clock in the afternoon."

"I was expecting that question. I got up at six in the morning, worked out, got ready for work. I spent about an hour in the office then headed to court. I was there for several hours then picked up Lindsay for a long lunch."

"Where did the two of you have lunch?" I asked.

136

"At Le Petite."

I looked up from the notebook. "Isn't that in the lobby of the Miami River Hotel?"

"Yes, it is, and to answer your next question, yes, we went upstairs for a little over an hour before returning to the building."

"Do you happen to have any proof that the two of you were together during the time of the victim's murder?"

"Yes." He opened the top desk drawer and pulled out several receipts. I took them from his hand. The receipts showed purchases at the hotel, the restaurant, and a gas station for the day and times but that didn't mean that one of them didn't slip off and kill Brian.

"So you and Lindsay were together that whole time?" I asked.

"Yes, Miss Murphy, and I've already given my statement to Detective Tompkins."

"Okay. What about your clients, Brian's friends? Any reason any of them would want him dead?"

"Now you know I'm bound by client-attorney privilege."

"Yes, I know, but I wouldn't be doing my job if I didn't try."

He chuckled. "I understand and I'm glad you're working hard to help Lindsay. She could never do anything like that. It's just preposterous."

"Yeah, it is. Thank you for your time." I stood up to go. "Oh, one last thing. Does your wife know about you and Lindsay?"

"No, and I have no intention of her finding out."

"Not now or not ever?"

"I think we're done, Miss Murphy."

Yeah, I kind of figured we were. During the elevator trip down to wonderful terra firma, I focused on what should be my next move. Since my office was as good a place to be as any I headed there to do some thinking. Inside, the machine was taking a message. I grabbed the phone and said hello but it was too late, the caller had hung up. I pushed play and was surprised to hear Brian's sister, Sara, leaving a message. She said she had to talk to me about her brother's murder. She claimed she couldn't go to the police and I was the only person she could talk to.

I called her back but, unfortunately, the call went to voice mail. After the way she had acted when I was at her mother's house, it didn't make sense she would want to talk to me. She had been dealing with the loss of her brother so that had possibly played a large part in her attitude. I never wanted to feel what she had been going through. I left a message for her to call me back. Since I had forgotten to charge my cell phone, again, I gave her my home number.

I pulled the prescription bottle and mangled picture out of the desk. Something about these things still bothered me. Why would Angie hide them? Did they have anything to do with Brian's and Adam's murders or Angie's disappearance?

The phone rang, jarring me from my thoughts. I put the items down and answered the phone. "Murphy Detective Agency."

"Yeah, this is Sara Lewis."

"Sara, how can I help you?"

"I need to talk to you about Brian."

"Okay, you can come to my office now if you'd like, or I could meet you somewhere."

"I can't now, I'm on my way to a client's."

"Well, you tell me what time is good for you."

"I'm working late, so is eight o'clock okay?"

"Sure, where?"

"My place, I have something to show you."

"That's fine."

She gave me her address and ended the call.

Somehow I must have earned her trust; that or she was so desperate she was willing to take a chance with me. Gee, wonder which it was? Not that it mattered. If she had information that could find her brother's killer, I'd be forever grateful, as would Lindsay. Okay, maybe not Lindsay, but I sure as heck would be.

Since I had dodged a certain client's calls for the past two days I figured that was one job I may as well get out of the way. I turned on the laptop and typed up a report, excluding the location of the meeting and the confessions of the other members of the group. I printed it up and wondered if I was taking the cowardly way out. I was and I was better than that. At least my parents always thought so. Instead of putting it in an envelope, I left it on the desk, grabbed the phone, and called her.

"Hello."

"Mrs. Pollowitz, it's Kim Murphy."

"Kim, it's nice to hear from you but I can't really talk right now. I'm on my way to the airport. My aunt passed away and my husband and I are leaving for the funeral."

139

"I'm so sorry."

"Thank you. She was in her eighties and had a wonderful life. So, how about I call you when I get back?"

"That'll be fine. Have a safe trip, and again, my condolences."

"Thanks."

Oh, thank God. I didn't have to tell her, at least not yet. My relief was short-lived. An old lady had died. Granted I hadn't known her, but she had loved ones who would miss her. I did a silent prayer for the deceased and her loved ones.

I leaned back in my chair and closed my eyes to consider my next move.

***

"Busy at work I see."

I jumped up and opened my eyes. Brandon was seated across from my desk; a grin on his face that looked a lot like Garfield's when he was presented with a pan of lasagna. "What are you doing here?"

"Nice to see you too."

"Sorry, I meant—"

"I know what you meant. I'm here because you seem to have forgotten something."

"Yeah, what was that?"

"You forgot to tell Tompkins I was at the restaurant with you."

"Oh crap. How did you find out?"

"Does it really matter? Don't you ever do something that stupid again!"

"It wasn't stupid. I was protecting you."

"And just who the hell was protecting you?"

"I don't need protection."

"Really? That's funny, 'cause you're the one with a target on your back."

"What are you talking about?"

"Angie's missing and you're one of the last people to see her."

"Oh, come on. No one believes I had anything to do with Angie's taking off. Do they?"

"Not seriously, no. We both know Tompkins won't ignore something that big. Or have you forgotten the last time?"

"No, I'll never forget that. Spending the night in jail was hell."

"I bet. So what do you think twenty to life will feel like?"

"Okay, I get it."

"Do you?"

"Yes."

"Good. So what's going on with our case?"

"Our case?"

"Yes. I'm involved whether you like it or not."

"Not."

"Too bad."

"If Dad or your boss find out, you're toast."

"Let me worry about that."

"Brandon..."

"Kim..."

"Agh. Fine." I put the empty pill bottle and picture on the desk in front of him.

"What's this?"

"Don't know."

"Where'd you get them?" he asked.

"You don't want to know."

"Yes, I do."

"No."

"Kim!"

"Okay, I may have found them in Angie's apartment."

"What? Are you crazy?"

"Stop yelling at me. I'm not crazy."

"You could have fooled me. Do you have any idea what you've done?"

"Look, it isn't as bad as it seems."

"Want to explain that?"

"Well, I went over to Angie's after she was a no-show at Max's Diner."

"Then what? Broke into her apartment?"

"No, the door was open."

"Oh, so you just let yourself in. Much better."

"Sarcasm much?"

"Stupid much?"

"Ouch."

"Too bad. All right, go on. You let yourself into Angie's apartment and…"

"It was small but very clean, like OCD clean."

"I hope you got more than that."

"Not really. I looked around. These were the only things I found that didn't seem to make sense. She was hiding them in a shoe box, under her bed."

"An empty pill bottle and a damaged photo? This sure isn't a heck of a lot to go on."

"I know."

"Is this all you've got?"

I chewed on my lower lip, debating if I should tell him about the phone call from Sara. I knew he'd be pissed if he found out about everything else, but I still didn't want him involved. He may not have been concerned about his well-being, but I sure as heck was.

"No, that's it." I tried looking him in the eye but couldn't quite do it so I stared at his nose.

"Okay, well, I've gotta go. If you find out anything else, give me a call. I don't want you doing something stupid on your own."

"So, if I'm going to do something stupid, you want to be there?" I laughed.

"You are such a pain."

That seemed to be a common opinion of me lately. "Right back at ya," I said.

He grabbed the pill bottle and put it in his pocket.

"Hey, what are you doing?"

"I have an idea. I'll let you know if it pans out."

"Brandon…"

"See ya." With that he was gone.

Brothers. Before he arrived I had two clues, now I was down by one. Not that it really mattered at this point. I was at whatever was worse than a dead end. The picture was too badly damaged to make out the faces of the people. The fancy clothes worn made it appear they were attending a party.

This was no help, at least as far as the case was concerned, but it had reminded me I needed a dress for my mom's party. Since I was my own boss I decided to give myself the rest of the day off so I could go shopping. I shut off the laptop then heard someone knocking on the front door. If it was Lindsay or that reporter, I wasn't going to answer the door. Instead, on my doorstep stood someone who could be an even bigger problem. I calculated the amount of money in my checking and savings accounts to see if a short vacation, taken immediately, was doable. Unless my dream vacation was spending several days in Cincinnati, it wasn't. I was stuck here. More out of curiosity than anything else, I opened the door and plastered on a smile.

"Sorry, I thought I had unlocked it."

"Oh, that's fine."

"So, how can I help you?" I asked.

"I was hoping we could go inside and talk."

"Oh yeah, of course, follow me."

In my office I motioned for her to have a seat. "I guess I should introduce myself, I'm Kim Murphy."

"Yes, and I'm Elizabeth Hardin."

"Well, Mrs. Hardin, what can I do for you?"

"This isn't easy to admit but I believe my husband is having an affair."

Oh, for the love of Hershey's. How the hell did I manage to get myself into these things? "Well, I'm…sorry about that, truly, but I'm…kind of busy right now. I can give you a list of agencies that would be able to help you."

I grabbed a Post It note and a pen then jotted down the information.

"Here," I said, handing her the paper. "You should be happy with any of these."

She looked at the paper then back at me. "I'd really prefer to hire you."

"Thank you, but, like I said, I can't really handle your case. I'm sorry." I tried to make eye contact so

144

she would not think I was lying, but she was staring at the crumpled picture on my desk. I picked up the picture and tucked it into the top drawer, then stood up. I hoped she would take the hint. She did.

"Well, thank you for your time and for the recommendations."

"Sure, no problem," I said, feeling like a jerk. I wanted to shout, "Hell yeah, your hubby's cheating on you," but I couldn't. Lindsay was my client and I had an obligation. I wouldn't break it, no matter how I personally felt.

I locked the door behind her and sighed in relief. That was just too close.

Since there was nothing more for me to do until I met with Sara tonight, I locked up the office then got into my car and headed straight for the Fairfield Mall. As much as I loved clothes, I usually avoided the malls thanks to my budget. But this was for my mom and I wanted to look nice, and if the dress emphasized my assets, then that was a bonus.

The clothes in my closet were all labeled a size six. Unfortunately, the first three stores I went into only went up to size four. If I'd been a size zero, there would have been plenty to choose from. Just exactly how many size zero women were there walking around? None, unless they were walking skeletons, in which case we had much bigger problems to worry about. Two hours and eight stores later I emerged from the mall with my purchases. Thanks to a thirty percent off sale I was able to buy new shoes and a purse to go with the green dress.

Back home, I hung the dress on the back of my

bedroom door then tucked the shoes and purse in my closet. It was six o'clock and my stomach gave a little friendly reminder it was empty. I grabbed the containers of leftover Chinese food out of the refrigerator and piled it onto a plate, stuck it in the microwave, and reached for a beer. I remembered my late meeting with Sara and switched to a Diet Pepsi.

When the food was ready I took it into the living room and sat on the couch. The news was on and, lucky me, I was just in time to see the stories about Brian's and Adam's murders. They showed a short clip that was taken in front of my apartment building. Surprisingly, my name was not mentioned in either story. Either God was looking out for me or someone a lot closer was. I was grateful for whoever was responsible. There wasn't anything about Angie's disappearance, so it seemed the police had managed to keep it from the press so far. That wouldn't last long. Once she was missing for forty-eight hours it would be released to the press. I wondered about her family. Would they ever see her again?

I finished dinner, washed the dishes, and took out the trash. Upstairs, I turned on the laptop and searched for information on Angie. Like other twenty-somethings she had a Facebook page. Angie had chosen a public setting, which meant anyone could look at her page, see her comments, and any pictures she posted. You could also see her list of friends and family, similar to Lindsay's. Though this wasn't safe, for my purposes I appreciated how easy it was to get information. I took out a notebook

146

and a pen and started jotting down notes. Inspiration struck and I did the same for Brian, Adam, David, Kevin, and even threw Sara in for good measure.

Though broken up, Angie and Brian were still on each other's list of friends. Both had also left their status as "in a relationship." So maybe they weren't as broken up as everyone had thought. Brian and group seemed to have a lot of the same friends and spent a great deal of time playing games. Each had friend lists that exceeded twelve hundred people. Jeez, I didn't think I knew twelve hundred people. I certainly wouldn't consider them all friends. Ahh, the life of a gamer. None of that was useful, but I was able to get contact information for several members of Angie's family. They were all local; one sister, two brothers, and a cousin. I jotted down the information on her list and moved on to Sara's profile. Her last update had been shortly after the police had informed her and her mother of Brian's death. She posted a picture of her and Brian when they were kids. As sad as that was, Adam's profile had brought tears to my eyes. He had the same large list of gaming friends but the only relative was a great-uncle out in Arizona.

My own profile had nearly a hundred family members. The friends list I had insisted contain only real friends was small, but the people on it were the ones I called when I wanted company, which, to me, was the point of friendship, but what the heck did I know.

David's and Kevin's profiles were similar to Brian's—a large list of friends and a scattering of family. The difference was where Kevin posted comments several times a day, David seemed to post updates no more than once a week.

I'd kept myself busy but all I'd learned was their favorite movies and video games. I'd also learned that David, Kevin, and Brian had all been proud enough to post their mug shot pictures on their accounts. Not exactly something I would have been eager to show to the world. Six months later and I was still grateful my interrogation with Grant never progressed to the booking and fingerprinting stage.

At the time I had avoided television, newspapers, and the web. Now out of some morbid curiosity I Googled my name. There must be quite a few more Kimberly Murphys in the world; if not, I was responsible for ten thousand articles. I exited the search without opening any of the sites. The last thing I needed was to dredge up all that crap.

I glanced at the clock. If I was going to meet Sara, I had to leave now to make it on time. I turned off the laptop and stuffed the papers in the desk drawer. I locked up and got in the car. Sara lived only a few blocks away from her mother. What a difference those blocks made. This side of town was low income housing. Most of the residents here were families struggling to make ends meet, good people in bad situations. Then there were the drug dealers and the users who would do whatever it took to get their drugs.

Street lights no longer worked on this block and the city wasn't in any hurry to have them fixed. What was the point? They wouldn't last twenty-four hours. This lower income section was at the north end of town, a few streets over and you were in

Dayton.

I parked in front of the dark apartment building and wondered how long my car would be safe on the street. There were six apartments in Sara's one-story building. Hers was on the end. I stepped over trash and abandoned toys to get to her front door. I knocked then waited. Televisions blared and several different food smells swirled around in the air. I knocked again. Just because I was on time didn't mean Sara wasn't running behind. Too bad that annoying voice in my head insisted this felt too much like the visit to Angie's place.

This was different, I told myself. Sara called me. She wanted to talk. Didn't she? This was stupid. I was letting the neighborhood and everything that had happened get to me. If Sara said she'd be here, she'd be here. I went back to my car to sit and wait. She'd be along any minute. *Yeah, right.* I spent the first minutes reading the romance book I had stuffed in my purse, glancing up every so often to see if Sara's light in the front window was on. No longer able to concentrate, I put the book back in my purse and tried listening to the radio. After another fifteen minutes, I pulled my phone out of my purse and tried Sara's number—no answer. I tried her mother's number and again no one answered.

A knock on the passenger window elicited a small scream. I looked over to see a face pressed to the glass. I lowered the window an inch. "What?"

"You gonna sit here all night?"

"Jeez, Brandon, what are you doing here?"

"Following you. If I'd known it would be so boring, I would have gone with the guys to play darts and drink beer."

"Then go do it."

"Are you gonna let me in or not?"

"Not."

"Funny. I guess I could go back to my truck and wait with Michael."

"You brought Michael? Are you insane?"

Brandon chuckled. "Look who's talking."

"You shouldn't have involved him. You know he'll rat me out to Dad."

"Thanks for the confidence," Michael said, his face joining Brandon's at the window.

"Hell," I muttered, flipping the locks open.

Brandon sat next to me while Michael sat in the backseat behind me.

"Aren't you afraid someone will steal your precious truck?" I asked Brandon.

"We're right here and the alarm is set."

"Oh, and you've never written up a report for a stolen car that had an alarm?"

"It's only five feet away."

"Well, it's so dark out there you can't see a few feet in front of you."

"Knock it off, Kim," Michael warned.

"So, what are you doing here?" I asked.

"Same as Brandon, trying to keep you out of trouble."

"Sorry, Kim, but it seems to have become a two-man job." Brandon chuckled.

"You both think you're so funny."

"We are. Right, Brandon?"

"You bet."

"Could the two of you shut up?"

"What's the matter? Your date stand you up?" Michael asked.

"Jeez, you must be pretty desperate to be picking up guys from down here," Brandon said.

"Actually, Mom is so worried the two of you won't find anyone, I was trolling for women for you."

"Now who thinks she's funny."

"Yeah, right, as if we can't find women for ourselves," Brandon said.

"You both forget. I've seen the type of girlfriends you bring home."

"Ouch. So, are we going to discuss the real reason you're here?" Michael asked.

"I have nothing to say to either of you."

"Kim, we all know it has something to do with the dead guy in your apartment," Michael said.

"He was not in my apartment!" I said through clenched teeth.

"Sorry, your neighbor's apartment. You're stuck with us so you might as well spill and tell us what you're up to. We'll figure it out anyway."

I hated to admit Michael was right, but he was. Seeing no harm in being honest, I explained to them how Sara had asked for me to meet her here to discuss her brother's case.

"So, where is she?"

"Jeez, Michael, don't you think if I knew that I wouldn't be sitting here having such stimulating conversation with the two of you?"

Brandon chuckled. "You two want to put on a pair of boxing gloves and go a few rounds?"

"No, it would be too embarrassing for Michael

when he goes back to work and admits he got beat up by his younger sister."

That got a chuckle out of them both.

"So let's try knocking on the door again," Michael suggested.

"Uh, hello, the light is still off," I said.

"Well, this chick is forty minutes late. Are you going to spend all night waiting?" Michael asked.

"No, but I don't think there's any point trying the door again. She isn't home."

"Or maybe she isn't able to answer."

Brandon had just expressed my greatest fear, at least the greatest fear this moment. What if the killer got to her? Before I could decide what to do, Michael got out of the car and walked toward Sara's door. Brandon and I looked at each other before following after him.

I got to the door and knocked. Surprise, surprise, there was no answer. My hand closed on the door knob and turned. The door opened and Michael grabbed my arm.

"You can't do that. You want to be charged with breaking and entering?"

"Technically it would just be entering."

"I can't watch you do this. Let go of the door."

"If you don't want to watch, leave."

"Hey, Kim, did you hear that?" Brandon asked.

"Hear what?"

"Someone calling for help. Don't you hear it?"

"Brandon, what is wrong with you?" Michael asked.

"Look, Michael, she's going to do this whether we're here or not. I'd rather she did it with us here to protect her. I get it, though. If you want to take off, take my truck. We'll meet up later."

"Just great, now you're becoming as reckless as Kim is."

"Hey, I'm not that bad."

"Excuse me, but could the two of you stop talking about me like I'm not here? Besides, all this talking is getting us nowhere. If Sara's in there hurt, we need to get her help."

"Fine, but I'm going in. You two wait out here," Michael growled.

Brandon and I stood listening for any sounds coming from inside the apartment. Michael returned, a grim look on his face.

"I'll call this in," he said.

"What? What is it? Is she in there?" I asked.

"No, but the place has been trashed. We'll need the tech geeks out here."

"Maybe she's just a bad housekeeper," Brandon offered.

"Nobody's that bad. The place has been searched and they didn't mind leaving a mess."

"Not again. That's what happened at Lindsay's place."

"Kim, whoever did this wasn't messing around. Give me your keys." Michael then turned toward Brandon. "Drive her home; I'll meet you guys there after I'm finished here."

"No," Brandon and I said in unison.

"The two of you can't be here."

I looked at Brandon and he nodded. "We're staying," I said.

Michael muttered something then stormed off to

call for help. With his back turned I figured this was my only chance to see for myself what had happened. I rushed in before either of them could stop me. I pulled a flashlight from my purse and turned it on. The apartment was not quite as small as Angie's but it had been decorated with pictures on the walls, an afghan on the back of the couch, and knickknacks on every flat surface. All of this seemed to have been done to chase away the drab feeling of the place. It would have worked if not for all the destruction. With nothing more to see I turned to leave and spotted a piece of paper sticking out from under the couch. I leaned down and picked it up.

"What the hell are you doing in there? Get your butt out of there now!" Michael shouted.

I stuffed the paper in my pocket and hurried out just in time to see two patrol cars pull up, followed by an SUV. I nearly fainted when my dad stepped out of the vehicle and headed straight for us. "Oh, dear sweet buttercream, we're in so much trouble."

"What do you mean, we?" Brandon asked.

"Both of you, shut up and let me do the talking."

"But, Michael…"

"I mean it, shut up."

"So I was just about to head home to spend what was left of my evening with your mother, when I get a call that not one, but three of my children are at a crime scene. Someone care to explain what the devil is going on here?"

"It was me. I called in a break-in."

"Correct me if I'm wrong, but aren't you off duty tonight?"

"Yes, sir, but as you taught us, if there is evidence of a crime, we must secure the scene and call it in and wait until assistance arrives."

"Well, you got me there, but that doesn't explain what the three of you are doing here."

"Yes, well, you see…"

"It's my fault, Dad."

"Shut up, Kim," Michael said.

My dad raised his hand and looked away. He turned around and headed straight for one of the officers standing by Sara's door. After a brief conversation, he returned.

"We're going to finish this conversation at home. Let's go."

"Yes, sir," Brandon said, speaking for the first time since our dad arrived.

Brandon and Michael drove together, following behind the SUV. I brought up the rear, following behind the two of them. I knew my dad was mad.

At my parents' house, my brothers and I took seats in the living room and waited. I could hear my mom and dad talking but could not make out the words. A few minutes later they entered the room together. They sat on the couch and my mom nudged my father.

"Okay, I'm ready to listen."

I looked at my mom; she smiled and nodded at me. That was all it took. I told them everything, from the moment Lindsay banged on my door, the first time, to what happened tonight. Well, almost everything, I neglected to mention my going into Angie's apartment. I didn't think that little detail needed to be shared with anyone, certainly not with

155

my parents. The whole time I talked I stared at my hands, folded in my lap. I stopped talking and looked up at my dad. I could have sworn his eye twitched. I waited for a response. There were a few minutes of silence, then he asked my brothers and mom to wait in the kitchen for a few minutes. Brandon and Michael moved so fast they looked like jets taking off from an aircraft carrier. My mom, however, stayed right where she was.

"Sweetheart, I think it would be best if I spoke with Kimberly alone."

"I'm sorry, but I disagree."

Oh no, I did not want my parents to have a disagreement over me. "It'll be okay, Mom, I'll be fine."

"Of course you will, Kimberly, your father and I want nothing but the best for you."

My father sighed. If it was obvious to me, then it had to be to him as well—my mom wasn't going anywhere.

"Yes, well, I know that you've been hired to look into Brian Lewis's murder, but this is Detective Tompkins's case. Now I don't want any more interference from you. Is that understood?"

"Yes, sir."

"Now, dear, she's been hired to do a job, and it isn't her fault if she and this detective of yours are running into each other, so to speak, while doing it."

"Yes, but she isn't a cop."

"I know, but six months ago, that…monster would have gotten away with…"

My mom shuddered and looked up at the ceiling as if seeking assistance from a higher power. My

156

dad reached over and clasped her hands. A smile passed between them.

"If not for Kimberly that monster would have been walking around, free to hurt more people."

"I know and I'm grateful, but she also put herself in harm's way. I'm sure neither of us wants that again."

"Of course, but every day people I love go to work and put their lives on the line for people they don't know. It is something I've learned to live with."

What she hadn't said was all those *people* were men.

My dad looked at me and back at my mom. "Okay, I understand."

"Good, now I'm going into the kitchen and check on the boys."

After she left my dad gave me a friendly reminder of what was acceptable and what wasn't for a private investigator. He also made me promise to be careful and ask for help if I needed it. I promised and was grateful when the lecture was over. He stood up and gave me a hug.

We walked into the kitchen and found my brothers stuffing their faces with leftover parmesan chicken, pasta, and warm bread my mom had reheated for them. She offered me a plate and for once I actually declined. From the shocked expressions on everyone's faces you would have thought I never turned down food in my life. Okay, well, maybe this was a first.

"After you're all done here, I want you to go to the station and fill out reports about what happened tonight," my dad said.

It didn't take long for Brandon and Michael to finish off the pile of food and then we were off to the police station. The whole drive over, all I could think was please, please don't run into Grant. My brothers and I were out of there in twenty minutes, and Grant was nowhere in sight. Yay.

"Well, it's been fun," Brandon said.

"I can't believe I wasted my evening."

"You know, if you two hadn't followed me, none of this would have happened."

"You're blaming us?" Michael asked.

"Yes. No, no, I just meant if you hadn't followed me, I wouldn't have had to get a lecture from Dad and I wouldn't have had to come here to fill out reports that could have been done at the scene."

"You are unbelievable."

"Michael, she's sort of right. I mean, she didn't ask us to go with her."

"Jesus, you," he said, pointing at me, "are a bad influence. Brandon, don't get involved in any more of her messes."

"Thanks, Michael, I'll remember that the next time you need help," I said.

Michael stormed off and got into Brandon's truck.

"It'll be okay. You know Michael, he's a hothead. After he cools off, he's gonna feel real bad about what he said. You'll see." Brandon gave me a quick hug then walked to his truck. I climbed into my car and started the engine. I smiled as I watched them leave the lot. No matter how angry, they hadn't left until they were sure my car started.

It felt so good to be home. Inside, I headed straight for the freezer and the pint of mint chocolate chip ice cream I had bought at Wal-Mart. Thankfully, its time in the frozen rectangle had restored the minty goodness after its melting in the parking lot. I grabbed a spoon, kicked off my shoes, and curled up on the couch. When the container was empty I set it on the coffee table and grabbed the phone. I called Sara's number and got her voice mail, again. I left another message, adding the part about the break-in at her apartment. I asked her to call me as soon as she got the message.

With that there was nothing else to do, at least for now. It had been a long day and it was time to call it quits. I tossed the container in the trash and the spoon in the sink, and then headed upstairs for bed. I stripped out of my clothes and pulled a men's large Scooby-Doo t-shirt over my head, spent a few minutes in the bathroom, then crawled under the covers.

My head had just hit the pillow when the doorbell rang. I didn't move and hoped whoever it was went away. I was in no mood to deal with anyone. When the doorbell rang again, I threw off the covers and stomped my way down the stairs.

I threw open the door and yelled, "What?"

"Are you going to invite me in?" Grant asked.

"No."

"You've got such nice manners."

"Grant, I'm tired and cranky. Plus, every time I turn around there you are. It's annoying. So just say whatever you were going to say and leave."

"I'm worried about you."

"I can take care of myself."

"Hah."

"I can, and you could have called and saved yourself a trip."

"If I'd called, I wouldn't have been able to see you in your Scooby shirt."

"Don't dis Scooby."

"I wouldn't dare. I was just trying to decide if you were Daphne or Velma."

"Wow, and what did you decide?" I asked.

"You're like a spicy combo platter. You've got the Daphne hotness and Velma's brains but sadly you've also got Fred's whacky schemes on how to solve a case."

I hated to admit that my nipples tingled at the hotness and the brains comment but then he just had to go and blow it. I certainly didn't go around town setting up traps for people. The little voice in my head begged to differ. I quietly told it to stay out of it.

"Well, I guess I should go so you can get some rest," he said after I yawned.

"Good idea," I said while the voice was back and calling me a liar. "Shut up."

"Excuse me?" Grant was looking at me like I imagined I looked at prunes.

"Sorry, just talking to myself."

"Okay." Grant lifted his hand and brushed a strand of hair from my face. Our eyes locked and I held my breath. "You are so infuriating, and yet I can't stop thinking about you."

I sighed. "Wait. What?"

"I have to go." He leaned down and placed a kiss

on my forehead. He then placed one on each cheek. My skin burned in the places his lips touched. My hands ached to trace along each and every inch of his preferably naked body.

He turned and walked away. I could have sworn I heard him muttering something about another damned cold shower. Good, I hoped he was as frustrated as I was.

CHAPTER NINE

Thursday

The next morning, I was jarred awake by something the radio station insisted was music. To me it just sounded a lot like chain saws, dental tools, and the lawn guy's leaf blower. I turned the alarm off and considered staying in bed. After Grant left I eventually fell asleep and was plagued with nightmares. In the light of morning I couldn't remember them and for that I was grateful. I jumped out of bed and got dressed in workout clothes, making sure to put my favorite sports bra on underneath. With a 36C chest there was no way I was going to exercise without one. I rushed down the stairs, grabbed my purse, and took off for Lakeview Gym.

Over the next hour, I was tortured by several evil machines. I wasn't sure who the lying piece of crud was who had claimed some bull about endorphins. I did know if I ever got my hands on him, I'd beat the crap out of him. I assumed it had to be a guy because, let's face it, a woman wouldn't lie to other women about something that important. As I walked toward my car I wondered just how many calories I'd burn beating his sorry ass up.

Back home, I took a quick shower before getting dressed and putting my hair up in a ponytail holder. Before leaving I took a few minutes to apply lipstick and mascara. Not satisfied with the results, I went ahead and finished putting on my face. At the office I headed straight for the small kitchen. It was eight o'clock and I was desperate for caffeine. Not in a hurry to start the workday, I stood staring at the coffee maker, willing it to work faster. Finally, I filled my mug and walked into my office, flipping on lights as I went.

Settled as comfortably as possible in a desk chair, I flipped on the computer to find out what was happening in the world, or at least my little part of it. While I'd slept there'd been a garage fire, two driving under the influence, otherwise known as drunk driving arrests, and a domestic disturbance call. Not bad for a Wednesday night.

Lindsay's idea that because she was getting her apartment back meant the whole thing was over for her was just stupid. She should have been asking her lawyer boyfriend about what happened next. Though I doubted they did a whole lot of talking. An image I fervently wished I could push the delete button on popped into my head. I just hoped it wouldn't start a vomiting marathon. At the very least I wasn't likely to eat anything for at least a whole hour.

"So, this is what the private investigator, busy at

work, looks like."

"Mr. Abraham, what are you doing here?"

"Kim, you know what I want."

"That's Miss Murphy to you and what I want is you gone."

"Is that any way to treat the guy who's been helping you?"

"You must be delusional if you think following me around and badgering me is helping."

"We both have jobs to do. I don't see why we can't help each other."

I stood up and pointed at the door. "I'll agree to help a reporter the day Paris Hilton earns a PhD."

"Funny, can I quote you on that?"

"Get the hell out of my office."

"Or what, you'll call the cops? I can't imagine you'd want their help at the moment."

"You'd be surprised at what I'd do."

"Oh really, do tell."

"Get out!" I reached for the phone.

"Okay, okay, I get it. You don't have to make this so hard."

"I'm dialing."

"Fine. Just remember me when you're ready to talk."

"Sure, you'll be the first one I call."

Without another word, he turned and left. I guessed he didn't appreciate sarcasm. I grabbed my mug and headed for the kitchen. Skipping breakfast had been a mistake. My stomach growled and I wished I had stopped at McDonald's on my way into the office. A quick look at the clock and I groaned. Breakfast was only available for one more minute. Not even with my driving could I manage that. If Abraham hadn't shown up, I could have made it in time for a Sausage McMuffin, yet another reason to dislike him. On the plus side, I could get a Big Mac, fries, and a large Diet Coke. When my stomach growled again I took it as a sign I was meant to go.

Round trip took eight minutes, five of which were spent in line. The smell of fries had been too tempting to wait. I dug into the bag while the nice drive-thru lady was warning me they were hot. I would sure as hell hope they were. Cold fries were disgusting.

With my breakfast of lunch foods over, it was time to get to work. Since I was getting nowhere on Brian's and Adam's murders, I needed a break. I also needed to do a job that would pay the bills. I had a small cushion in the bank but refused to touch it unless there was an emergency. Some women spent a fortune on shoes but I preferred to spend my money on a new gun. A girl could never have too many Glocks, or maybe that was just me. I opened the file cabinet and pulled out a sheet of paper filed under A for Mrs. Janet Mitchell-Weaver-Evans-Adkinson. I grabbed my purse and headed out.

I got in my car and entered the addresses into Mapquest on my phone. It was maybe less efficient than putting the info into the GPS but I feared hearing that voice one too many times would cause me to take out my gun and shoot it. My trip ended on the east side of Lakeview in one of the more affluent neighborhoods. In other words, these people had bought mini mansions on lots the size of

165

an iPhone. Sure the miniscule lots meant less yard work, but spending that much money on a house and being able to shake hands with the neighbors without even having to leave it was just plain stupid.

I parked several houses away from my target and did a silent prayer I'd be done before someone called the cops on me. To help sell my innocent vibe I grabbed my cell phone and pretended to talk. Ever since Ohio passed the law making it basically illegal to use a cell phone while you were driving, more and more people were pulling over to take calls and texts. I had done a bit of research and found out the lady I was watching had been married for twenty years—to four different guys. Each one had been more successful or wealthy than the one before. It seemed much like Maria. This lady slept with and married any guy with a big enough bank account and a working penis. The last part was purely conjecture on my part. Despite the heat I shivered. The last thing I wanted to be thinking about was anybody else's sex life, especially when my own had been rather bleak for longer than I would have admitted out loud.

It wasn't long before my target made an appearance. Dressed in a purple sweat suit and gym shoes, Janet got behind the wheel of her bottle green Jaguar and zipped out of the driveway without a glance my way. I tossed the cell phone onto the passenger seat, started the car, and turned around in the nearest driveway.

On the freeway I had a habit of considering speed limit signs as merely suggestions. In neighborhoods with kids and pets likely to dart out I considered them the law. Which, of course, they were, but I actually treated them that way. As Janet zoomed through her neighborhood it didn't appear she considered others in her rush to wherever the hell it was she was going. I said a quick prayer to God, Jesus, and Mary before stepping on the gas pedal. Asking all three was a bit extreme but I figured it couldn't hurt.

We drove through town, turning left and right until finally Janet pulled into the parking lot of a hotel just over the city line in Deer Creek. At one time Deer Creek had lived up to its name. Now, thanks to all the construction projects over the past fifteen years, the deer had been forced to live in a small area to the south or had been driven out completely.

The hotel Janet walked into had fireplaces in the suites and offered real food for room service. This was about as far as you could get from one of those dumps that charged by the hour.

I parked close enough to have a view of her car and prepared myself to wait for her return. In recent months I had made several attempts to get inside the hotel and get information about their guests. Now, my picture, taken by an employee with a cell phone, was posted at the front desk. It had been strongly suggested I not return as anything other than a paying guest or I would be arrested for trespassing. I figured as long as I stayed in the car I wasn't committing any crimes. At least I sure as hell hoped not.

A large part of my job required patience, not

exactly something I was particularly known for. Just ask my friends and family. Though when tied to keeping me supplied with Hershey's chocolate, a roof over my head, or my very existence, I could somehow manage it. I rolled down all the windows before shutting off the engine. I grabbed my iPod from my purse prepared to settle in. If it was a quickie, I figured that would give me twenty minutes or so to enjoy the awesomeness that was Kelly Clarkson. If they actually bothered to have a conversation, then I could *enjoy* the free sauna in my car. I was so glad I'd spent time putting on makeup this morning.

Fifty-five minutes and two bottles of water later, Janet and an older gentleman exited the hotel. I grabbed my camera and was able to get several nice shots of the two of them swapping spit in front of the hotel. Nice, but I had to swallow the urge to gag. Though Janet wouldn't be carded for cigarettes ever again, this guy was old enough to be her father, or worse, grandfather. Yuck. I stuffed my iPod and Racy Red nail polish into my purse and started my car, grateful to once again have air conditioning. I even welcomed the blast of hot air that shot out of the vents, knowing that soon it would feel like a winter day. Awesome.

Janet's next stop was only three blocks away. She parked in front of the dry cleaners and went inside, returning a few minutes later with an armful of clothes. Once again I was able to get several shots of her. Next Janet and I parked in the lot of a local organic grocery store that charged three times the price for a gallon of milk than my local Wal-

Mart. I had made the mistake once of running into their sister store near my apartment, desperate for a can of mushrooms. Sadly my spaghetti sauce seemed lonely and sad without them. There was no way in hell I'd pay eight dollars for ten ounces when I normally paid a dollar fifty.

This time I parked under a tree that was kind enough to provide shade, and, as an added bonus, a small breeze kept me from baking in the car. Janet returned pushing a half-filled cart in half the time she had spent inside the hotel. This was going so much better than I'd thought it would. Before returning home, Janet went next door to the smoothie shop and got herself a treat. I hoped she enjoyed it because once my client got these pictures she'd need to add a bit of alcohol to that smoothie, though I wasn't sure she'd be able to afford it soon. Not my problem, I reminded myself.

Back at her house, I got another dozen pictures of Janet carrying grocery bags and a case of bottled water into her house. It had been so kind of her to leave the garage door open. I'd have to remember to thank her. Huh, probably not. My client would be thrilled. Janet had supposedly slipped and fell in a jewelry store and *injured* her back. At least that's what her lawsuit had claimed. I'd been hired by the jeweler's insurance company and attorneys to get proof she was quite capable of lifting heavy items and running her own errands. My pictures would prove her claim of being unable to lift anything heavier than a hair dryer was a lot of hot air.

"Hey, what do you think you're doing?"

I jumped at the booming voice coming from a

man who would have to use a step ladder to reach the top shelf in my kitchen cabinet. So did I, but, well, I wasn't a guy. I pressed the buttons and rolled up the windows. Though he couldn't do anything about his height, he could have chosen something other than a red track suit and an absolutely horrendous toupee.

"Hey, I'm talking to you." He tapped on the glass window as if I hadn't heard his yelling. "You can't take pictures of people's houses. I'm calling the cops."

Since he was leaning against my car, I couldn't drive off. A bit of diplomacy seemed in order. I rolled the driver's side window halfway down and politely informed him I was not breaking the law.

"That's bull. Give me that camera!"

There was no way I was about to hand over what could possibly be my only chance at catching Janet in her lies. I turned the key and started the car. He grabbed the car handle and tried to open the driver's side door. With the car still in park, I gunned the engine, hoping to scare him off. Mr. Nosy Napoleon Complex's shouts drew the attention of several neighbors, including Janet. I put the car in gear but he refused to let go of the handle. It took several seconds to do the math in my head to see if my driver's license could handle the points I'd get for running over this idiot's foot. To my dismay I had way too many points to risk my license for the momentary satisfaction I'd get.

Unsure of my next move, I looked around and spotted a group of neighbors huddled close by, taking in the commotion. Desperate to get out of there, I released the door locks and shoved my door into Mr. Nosy Napoleon, knocking him back just enough that he let go of the door handle. If I was careful there was just enough room for me and my car to squeeze through. It should have worked, and would have if a giant tanned wall of a human hadn't taken advantage of the unlocked door and plopped into the passenger seat, knocking my camera onto the floor. I grabbed the camera, took out the memory card and put it in the only safe place I could think of—my bra.

"Get the hell out of my car!"

"Not until you tell us what you're doing in our neighborhood," said the giant man.

He reached over and tried to take the key from the ignition. I tried slapping his hand away but was about as successful as a Prius driver playing chicken with an eighteen wheeler. As I was fighting with Mr. Humungous my door opened and hands grabbed at me. My elbow connected with Mr. Humungous' nose. The giant intruder let go of the key and put both hands to his nose.

"Oh man, I'm bleeding."

Hesitant hands became aggressive and yanked me from my seat.

"Get out. I don't want you bleeding inside my car."

Suddenly I was spun around and shoved against the side of my car. Mr. Nosy Napoleon along with several others stood in front of me. A gentleman dressed in jeans and a t-shirt held me fast to my car.

"Get your hands off of me!"

"Don't let go of her. The cops are on the way."

"Let go of me, or I'm having you arrested for assault."

"The only one getting arrested for assault is you," said Mr. Nosy Napoleon.

"I didn't do anything."

"You hit me in the nose."

I turned my head and was grateful Mr. Humongous was doing his bleeding outside of my car. "I'm sorry. That was an accident. You know you should really put some ice on that."

"Oh, right. Thanks."

I blanched and turned back around, much more willing to face an angry crowd than watch blood drip from that guy's nose. Though to be fair, I wasn't sure three people qualified as a crowd. Figuring the best thing to do was to not resist and remain quiet. The police would arrive soon and then I'd be on my way. I hoped.

"What the hell were you doing taking pictures of our houses?" Mr. Nosy Napoleon asked.

Instead of answering, I glared at him, and was pleased when he flinched.

"She put the memory card in her bra," said Mr. Humongous.

"Give it to me," Mr. Nosy Napoleon demanded.

I laughed. "Not a chance."

Unhappy with my answer, he reached forward as if to get it himself. "Try it buddy and I'll knock your teeth out."

A woman with gray hair and purple eye shadow that matched her shirt smiled and waved at me. I liked her.

Before Mr. Nosy could touch me, he was yanked

backward and a familiar voice said, "Try it and I'll lock you up for sexual assault."

"You can't do that. I've done nothing wrong," Mr. Nosy Napoleon sputtered.

Why oh why wasn't there a zombie apocalypse when you needed one? I looked around, desperately searching for a zombie or a hungry werewolf. Hell, I'd have even settled for a cranky Chihuahua, but, alas, it was not to be. Instead, I suffered the humiliation of being rescued by Brandon and Grant.

"You need to step back. Now."

"No way. We caught her taking pictures of our homes. She's probably going to come back at night and rob us or kill us in our sleep. Besides, who the hell are you?" said Mr. Nosy Napoleon.

"I'm Detective Tompkins and this is Officer Murphy. Now, if I have to tell you again to get your hands off of her, you'll be wearing a set of cuffs and explaining to your lawyer why you disobeyed an order from the police."

In Nosy Napoleon's haste to get as far away from me and, I assumed, Grant, he trampled over two of his neighbors.

"Finally. Now all of you go on back to your houses. We've got this," said Brandon.

Not ready to admit defeat, Mr. Nosy Napoleon shouted, "We have a right to know what she's doing here."

"If your only complaint is she took pictures from the street, then she didn't break any laws. If she had trespassed on your property, that would have been different, and I don't think any of you are saying she did that. Are you?" Grant asked, staring directly at Mr. Nosy Napoleon.

"No, but she did break his nose."

Everyone turned to look at Mr. Humungous, whose nose, I was grateful to observe, no longer leaked the gooey red gunk like a faucet from a horror movie.

"Nope, it's all cool. The bleeding's stopped. Besides, it's my fault. I never should have scared the little lady."

I didn't think I'd ever been called *little lady* in my life. I wasn't sure if it was a compliment or an insult. Either way, he wasn't going to press charges so I would just take the win.

"Now that that's all settled, everyone can go back to their business. Have a nice day," said Brandon.

After a few mumbles and grumbles the small crowd dispersed. I even waved a cheery goodbye to Mr. Nosy Napoleon, who glared in return. Oh well.

"Thank you, both, but I don't want to talk about this."

"Jeez, Kim, what the hell?"

"Brandon, what part of don't want to talk about it did you have trouble with?"

"The don't part."

"Hey, wait a minute. What are you doing on duty? It's daytime."

"Figured that out on your own, did ya?"

As an answer to his question, I glared at him.

"I switched with one of the guys for the rest of the week. That way I can be off for Mom's party."

"I don't want to hold you up so you can go now."

"Lighten up. We did just save you from an angry mob."

"Oh please, that group of uptight, loaded snobs. They would have probably stuffed me in a track suit and tried to force lemongrass or foie gras on me."

Brandon chuckled. "I don't know, the short guy looked tough."

"Please, if I'd wanted to, I could have sent him home crying to Mommy or his wife or maybe his maid. The guy was a jerk," I said. "So, what are the two of you doing here together?"

"Saving your ass," Grant replied.

"Well my ass and I were just fine, thank you very much."

"Gross. I'm outta here. Try to stay out of trouble." Brandon slung his arm over my shoulder and whispered, "Be nice."

Brandon got into his police cruiser and took off.

"I guess I'll be going too. See ya." I turned to leave but Grant stepped to the side, blocking my car door.

"Not yet. We've got to talk."

"I can't imagine we have anything to talk about." I tried to ignore how my pulse had suddenly picked up.

"For starters, you can thank me for saving your, as you put it, nice ass." He glanced down at said ass and back up, waiting for a response from me.

"I did, didn't I?"

"It was pretty pathetic."

"Fine. Thank you, Detective Tompkins. How's that?"

"Better, I guess. What are you doing here?"

"My job," I said, trying to ignore just how close we were standing.

"Does your job include pissing people off?"

"Unfortunately it's in the job description, somewhere between prying into other people's business and spending hours in my car taking pictures of people."

"Then you're in the right job. You have a natural ability to piss people off."

"Not always."

"You always get me angry."

"Maybe it's just you."

"No way. Most people find me easygoing and quite good-looking as well."

"Oh, is that all the guys you arrest, or just the special ones?" I asked, not wanting to admit my own opinions of his looks. The man was arrogant enough already.

Grant frowned.

"Although, I'm sure some of the ladies you arrest would love to have you strip search them."

Grant's eyes locked onto mine. For a brief moment I forgot how to breathe as an image of Grant and me naked popped into my head and wouldn't go away. Especially when he leaned down, his warm breath brushing against my ear.

"Don't worry, Kim, I'll make sure there's a female officer to handle yours."

"Asshole!" I tried to push him away but the big jerk didn't even budge an inch.

I had an urge to remove the smug look on his face. The only thing that kept my hands at my sides was the very real fear he would carry out his threat.

176

The thought of getting felt up by a female officer didn't do anything for me, but the thought of Grant handling the task got me tingling in all the right places, though I'd admit that the day one of my brother's won the Miss Universe Pageant.

"No, thanks, but there is one guy there who could definitely give me one. Hell, it might even be worth making a false confession to get some alone time with him."

Grant pushed me backward so I was once again being held against my car, only this time I didn't seem to mind as much. Several body parts were interested in a bit more bodily contact.

"Don't even think about it."

"Why? What do you care?"

"If anyone is going to strip search you, it's going to be me."

Of course my cell phone chose that moment to ring.

"You should get that," Grant said, taking a step back in more than just the physical meaning.

"It can wait."

"Go ahead."

He moved a couple feet away and I knew that whatever else he had been about to say was now safely tucked away. I'd never get it out of him now, short of an interrogation room and a pair of handcuffs. Ignoring the thrill the image of Grant in handcuffs gave me, I grabbed my phone from my pocket and answered. "Hello."

"I have a job for you."

"Dimitri Fortunato, are you so busy you can't waste time on hello?"

"Hello, Kim. Is that better?"

"Much. What's up?"

"I have a job for you tonight. It pays fifty bucks," Dimitri said.

"Fifty?"

"Okay, okay, a hundred."

"What is it?" I asked.

"I've got another cheater. What else?"

"Just the thought of some loser hanging on me makes me want to take a shower in hand sanitizer," I said.

"Okay, one fifty and that's as high as I can go," Dimitri said.

"What about your regular girls?"

"He only goes for brunettes. I've got a blonde and a redhead. My brunette can't do it 'cause the babysitter had to have her appendix removed last night."

"Ouch."

"Well, it's pretty bad timing for me. So, will you do it?"

"Sure."

"Great. I'll meet you at Indiscretions at eight."

"A strip club? No way."

"Don't forget to wear something slutty."

"Dress slutty how?" I asked, but it was too late, he had already hung up. I looked up and found Grant staring at me. "What?"

"Nothing." He raised his hands and stepped back.

"If we're done, I'm out of here."

"Sure."

I opened the car door and slid behind the wheel.

"Hey."

"Yeah?"

"Short, tight, and see-through." With that he turned and strode off to his car.

Instead of going back to the office I went home. With my evening assignment I had to do a quick check of my closet to see if I had anything that could be considered slutty. I parked in the back and tried not to stare at Lindsay's apartment. If I hadn't known better, I would have sworn the thing was taunting me. I shook my head at my brief trip to Insanity Station and walked into my apartment. Upstairs, I dumped my purse and keys onto the bed. I opened the closet door and stared, not seeing anything that resembled what Grant had suggested. My everyday wardrobe consisted of comfort clothes made up of t-shirts and jeans. For dress up I did have several nice dresses deemed appropriate by my family. I even had a sexy number that had received my friends' seals of approval, but I was missing the slutty factor.

I hesitated briefly before grabbing my cell phone and punching in speed dial number one. A male voice answered on the second ring. "Richie residence."

"Hi, Elijah, it's Kim. Is her highness available?"

He chuckled. "How are you today, Miss Kim?"

"No worse than usual. How about you?"

"Just fine and dandy. Wait just a moment while I get her."

I waited while Melissa's combination housekeeper, chef, personal assistant, bodyguard, and chauffer bravely invaded her office where she was enjoying killing people off while her other characters were busy getting laid in ever explicit and glorious detail. The latter was why I had called her for her assistance. Though if I ever decided to go on a killing spree, she'd also be the person I called for advice.

A few minutes of silence was broken by the sound of my best friend shouting, "Hell yeah, I want to talk to her."

There was a muffled sound and then Melissa said into the phone. "What's wrong?"

"Hello to you too," I said.

"I repeat, what's wrong?"

"Just because I'm calling during your self-imposed 'do not disturb because I'm on a deadline' time, doesn't mean anything is wrong," I replied.

"While it's the beginning of my day, you, I assume, have been a busy little investigator so I know there is something important going on in that adorably obnoxious head of yours. So spill it."

"I am not *adorably obnoxious*. I don't even think that makes sense."

"Trust me, sweetie, it does. So what do you need help with? Fess up," she said.

"Fine. I do need your help."

"Ha."

"I have a job to do tonight and I need your advice," I said.

"Ask away."

"I have to dress slutty."

"Okay, are we talking hooker slutty or desperate single and approaching thirty slutty?"

"Melissa…"

180

"Okay, okay, don't twist your panties up. Well, you can forget finding anything in that thing you insist is a closet. Ooh, I've got it. When do you need this?"

"I need to be at Indiscretions at eight."

"Perfect. I'll meet you at your place at six."

"Thanks."

"No problem. I love playing dress up. Bye."

With Melissa taking care of the evening's attire, I was freed up to go back to the office and accomplish something, namely work for my client. I had to take a moment to appreciate the fact that I had a friend who didn't ask a bunch of stupid questions or judge me, she just started handling it. That was awesome.

I stuck the cell phone in my purse and grabbed the keys. I drove back to the office actually excited at the prospect of getting real work done. It seemed forever since I had felt like I had accomplished something. At my desk I flipped on the computer and removed the memory card from my cleavage. It was with a great amount of restraint that I refrained from getting up and doing a happy dance when the images of Janet appeared on the screen. They were fantastic. I printed out four sets of pictures. Two were going to the lawyer and the store owner, while I kept one for my own records. Inspired on the drive over, the last set, containing only the photos taken at the hotel, would be sent to Janet's current husband.

Janet hadn't limited herself to just cheating on her husband. She had gone beyond that when she'd filed a bogus lawsuit. Cheating of any kind had a

181

way of pissing me off. I always rooted for them to get caught, even when I was just a kid playing Candy Land with my sister. When I'd found out the sack of crap I'd married was cheating on me, I hadn't realized at the time he'd actually done me a huge favor. If I hadn't caught him cheating, I may have still been married to him. I shuddered at the thought. Though it had hurt like hell at the time to find he had continued to date other women after we said "I do," it turned out to be for the best. One day when I didn't feel like ripping his nuts off and feeding them to the neighbor's pit bull, I'd have to thank him.

In hindsight, I should have suspected something. For the whole three years we were together I never once had to worry about buying condoms. He had seemed to have an endless supply of the things and had always insisted on wearing one, even after we were married. For that I was truly grateful. If he had given me a sexually transmitted disease, they would have never found his body.

I stuffed the three sets of pictures into large envelopes and addressed the one for Janet's husband to his work address. With all of that done, I pulled the file on Lindsay and once again went over everything I'd jotted down about what had happened since finding Brian's body in Lindsay's apartment several days ago. I had hoped going over my notes would jog my brain, bring some small detail into focus and help this whole thing make sense.

It worked sometimes so I figured I'd give it a try. Twenty minutes of reading and rereading resulted in absolutely nothing. Frustrated, I stuffed the file in my desk drawer and decided to walk to McDonald's for inspiration in the form of a vanilla milkshake and french fries—a perfect combination for getting the brain cells working again. I stuck the memory card into my purse and made the short walk to McDonald's and back.

Once again seated at my desk, I took the crumpled picture I'd found under Angie's bed out of the desk drawer. The longer I looked at it the more I felt like I was missing something, something obvious, but I couldn't, no matter how hard I tried, figure out what the hell it was.

Disappointed my guaranteed, never to fail inspiration method had indeed failed, I put the picture in the file and locked it in the file cabinet. There was nothing else for me to do so I decided to call it a day. I dropped the envelopes into the mailbox on my way home.

Figuring the night would be a late one, I crawled into bed and set the alarm. Two hours later I turned off the squawking sound, grateful to be awake and away from the bad dream that was thankfully already slipping from my memory.

In the bathroom I stripped out of my clothes and got into the shower. Though I wasn't sure why I was bothering showering. I was pretty sure after spending the evening at a strip club I'd feel the need for several gallons of hand sanitizer. After my shower I slipped into a robe, dried my hair, and put on makeup. I was just finishing up the mascara when the doorbell rang.

Having finally learned my lesson, I remembered

to look through the peephole before opening the door. All I saw was what appeared to be a white trash bag and fire engine red nails that looked more like talons than human fingernails used on a computer keyboard every day.

I opened the door and was suddenly surrounded by the scent of White Diamonds perfume and Melissa's commentary of how long it took her to find just exactly what she had been looking for. The bags I had mistaken for trash bags turned out to be garment bags.

"After we pick out your outfit we'll do your makeup."

"I already did it."

"Oh please, that's way too understated for these outfits."

"Wait, how many outfits did you buy?"

"Just a few. Relax, I'll return anything we don't use."

"We?"

"Yes, we. Did you think I was going to send you out in the world all slutified and alone?"

"Slutified is not a word, and, besides, I'm working."

"First, it's a word because I just made it up, and second, of course you're working, duh. So let's get started, shall we?"

"Melissa…"

"Come on, let's get upstairs. This is going to take some time."

Resigned to the fact I'd be dragging my best friend to a strip club and have her watch while I came on to some guy, I followed her upstairs and filled her in on our evening plans.

"Sounds exciting. This could be excellent research for a book, which means I could write off the cost of the clothes."

"I plan on paying you for them."

"Don't even think about it. I will slap you silly if you try."

***

I looked at myself in the mirror and cringed. "Oh jeez, this is horrible."

"Really? I thought it was the best of all three."

If my parents or, God forbid, Father Steve saw me like this, I'd be in confession for hours. Though to be fair, the outfit would only get me a few minutes. Not much, when compared to all the other things I'd need to confess. It had been quite a while since my last confession when I'd admitted to putting my ex-husband's baseball card collection through the shredder.

It had taken nearly an hour but boy, had it been worth it. I finished off the bottle of wine about the same time I'd put the last card in. The first half of the bottle had been the encouragement I'd needed. The second half was because I hadn't wanted it to go to waste.

I had always felt there had been a divine intervention I hadn't woken up the next morning with a hangover, considering my oath to God about getting drunk. At the time I had figured he'd given me a pass considering the situation.

Satisfied the barely there black mini skirt and

185

red-hot halter top would have to do, I looked at Melissa and clapped my hand over my mouth. Gone were her designer clothes and expensive jewelry, and in their place were black leather pants and a matching bustier. "I can't believe you replaced your diamonds with that clunky gold colored costume jewelry."

"Everyone knows it isn't safe to wear real jewelry to a place like that."

"Oh."

"So are you sure you don't want any jewelry?"

"I'll pass, thanks."

"Suit yourself. Now let's do something with your face."

I sat on the toilet seat and let Melissa slather on so much makeup I feared I'd need a jack hammer to remove it all. She claimed she was finished with me and added a bit to her own already done up face. We stood next to each other in front of the mirror and, even made up to look like hookers, I felt like a store brand knockoff next to a name brand item.

I liked my brown hair but it wasn't the shiny mahogany like Melissa's. Her dark brown eyes with gold flecks went along with her olive skin, giving her a mysterious and glamorous feel. If she wasn't also one of the kindest, most generous people I knew, I'd have probably given in to the urge to kill her years ago.

We grabbed our purses and while I headed for the back door, Melissa headed for the front. "What are you doing?"

"Elijah is waiting out front. I thought it best if he drove us. Don't worry, he won't stay. I'll call him to pick us up."

"I don't want my neighbors to see me dressed like this. Besides, don't you think Elijah is going to be a bit shocked to see us?"

"Shocked? No. Amused? Absolutely. How could you deny him the joy?"

"Fine."

We stepped outside and the street suddenly seemed much farther away than it ever had before. Walking to the Mercedes, I prayed none of my neighbors would choose that moment to look out their windows. Melissa had been right. Elijah's eyes looked ready to burst out of his head but he merely smiled while he held the door for us. Though I could have sworn I heard a chuckle just before the door closed, shutting off the sound.

Indiscretions was on the other side of town, which in a city the size of Lakeview meant we were only a twelve-minute drive away. Once there, Elijah pulled the car up to the front and got out, offering his hand to assist us exiting the back of the car. We waved goodbye and I wished desperately I was once again back inside the car headed just about anywhere.

"Well, let's go."

"I don't want to," I said.

"What are you, two? Come on."

"Fine, but you have to promise to stop me from hitting any of these jerks if they put their hands on me."

"Promise." She placed her hand over her heart and smiled.

I was screwed.

We got in line and paid to go inside. They even carded us at the door. It would have been a compliment if they hadn't carded the old guy in front of me who looked like he'd been around when Orville and Wilbur took their historic flight in 1903.

Inside, the music was loud, as were the furnishings—the tables were black while the chairs ranged in color from blue to purple and orange to pink. To be fair, they matched the carpet as well as the multicolored flashing lights. Evidently their clientele wasn't too interested in fancy décor. Of course, to complete the picture, there were two women in their twenties onstage dancing around while they took off one item of clothing at a time.

Melissa and I made our way past tables of rowdy men hollering at the dancers. At the bar we each bought a beer and snagged a table as far from the floor show as possible, despite Melissa's objections that we were too far from the excitement.

"Wow, that girl's limber. If I could do that, I'd still be married to the mutant."

"No, you wouldn't. The mutant was also an asshole," I said.

"Oh yeah, good point. I don't know why I forget that."

"Denial can be a beautiful thing."

We had only been sitting down for a short while when the parade of losers began. The pickup lines were just plain sad. One of our would-be suitors was my contact pretending to hit on us. He slid a picture onto my lap and leaned down to whisper in my ear. "He's at the bar. Red shirt, blond hair."

"Got it. Now get lost."

"Your friend looks hot. Maybe she'd like to come work for me."

"Sorry, buddy, but you can't afford her."

"A damn shame." Dimitri grabbed the picture from my hand, straightened up, and walked back to where he'd been sitting at a table only a few feet away.

"So what's next?" Melissa asked.

"I'll watch him for a few minutes then I'll go over and make a move. Hopefully, this won't take long."

"Don't worry, I've got plenty of singles."

"Are you crazy? Put that money away."

"Oh, you're right. I shouldn't be flashing my cash around."

That, and I didn't want any of the ladies to get the wrong idea. I didn't know about Melissa, but there was no way I was going to put that money on any of the dancers.

"Too bad the guys aren't dancing tonight. Now that would be fun."

I smiled and nodded. Though for me, having a strange guy rub against me was too much like being back with my ex. You just knew he'd been rubbing those parts against God only knew how many other people. I wouldn't have sex with my ex if he covered his junk with an entire box of condoms.

A man in his fifties, with gray hair and a beer gut to rival Jessica Simpson's pregnancy belly, stumbled over to our table and offered us some wine and a good time if we both went back to his place with him. Though disgusted by the invite, we kindly turned down his offer. Unhappy with our response, the drunk called us dykes before stumbling off.

"What a jerk," Melissa said.

"Look around, the room is full of them."

I took my own advice. Most of the guys were dressed in jeans and t-shirts. There were several tables where the groups of men were in suits and ties. I guessed watching a bunch of women dance around half-naked was just what a busy businessman needed to unwind at the end of the day.

For a moment I thought I saw someone who looked familiar in the back of the room just past the bar. When I blinked he was gone. Convinced I'd imagined Kevin, I turned back around. The *charming* atmosphere had me eager to get the job done so I could go home and get out of the ridiculous outfit. I also wanted to spend about an hour in the shower to remove the grime I couldn't see or feel but was sure was there.

I stood up and was pushed back down into my seat.

"Don't go now. I want to play."

One of the strippers was standing over me, wearing a few strips of cloth, waving her boobs in my face. Over the music I could hear Melissa's laughter.

"Uh, I…I'm not…"

"I can tell this is your first time. Don't worry, sweetie, I'll be gentle."

"Don't, I'm not gay."

"Neither am I. I'm bisexual. There are just too many wonderful choices out there to limit yourself."

"Okay."

"So why don't you come in the back with me? I'll give you a private show."

"No, no, no. I can't. Sorry. Melissa…"

"Sorry, she's with me. I'm trying to loosen her up some."

"That sounds like fun. Here's my number. If the two of you ever want to make it a threesome, give me a call." With that she got her boobs out of my face and moved on to the next table.

I turned and glared at Melissa. "Stop laughing or I swear I'll give her your number."

"Okay, jeesh, lighten up. I do have one question—real or fake?"

"Bitch. Fake, I think."

Melissa laughed and tried to cover it with a cough.

"Okay, I'm going over to make my move."

"On the stripper or…"

"Tell me again, why are we friends?"

"Because not many others would put up with us."

"True."

I grabbed money from my purse and made my way over to the bar. As luck would have it, a spot next to my target opened up. I slid in, careful to gently bump into his knee. "Oops, sorry."

"No problem. Let me buy you a beer?"

"Sure."

He gestured to the empty stool next to him. I sat down and brushed my hand across his thigh. My new friend ordered our drinks and I watched the bartender open my bottle and set it in front of me.

For the next twenty minutes Mr. Possible Cheater's hands began to roam. I drank half my beer, getting the courage I needed to sit still and not dump it on his head. Besides, I figured it would be a waste of a good beer.

Having downed his own bottle of courage, he leaned forward and put his tongue in my ear while his hand groped my breast. I pushed his hand away and asked him if he wanted to go somewhere more private. In answer he grabbed my hand and rubbed it against his crotch. Oh, I had most definitely gotten his attention. If there weren't enough pictures already, then that was too freaking bad. As if on cue, my contact strode over and put his arm around my shoulders.

"Hey, baby, sorry I'm late."

"I thought you'd ditched me."

"So, what, you were heading out with this guy?"

"No, of course not, honey. I was just sitting here having a beer and I figured since you weren't here, I was going to go home."

"Well, now that I'm here, let's go grab a table."

"Yeah, great." I looked at Mr. Possible Cheater's face and smiled. "It was nice to meet you."

"Yeah, you too."

We watched him walk away and out the door.

"Now there goes a very frustrated man."

"Thanks for the rescue."

"No problem. I got lots of great shots."

"Thank God. Now if only I could go home and wash off the sickening feelings."

"Good luck with that. Here, this should help." He handed me a check for three hundred and fifty dollars.

"Wait a minute. This is more than we agreed to."

"Keep it. You earned it."

I walked back to the table and found Melissa talking to the guys at the next table. Eager to leave but not wanting to seem rude, I sat down and grabbed my now warm beer. I finished it off and waited for her to finish her conversation. Finally, Melissa introduced me, using a character name from one of her books, to her two new buddies. When it became obvious we weren't going home to have sex with them, they turned their attention back to the performances on stage.

"So I take it you got what you needed?"

"I sure as hell hope so."

"Great. Now we can celebrate."

"Celebrate what?"

"Well, your job is done and I turned my latest book in to my editor this afternoon."

"Congrats."

"Thank you. Where are the waitresses? Oh, heck with it. I'm going to go to the bar and get us a couple beers."

Feeling weird, I grabbed my purse and headed for the bathroom. On my way I bumped into someone I could have sworn was Brian's jerky friend, Kevin.

I opened my eyes and winced. I squeezed my eyes shut to keep out the bright light.

"I think she's waking up."

"Oh, thank God."

"Maybe you guys should wait outside."

I recognized the voices as those of Melissa, my

dad, and Grant. I opened my eyes and squinted. Sure enough, the faces staring down at me matched the voices. That was good but I could have done without the worried expressions. "What happened?"

"You're in the hospital. Everything is going to be all right."

Normally my dad's voice put me at ease, but not this time. I looked at Melissa. Seeing her tear-streaked face, I began to cry. She grabbed my hand and refused to let go. Not even when a female officer named Gonzalez shooed everyone else, including my father, from the room.

It seemed despite my vigilance I had somehow been slipped a date rape drug. The last thing I remembered was getting up and walking toward the bathroom. The next was waking up in the hospital. Everything between now and then was a complete blank. Melissa explained she'd waited for a few minutes at the table but when I didn't return she had gone looking for me. She had found me slumped over the table in the back. She had called 911 and rode in the ambulance with me to the hospital. Once here she had called my dad. She had no idea why Grant was here. I'd have to worry about that later, much later, like maybe never.

There was good news. The doctor who stitched up my hands several days ago had evidently examined me and found no evidence of sexual assault. I was grateful. I was also a bit embarrassed. This guy was seeing way too much of my person without having bought me dinner first. Yeah, he was a doctor, but still. Officer Gonzalez asked me about a million questions. I was only able to answer six of them. When it became obvious I was going to be of no help, she left. My father returned to the room without Grant, for which I was grateful.

I was confined to the hospital bed for several hours before I was finally released. My dad drove Melissa and me back to my place. Once there he insisted we stay in the car while he checked out my apartment. Once he deemed it bad guy free, Melissa and I went inside. He left after she promised to stay the night. Too tired to argue or traverse the stairs, I curled up on the couch.

CHAPTER TEN

Friday

I awoke to the smell of bacon and coffee. If there was a better way to start the morning, besides great sex, I couldn't think of it. For a brief moment I thought maybe I was imagining the smell. Melissa certainly couldn't cook breakfast, or anything else for that matter, and I didn't think someone broke into my apartment to cook me breakfast. Who would do that? Then it came to me, my mother.

Normally I would be thrilled at a free meal cooked with love by her. The downside was my dad had obviously told her what had happened last night. Cooking was her way of dealing with stress, plus she was just so good at it. I closed my eyes and wondered how long I could pretend to be asleep. It took all of about thirty seconds before my growling stomach had me off the couch and walking into the kitchen.

"Oh, good, you're awake. Have a seat at the table and I'll bring you some breakfast."

"Okay."

A minute later I was seated across from Melissa and my mom. Each of us had a heaping plate of food and mugs of coffee. I gulped down half the cup before stuffing a piece of bacon in my mouth. I could have wept. Two eggs, over easy, and two pieces of white toast completed the meal. Not wanting to answer any questions and spoil the moment, I ate staring at the table while they talked about unimportant things like the weather, gas prices, and the annoying news anchor on one of the local TV stations.

When our stomachs were full and our plates empty, at least in my case, I pushed back in my chair and prepared for the onslaught. Instead, what we got was a reminder to take it easy, hugs all around, and then my mom was off to do whatever it was she did with her days.

"So what are we going to do today?" I asked.

"I don't know, but we need to do something fun," Melissa said.

"Jeez, have you already forgotten what happened to me last night?"

"No, of course not, but nothing horrible like that is going to happen again. I promise."

The decision was sort of made for us. Just after my mom left the vultures arrived. News vans from all the local TV stations were camped out in the front of the apartment building. Melissa peeked out the sliding door and found a few camped out in the back lot. I grabbed the phone, called the police station, and asked for Jackie.

"Hey, girl, what's up?"

197

"There are news vans in the back lot. They're parked in a tow away zone," I said.

"So what do you want me to do about it?" Jackie asked.

"Hello?"

"Oh man. No way."

"Come on. Please," I said.

"Fine, but I'm telling that man my sister insisted on marrying that you owe him a favor, not me. Got it?"

"Got it. Thanks."

"Fine. Whatever."

"So, do you want to go shopping?" Melissa looked at me and grimaced. "Guess not."

"Thanks to that jackass reporter, I can't go anywhere. Even if we get away, people are going to recognize me—again."

"Oh please. Less than half the town watches the news. Of those who do, only about five percent will recognize you and only one percent will realize it's from the news. The others will just think you go to the same church or whatever."

As much as I hated to admit it, she was probably right, and even if she wasn't, I had to escape or I'd go mad. "I like your math."

"I thought you would." She grabbed her cell phone and called Elijah and asked him to meet us on the other side of the park by my apartment.

Melissa and I kept watch and fifteen minutes later several tow trucks pulled into the parking lot. Three large guys, who looked like they could carry small cities on their backs, got out and walked over to the offending news vehicles. Finding them

198

empty, they didn't waste any time. All the vans were loaded and on their way out of the lot before the drivers realized what was happening.

There was a bit of shouting but the drivers were out of luck. They stood staring at the signs warning drivers of just such a fate to anyone dumb enough to park in our lot who did not belong. Amid the chaos, Melissa and I slipped out the patio door and walked casually across the lot to the park. It was filled with parents and kids, making it much easier to blend in. Fortunately for us, Elijah was waiting when we finally made it to the parking lot on the other side of the park. We got in the car and went straight to Melissa's house, conveniently located in a gated community. Unlike the many other such neighborhoods in our town, this one actually used the gates.

House was such a small word for such an enormous place. Melissa's home was big enough to fit my entire apartment building a couple of times over with room to spare. She parked me on her patio with a nice view of the in-ground pool and a glass of ice cold lemonade. She left and returned with a stack of paperback mysteries.

"Don't you think it's a bit early for that?" I said, pointing at the bottle next to her.

"After the night we had I'd say we're entitled to do a bit of vodka."

"I'll pass for now but keep it handy."

"No problem. While I was inside Charmaine called. She's coming over later."

"Oh jeez, I don't need two babysitters."

"Of course not. I don't think she knows about

what happened."

"Good."

"Kim…"

"I just mean if she doesn't, then a whole lot of other people don't know either."

"Absolutely."

"Wait a minute. What aren't you telling me?" I asked.

"Nothing."

"Bull. You always stare at the ground when you lie, and you fiddle with your jewelry."

"I do not," she said.

I laughed as she dropped her necklace and put her hand back down at her side.

"Well, hell," she muttered.

"The truth is easier. Fess up."

"All right, just remember you wanted to know."

"Okay."

"Your favorite reporter is at it again."

"Now what?"

"He reported about your trip to the hospital."

"Since when did a hospital visit become news?"

"I don't know, but I must say, Kim, I'm impressed with how calm and mature you're being about this."

"Screw you."

"Sorry, I would, but you're not my type, you being female and all."

"Wow, what a relief."

Melissa laughed and I laid my head back against the lounge chair and closed my eyes. I opened my eyes and stretched. Ever since I'd been found with the body in Lindsay's apartment I hadn't managed to get a full night's sleep.

***

I looked around. Melissa was nowhere in sight. The pool was a shiny, wet temptation. Though it was one temptation I'd have to ignore. Invigorated from my nap, I got up and went in search of Melissa. I found her in the kitchen and she was not alone. Charmaine, dressed in a pair of white pants and an emerald green blouse, stood pouring soup into bowls. She managed to look completely comfortable in Melissa's state of the art kitchen where the appliances cost more than my car and a weeklong vacation in the Bahamas.

"Hey, you, good timing, lunch is ready," Charmaine said.

"Kim, go sit down in the sunroom. We'll bring everything out there," Melissa said.

"What can I help with?"

"Plenty," Charmaine said.

"Nothing right now. Go sit," Melissa ordered.

Lunch was a salad, baked potato, Diet Coke, and a bowl of chicken noodle soup—the homemade kind, not the stuff in a can that everyone claimed was chicken noodle but tasted more like how my brothers' feet smelled.

I pushed back from the table. "Okay, I've gotten some sun, had a nap, and eaten lunch. So, what's up?"

Melissa looked at Charmaine and shook her head *no*.

"Spill it."

"My sister, Shandra, is being blackmailed by her no good ex-boyfriend, Irving the Third. We need your help."

I wasn't sure what I was expecting her to say but that sure as heck wasn't it. "What?"

Charmaine went on to explain how her sister's ex-boyfriend had taken nude photos of her while she slept and now wanted money for the revealing pictures or he'd put them on the Internet. Shandra was an assistant district attorney. If those pictures were leaked, they would be extremely damaging to her career.

"What does he want?" I asked.

"Five thousand dollars."

"Well, he sure is a greedy bastard."

"I'll gladly give her the money," Melissa said.

"You know my sister wouldn't take money from you or anyone else."

"She's going to have to. There aren't any other options. She has to pay this jerk."

"No," Charmaine and I said in unison.

"Why not?" Melissa asked.

"Because if she pays this jerk, what's to stop him from coming back next month? Or the month after that and the next month?"

"Okay, I get it, but what else can we do?"

"Simple. It's time for a little breaking and entering."

"Nice," said Charmaine.

"Well, we'll need help," Melissa said.

"Sorry, but there's no we, it's just me," I said.

"Come on. Let me help. She's my friend too," Melissa said.

"What about me? She's my sister."

"Which is why you will be nowhere near his place," I said.

"But—"

"Because, you'll be busy providing her with an airtight alibi, a very public alibi," I interrupted.

"Ooh, nice. I like the way your devious mind works," Charmaine said.

"Thank you. I think."

"So when does he need the money?" Melissa asked.

"He's giving her until the end of next week."

"Wow, how generous of him to give her time," I said.

"We did try to warn her about him."

"Not now, Melissa."

"You're right. Sorry."

"Okay, I'll want to go in at night. Not too late or too early," I said.

"According to his Facebook page, he's going to be at a bachelor party tonight."

"Tonight? That doesn't give us much time," Melissa said.

"Me. It doesn't give me much time. That's okay, it should work."

"Fine, but I'm coming with you, and I don't want to hear a word about it."

Taking Melissa anywhere was like trying to sneak the entire football team into your bedroom without your parents noticing. I was about to tell her this but stopped once I looked at her face. As was typical with my friends when one of us was in trouble, we could always count on the others to be there for us. How many people were lucky enough to have a friend willing to do a little B and E with them on such short notice?

"Sure."

"Yay. I have the perfect outfit."

Of that I had no doubt.

The three of us spent the next twenty minutes gathering as much information as we could. Charmaine called and convinced, or rather harassed, Shandra into having dinner at a restaurant conveniently located across from the Lakeview police station. When in need of an alibi, what better place than a restaurant filled with cops?

With our plans for the evening in place, Charmaine hugged us goodbye and headed back to her store. While Melissa fiddled with a new story idea, I spent the rest of the afternoon sitting by the pool and finished one of Toni McGee Causey's books. I lasted an entire fifteen minutes before I picked up another book and began to read again. Paranormal romance wasn't really my thing, but I found my face glued to Jennifer Lyon's latest one.

At four o'clock Melissa drove to my apartment. She was back half an hour later with everything on my list. A nice surprise was that all the news vans were gone, not just the ones I'd gotten towed away. Hopefully, they were off to bigger and better stories, which was good for me but completely horrendous for whoever they had swooped in on now. With enough problems of my own to fill a dinner plate and the entire salad bar at Wendy's, I didn't have much time or energy to worry about who that other person might be. At least not right now.

Melissa hurried off to her room to get changed while I used one of the six guest bathrooms. A few minutes later I stepped out and screamed. Standing five inches from me dressed in black pants, a black turtleneck, and a ski mask was, I dearly hoped, Melissa.

"Jesus, what the hell is wrong with you?"

A hand reached up and yanked off the mask, revealing my friend.

"Lighten up, Kim. I thought this was appropriate for a cat burglar."

"First, we're not cat burglars. We're going to the loser's place to get the pictures, that's it. Second, it's summer and it won't get dark for another three hours. And third, a ski mask is going a bit too far. Don't you think?"

"I guess. You know you used to be a bit more fun."

"I guess I'm having a bad week."

"Really? It seems pretty typical for you lately, anyway."

"Thanks for the reminder."

"Sorry."

"Why? It's not your fault I've become a trouble magnet."

"Well, we all have our strengths."

"True. I guess yours would be looking like a bad guy in a comic book." I pointed at her outfit.

"Funny. Fine, Kim, I'll change. I can take a hint."

A few minutes later and dressed in normal clothes, jeans and a shirt, Melissa led me to the garage. For a brief moment I feared she intended we take the Rolls Royce, but instead she led me to a newer model white Toyota Corolla.

"Where did this come from?"

"A friend of a friend's cousin's brother-in-law."

"What?"

"Trust me. You don't want to know."

She was probably right so I let it go. Besides, there was a more urgent matter at hand. "Fine, but I'm driving."

"Kim, that's not fair."

"What wouldn't be fair is if your driving got us killed before we could help our friend."

"I'm not that bad."

I covered my mouth with my hand and coughed the word *bullshit*. She simply rolled her eyes at me then handed me the keys. "Thanks."

The loser's apartment was ten minutes south of Melissa's house and just past the Victoria's Secret call center. Now, I appreciated a good push-up bra like anybody else, but how much underwear could the world's women order that kept that parking lot packed twenty-four hours a day?

We parked on the street two buildings down from the one we needed. Trying to walk casually down the street when you knew you were about to do something illegal was a bit easier than one would imagine, especially if you've had lots of practice. You just needed to get yourself in the right frame of mind. What almost always worked for me was the terrifying thought of getting arrested and having to share a toilet, out in the open, with a cellmate named Big Betty, and I didn't mean Betty White. I had no idea what Melissa's motivation was, but since she wasn't giving off any scared shitless vibes, she must have been okay.

The loser lived in a three-story, orange brick building with beige siding and matching shutters. Three white steps led up to the front door. Inside the entryway the walls were painted a pastel blue with a flower wallpaper border. Irving had invited Shandra's friends over for a small party shortly after they started dating. I hadn't been all that impressed but had kept my opinion to myself. He had seemed friendly enough, but, for whatever reason, in the seven months they had been together, I'd never changed my mind about him. I only wished for Shandra's sake I'd been wrong.

The apartment we needed was on the top floor, but since the building didn't have an elevator I gladly led the way up the three flights of stairs. When we got to the top I was pleased to be able to talk and breathe without huffing and puffing. It appeared the workouts were actually working. Damn, now there was no excuse to quit. I glanced over at Melissa and my impressive feat no longer seemed quite as impressive as she appeared ready to climb a few more flights.

Melissa knocked on the door and waited. No one answered. She tried again just to make sure. When again there was no answer, Melissa moved to stand behind me as both a shield and a lookout. I used a set of tools that if found in my possession would be an automatic trip to the pokey. In less than thirty seconds I had picked the lock, gotten us both inside, and deactivated the alarm.

207

"Wow, Kim, how did you do that so fast?"

"Practice. Lots and lots of practice."

She arched her eyebrows at me.

"Here, put these on," I said, handing her a pair of latex gloves."

"Ooh, thanks. With his obvious lack of housekeeping skills, I was a bit worried about catching something."

"They're so we don't leave any fingerprints. Also, be careful not to disturb the dust."

"You know, this takes a whole lot more than I thought."

"Exactly. Now, let's get this done before he comes home."

"Kim, relax. He's at a bachelor party. He won't be home for hours, and when he does make it home he'll be too drunk to notice us. Hell, he'd probably think we were the strippers."

"Oh, wow, getting mistaken for a stripper. What a lucky day."

The apartment was just how I remembered it, except now there was a thin layer of dust on everything, dirty dishes were piled in the sink, and a laundry hamper overflowed with dirty clothes.

"Yuck. This guy lives like my ex," Melissa said.

"Which one?"

"Number two, Miss Smart-ass."

"Nice mouth."

"Thanks."

I sent Melissa off to search the bedroom and bathroom while I tackled the living room, kitchen, and dining room. The place was small and unlike my great aunts', who insisted every flat surface was a place to show off some piece of crap they had picked up from a flea market. Without having to pick through a ton of knickknacks and crap, I made quick work of finding the loser's camera and laptop.

"Hey, Kim, come here."

"Hold on a sec."

"I really need you to come here. Now."

"Okay, okay."

I walked back to the bedroom and found Melissa standing in front of the dresser with the bottom drawer open.

"You are not going to believe this."

"What?"

Instead of answering, she pointed at the open drawer. I walked over and leaned down to take a look.

"Oh jeez!" I straightened up and took two steps back, trying to put some distance between myself and the drawer full of sex toys. I didn't consider myself a prude but that didn't mean I wanted to be up close with someone else's things. I also didn't want to consider my friend and that drawer, but what really bothered me were the photos of women—some were naked, others were wearing costumes. "We need to take those."

"You mean we need to destroy those."

"That too. Did you find anything else?"

"Nope."

"Okay, let's get out of here."

"Thank God." Melissa grabbed the photos and we left the bedroom.

I did a quick look around. Seeing nothing amiss, we let ourselves out, but not before I grabbed the camera and the laptop. Neither of us said a word until we were in the relative safety of the car.

"Holy crud."

Leave it to the writer to come up with the perfect words for the situation. Unsure of what to say, I chose to say nothing.

"I need a drink," she said.

I looked at the clock, then at her. "Too early."

"Are you sure?" she asked.

"Nope."

"Thank God."

"Don't get too excited, we have a couple of stops to make first."

"Swell." She groaned.

"Just suck it up."

"That was my intent, or rather, suck it down."

We took off the gloves and stuck them in an empty Wal-Mart bag. I yanked my cell phone out of my pocket and punched in some numbers. After two rings Ryan answered the phone, not with a usual greeting one expected when placing a call. Instead, I was instructed to bring a six pack of beer and a bag of Cheetos. I pushed *end* and stuck the phone back in my pocket.

"So where are we going next?"

"You'll see."

Four blocks away I pulled into a drive-thru. I bought the requested items and added two Diet Cokes, two Hershey's Bars, a bag of Doritos, and an additional six pack of beer. While I waited for my receipt I found myself once again thinking about how odd it was you could buy alcohol without getting out of your car. It was kind of like those fireworks sales where you promised not to use them in the state in which you were buying them. What the hell was up with that?

I handed my purchase off to Melissa with strict orders not to open a beer. The last thing either of us needed right then was to get pulled over with stolen property and an open container in the car. With my chronic case of lead foot, getting pulled over was a very real and common possibility.

Ten minutes later I pulled up to a mansion in the ritziest part of town. It was the neighborhood next to Melissa's. These places made a modest three-bedroom, three-bath brick ranch house look like a house for Barbie, only not as fancy and without the elevator. I parked in front of the guesthouse, which was an exact mini replica of the main house, down to the red brick, white pillars, and arched entryway. Melissa grabbed the Cheetos and one of the six packs while I slipped on another pair of gloves and grabbed the camera and laptop.

"What are we doing here?"

"You'll see."

Before either of us could ring the bell, the door was opened by the hottest geek God had ever created. He truly was a masterpiece. With piercing blue eyes, blond hair, and a six pack of his own that you could bounce quarters off of. You could almost forget about his need to attend Star Trek conventions in costume or the fact that he drove a powder blue Prius, but the deal breaker, for me at least, was that the twenty-eight-year-old's only source of income was a trust fund that he spent with abandon while living in his parents' guest house.

He ushered us inside. I had to give Melissa a gentle but firm shove to get her moving. He closed the door behind us.

"Ladies, have a seat."

Before I could take a step he put his hand on my arm and whispered, "If I'd known you were bringing a hot friend with you, I would have asked for a threesome instead." He chuckled to make it seem as if he was joking but we both knew better.

"Too late to renegotiate."

"Bummer. Maybe next time."

"Yeah, maybe."

Like never.

A threesome was beyond my comfort zone. I may not be the best Catholic girl on the planet, but figuring all the sins I'd already committed, I didn't think my eternal soul could handle much more. Although if Grant was an identical twin, I was almost positive God would understand.

I brushed past Ryan and sat in a chair instead of on the couch next to Melissa. I didn't think it wise to give him any visual stimulation. The last thing he needed was encouragement of any kind.

"So, what do you have for me?" Ryan asked.

"I need some pictures on this laptop and camera deleted," I replied.

"Cool. What kind of pictures?"

"Some adult photos."

"You brought me porn? Awesome. Maybe it isn't too late to renegotiate after all," Ryan said.

"Wipe the smirk off your face. It isn't porn. These pictures were taken without the woman's knowledge or consent. Got it?"

"Oh, sure, no problem."

He walked over to me and took the camera and laptop before heading into his tech geek cave, which was really just a big room with dozens of electrical gadgets, computers, monitors, and a giant, flat screen TV with an Xbox 360, a PS3, and a Wii U. Not quite as sexy as the Batcave but it would have to do.

"So are we just supposed to sit here and wait for him?"

"Yes."

"Great."

"Sorry this part isn't exciting enough for you."

"That's okay. Besides, I'm not supposed to have fun. We're helping a friend."

"I'm glad you remembered that."

"Of course I remember. I'm not selfish."

There were many adjectives that could be used to describe Melissa, rich, funny, annoying, and frustrating, but selfish was definitely not one of them.

"So what's his deal?" she asked.

"What do you mean?"

"He's hot but he dresses like a nerd," she said.

"There are hot nerds."

"Oh really? Name one besides this guy." Melissa looked over at me. "Well?"

"I'm thinking."

"So what's up with the two of you?"

"Nothing," I lied.

"Ooh, spill."

I looked to make sure he wasn't heading back. "Fine, we almost had sex once."

"What?"

"It was just too weird."

"Weird, huh? So, what, did he want you to dress up in Star Trek costumes?"

"Yuck, no."

"Then what?"

"I just kept thinking his parents were going to walk in on us."

"Oh jeez, that's sad."

"Tell me about it."

"So what's with the guesthouse with enough antiques to give my Aunt Jenny an orgasm?"

"Shh, he's coming back."

"Would you like me to leave the two of you alone?"

In response I glared at her. She covered her mouth with her hand, but I could still hear the laughter.

"Whoever owns this stuff has great taste in women, but he's a giant jerk," Ryan said.

Personally, I was thinking of something a lot stronger than jerk to call Irving. "Were you able to erase the pictures?"

"Sure, that was easy. The tricky part was loading a virus on his computer."

"You did what?"

"I put a virus on his computer. The next time he turns it on, he's going to wipe out everything on it."

"Wow. Why did you do that?"

"Taking pictures of ladies without their consent is crap. I'd be pissed if someone did that to one of my sisters."

"Well, thanks."

I took the things back from him and stood up to leave.

"Kim, it doesn't take two people to return those things. Why don't you pick me up later? That is, if you don't mind." Melissa had turned and addressed the last part to the grinning geek.

"I don't mind at all. We've got beer and we could have a little party."

"Melissa, he wanted us to have a threesome."

And just like that she turned and was out the door. It was as if I'd dunked her in a tub of ice cubes. Having lived through the experience when I was a little girl, I would never ever recommend it. My parents had rushed me to the hospital in the middle of the night. The doctor, desperate to get my hundred and four fever down, had me stripped down and covered in ice cubes. It was hell. My skin felt like it was on fire.

"Wow! What an ass."

"It's why I only ask him for help when I absolutely need it."

"No, I meant, like, *ooh what an ass*."

"Oh."

Back at the loser's place I had Melissa serve as lookout while I put the things back. I had considered just tossing them, but then he could accuse Shandra of theft. As for the pictures, he certainly couldn't tell the police someone had stolen pictures he had taken illegally.

I was eager to get this over with and get the heck out of Irving's apartment. I put everything back and did a quick look around to make sure I hadn't missed anything. I stepped outside and found the bane of my existence leaning against the wall, smiling.

"Miss Murphy, how nice to see you again," Mr. Abraham said.

"What the hell are you doing here?" I asked, looking around for Melissa.

"Oh, just enjoying a nice evening. What about you?"

"The same, and now I've gotta go," I said.

"So, what were you doing here?"

"You know, if people keep seeing us together, they may get the wrong idea. Maybe you should go stalk someone else for a while—like forever."

"Avoiding the question are you, Kim?" Mr. Abraham asked.

"We're not friends and we aren't related. So, I suggest you stick to Miss Murphy if you can't fight the urge not to speak to me. Better yet, how about if we don't talk again ever."

"So is that yet another 'no comment' for the record?"

"Absolutely." I stepped to the left to walk past him.

"It's a bit weird the police chief's daughter has become involved in so many questionable situations."

"I think if you have been reduced to following me around, you might want to consider a career change. I hear McDonald's is hiring. At least that is an honest profession."

Back at the car Melissa screeched when I stepped up next to her. "Nice job as lookout."

"Jeez, Kim, you scared the hell out of me. Hey,

the loser didn't show up. I was imagining being tracked by bloodhounds."

"Great."

"What took you so long?" she asked as we got into the car.

"That reporter showed up."

"Here?"

"Yeah. I'm not real comfortable about that, but there's nothing we can do about it."

"So what did he want?"

"He asked a bunch of questions, and I refused to answer."

"Thank God. The last thing you needed to do was to confess to breaking and entering."

"Well, we didn't actually break anything. So I say it should just be entering and we didn't steal anything." We both looked at the stack of pictures. "Those don't count."

"Absolutely."

Back at my apartment building we drove around searching for evil reporters with microphones lurking about. Finding none, we decided it was safe for me to make a run, or at least a fast walk, to the door. Once we were inside, Melissa texted Charmaine to let her know the deed was done. Charmaine texted back to let us know she had just left Shandra and was headed to my place.

I tried to ignore the flashing numbers on the answering machine but couldn't. I ended up pressing the delete button ten times in a row, accidently erasing a message from my dad. I called my parents and, after a short conversation with my mom, my dad came on the phone, and after a quick hello got straight to the point. Detective Tompkins would be contacting me soon. It seemed the ever annoying but hot as hell cop had more questions for me.

A few minutes later, Charmaine rushed in like a gust of wind. "Well?"

"It's taken care of and Shandra has nothing to worry about."

"Thank you both so much."

"All right, who's ready for some champagne?" Melissa asked.

Without waiting for an answer she jumped up off the couch and headed for the kitchen.

"Unless you plan on having some delivered you're gonna have to settle for a bottle of whatever's in the fridge."

Melissa returned a short time later with three wine glasses and two full bottles of white zinfandel and a half bottle of chardonnay.

It didn't take long before I began to feel the effects of the wine. I hustled Melissa into the guest room, and after grabbing some pillows and blankets, gave my room over to a very grateful Charmaine. Back downstairs I dumped my stuff onto the couch. I poured the rest of the white zinfandel into my glass and finished it off since it would have been a shame to waste it.

I curled up on the couch and turned on the TV, which was a big mistake. *Diners, Drive-Ins and Dives* was on, and, having skipped dinner, I was beginning to get a bit hungry, but with all the wine I'd consumed, food was out of the question.

The doorbell rang just as I was drifting off.

Kicking off the cover, I stumbled to the door. On the other side of the peephole I could make out Grant's face. I'd completely forgotten about my dad's warning. It was never wise to talk to a police officer while under the influence of too much wine. My plan was to make up an excuse and send him on his way. I plastered a fake smile on my face then opened the door. "Grant, what a surprise."

"Surprise? Didn't the chief tell you I was coming?"

"Yes, he did, but since it's so late I figured you'd wait until tomorrow."

Grant looked at his watch. "It's only eleven o'clock on a Friday night."

"Well, I'm really tired. So, if you don't mind, we should have this conversation tomorrow."

"Uh-huh."

"Hey, where do you think you're going?"

"You invited me in."

"No, I didn't" Did I?

"Just like I figured. Have a bit of wine, did you?"

"You're the defective. You figure it out."

"I think you mean detective."

"That's what I said."

"There are three wine glasses. Where are your drinking buddies?"

"Upstairs. Asleep."

"And you're sleeping on the couch?"

"Yup."

Grant picked up one of the bottles. I walked over to take the bottle from him and stumbled. Grant spun and grabbed me. The force of my forward motion sent us both over. We landed with a thud onto the carpeted floor, narrowly missing a table and lamp. The only sounds were our labored breathing and our hearts beating as if we'd just run a marathon or engaged in another physical activity that was a hell of a lot more fun and mostly done in the privacy of a bedroom or, say, the living room floor. Laying on top of Grant, my earlier appetite for food was replaced with a hunger for something not food related, though I wasn't ruling out the use of whipped cream.

"Kim, are you okay?"

"Yeah, are you?" I asked.

"Yes, except if you could move a bit. Your thigh is a little too close to my…"

Well, now that he'd mentioned it, that wasn't the only thing that was close. Our lips were mere inches apart. I could feel his warm breath on my face.

"Oh, sorry." I slid my leg down and Grant moaned. I shifted and found myself staring into his eyes.

I wasn't sure who moved first, but suddenly Grant and I were in a lip lock. Our tongues touched and I wanted more. I slid across him like a desperate horny sailor on his first shore leave in six months.

Grant shifted beneath me and reached his hand between us, but instead of heading for my southern region he pulled his phone from his pocket. Grant looked at the screen and began to swear and mutter something about annoying drug dealers. "I've got to go."

"Now?" I winced at the sound of desperation in my voice.

"Yes."

Frustrated in more ways than one, I rolled off of him. Grant stood up and like a gentleman helped me to my feet.

"Thanks." I straightened my clothes and avoided direct eye contact

Grant cleared his throat. "You should, uh, try to get some sleep." He raised his hand and brushed his thumb across my lips. "Lock the door behind me." He grabbed me and pulled me up against him. "You are too tempting." He kissed my cheek then left without another word.

I locked the door and curled up on the couch, convinced God had either a twisted sense of humor where I was concerned or he really hated me. Why else would he send Grant over here to get my engine revved up only to send him away again before I could get a tune-up?

The last time I'd had a partner that didn't require batteries was five months and two weeks ago. I didn't know exactly how many days, minutes, or seconds, but I did know it was too freaking long ago.

Sex with the hot geek could have done the trick but I was afraid my mother was right and I was reaching that point in my life where great sex with a guy wasn't enough. I shuddered at the thought. Just because thoughts of Grant popped into my head at inopportune times didn't mean I wanted anything more than some hot, sweaty sex. Right?

I tossed and turned, trying to ignore the sexual frustration as well as the mental aggravation Grant seemed to provoke in me like no one else.

CHAPTER ELEVEN

Saturday

"Oh for the love of Hershey's, who the hell is banging on my door?" I looked at the clock and groaned. It was four in the morning. Didn't anybody sleep anymore? Thinking it might be Grant returning to finish what we'd started earlier, I pried my eyes open and stumbled to the door. "What is so important it couldn't wait until a decent hour? Say, noon."

"I thought you'd want to know the fire department's putting out a fire at your office," Michael said.

"Shit! I've got to find my keys."

"You might want to put some shoes on too," he said.

I looked down at my bare feet. Yup, shoes were definitely in order. "Just give me a minute."

"One Mississippi, two Mississippi…"

"You're so not funny."

I grabbed gym shoes and my purse. In the

kitchen I jotted down a note explaining my absence just in case Melissa and Charmaine regained consciousness while I was gone. Then I told Michael I'd meet him there.

"No way, I'll drive."

"No, thanks."

"You're riding with me. We need to talk."

"Swell," I muttered.

We got into his Dodge Ram. I waited for him to talk. Finally, I couldn't take it anymore. "Well?" I demanded.

"Huh, oh, nothing."

"But you said we needed to talk."

"I just told you that so you'd get in without any more arguing."

"You're a jerk."

"Yup."

Michael glanced over at me and we both laughed. He parked in front of the apartment building next door to my office. Two patrol cars, a fire truck, and an ambulance filled the lot in front of mine. We walked up to the building but stopped at the police tape. One of the patrol officers noticed Michael and waved him in. I started to go under and the officer yelled for me to stop.

"It's okay. She's my sister and this is her office." Michael lifted the tape and let me through. I got to the back door and stopped.

"Kim, are you coming in?"

"Yeah, I think."

"Come on."

I followed him inside. The fumes attacked my eyes and nose. Taking a deep breath felt like I was breathing tar into my lungs. Three firefighters brushed past me on their way out. None of them stopped to give me a hard time, so it was safe to assume none of them were family.

In my office, the chair, desk, and computer had all been burned, then been soaked by the firefighters. Not that I was complaining, thanks to them the rest of the place was intact, sort of. Someone had searched my office. Drawers were open and knickknacks had been knocked over.

I checked the file cabinets in the little storage room next to the kitchen. All the cabinets were locked and did not appear to have been tampered with. Thank goodness. I would hate to think someone had gone through my client files. I went back to my office and found Michael talking with the fire marshal, Terran Barber.

"It's pretty obvious someone ransacked it then tried to torch the place," Terran said.

We'd met, so we skipped the introductions and got right to the questions and answers part of the conversation. I was of no help whatsoever. The only thing I could tell him was about the knife in my tire and that I wasn't sure if it was connected to this or not. He told me he'd be in touch and that I could have access to my office sometime tomorrow evening. I did learn there were signs of forced entry and that whoever broke in took out the alarm system.

Sometime during our conversation a man from the alarm company showed up, a bit too late to be of much use, or so I thought. He assured me he would board up the door and keep someone on the property to watch twenty-four seven until a new door and alarm system could be installed.

I thanked them both before Michael took me home. He parked on the street and asked me if I was okay. Not wanting to add to his worry, I lied and said I was right as rain. I didn't think he bought it but at least he was kind enough not to push it. He did, however, apologize for our previous argument without any prompting, which showed just how worried he really was.

I took two Tylenol with half a glass of water, hoping to prevent a hangover. I slipped under the covers and was asleep within a matter of minutes. It was nine thirty when I woke up. My head felt a little fuzzy but was pain free. Since I was nausea free, there was a decision to make—Bill's Donuts or McDonald's. Unsure of when my houseguests would rise, the donut shop was the winner. After a quick trip to the bathroom, I grabbed my purse and keys and headed out, careful to check for lurking reporters. Back home, I walked toward my door and noticed the police tape was missing from Lindsay's. Melissa and Charmaine were in the kitchen waiting for the coffeemaker to do its thing.

"Morning, ladies. That coffee will go great with these." I showed them the box of donuts, but instead of the happy face I got when offered donuts, they both frowned and backed away. "Not feeling the love for the jelly donut I take it."

"Kim, get those away from me," Melissa said.

"Sorry."

After the donuts were out of sight, I filled them in on the fire. They bombarded me with questions. I answered them as best I could over a cup of coffee. When we were all talked out we said our goodbyes.

When they were gone I settled down with more coffee and one too many donuts. When I felt like moving, I got up and did the dishes. Next to tackle was a week's worth of laundry. I got the hamper and took it with me to what the landlord generously called a laundry room, but was really a closet with a washer and dryer in the kitchen. First up, I started a load of t-shirts and went back upstairs into my at home office to begin making calls.

An hour later my ear was red and sore from having the phone pressed to it for so long, but the pain was worth it. I talked to the insurance company and set up an appointment for later this week. The agent had been pleasant. I just hoped they covered the cost of everything. The furniture was easy to replace with a quick trip to Wal-Mart but the carpet would need to be replaced and the walls in my office would need to be cleaned. I had also called my office landlord, who was less than thrilled to hear about the damage, but he did promise to replace the door after we got off the phone. I gave him the fire marshal's name and number. I also contacted the alarm company to give them a heads up about my landlord's imminent arrival.

From my bedroom I grabbed the basket of jeans and took it downstairs. I transferred the shirts to the dryer and started stuffing the jeans into the washer. As always I checked the pockets before putting them inside. In one of the pockets I found the piece of paper from Sara's apartment. In all the craziness I had forgotten about it. I got the laundry going and took it upstairs. It felt like déjà vu as I sat and tried to straighten out the picture, just like I had with the one from Angie's. This picture was more than just similar to the other. The two pictures had to have been taken at the same time. A woman in a red dress showed up in both pictures. In both, the pictures were too damaged to make out her face.

What the heck was up with these pictures? Why did Angie and Sara both have them? Why were they crumpled? All these questions and not a single answer to any of them. Frustrated, I stuck the picture in my desk. This case needed to be looked at with a clear head. Since I didn't have one I decided to take a break and catch up on chores. Over the next few hours, I got the laundry done and the entire apartment cleaned. The phone rang several times while I vacuumed, but I had chosen to ignore them all. With nothing left to do, stalling was over. I pushed play on the answering machine. After listening for a moment I hit *delete*. The message was from Mr. Abraham, the reporter from hell. It was the middle of summer but Miami had a better chance of getting two feet of snow than that idiot had of me returning his call.

I had also ignored a call from Lindsay. Not up to dealing with whatever drama she had lined up for me today, I skipped to the next message on the machine. It was from Brian and Sara's mom. I called her back, unsure of what she could want. She answered right away and asked for me to come to her place. We agreed to meet in an hour.

Sweaty from the workout and chores, I took a shower so as to not offend Mrs. Lewis. There was no point in bothering with makeup. As for my hair, I dried it and stuck it in a ponytail. With a twenty-minute wait before I had to leave, I sat down with Karin Tabke's latest book and lost track of time.

At Mrs. Lewis's home, she let me in before I had a chance to knock. We took the same seats we had a few days ago. She offered me coffee, but I took a pass. The last thing this woman needed to do was wait on me like a proper hostess.

"So, Mrs. Lewis, what was it you wanted to speak to me about?" I asked, dreading the answer while knowing what it would be.

"I know you're looking into Brian's murder. My daughter, Sara, is missing. I want you to help the police find her."

Sometimes it really sucked being right.

"Mrs. Lewis, I need to be honest with you. I'm not having any luck with your son's case. Sara called me and asked to meet with me."

"She did?"

"Yes, but when I went to her apartment she never showed. Did the police tell you someone broke into her apartment?"

"Yes. I don't understand any of this. Brian was a good kid who got into trouble, but he turned his life around."

"What about Sara?"

"She was an okay student in high school. She hung out with a wild bunch but then she went to college and got a job as a home health nurse. She's doing well."

"So you can't think of any reason someone would want to hurt them?"

"No. Like I told the police, none of this makes any sense. Miss Murphy, I don't have a lot of money but I have a decent job and I can make monthly payments. I could give you a few hundred dollars to start."

"Mrs. Lewis, I'm sorry, I can't take your money."

"Please, it's all I have."

"No, I'm sorry, I meant, I'll look for Sara. You keep your money."

"But…"

"Don't worry about it. So, let's get started. I want a list of her friends, boyfriends, exes, place of employment. The faster you get that for me, the better."

"Here, I stayed up all night. I wrote this up in case you agreed. Her boss's name is at the bottom."

"Okay, well, thanks for this. I'll get started on it right away." I stood up and Mrs. Lewis walked me to the door. Before she closed it I told her to try to take a nap, that wearing herself out was the last thing she needed right now. She smiled and nodded her head but we both knew sleep wasn't going to come to her anytime soon.

A part of me had wanted to turn her down, but I couldn't. The poor woman had already lost a son and now her only other child, a daughter, was missing. The kind of hell she was going through I couldn't begin to imagine and hoped I never could.

Walking toward my car, I veered off, headed straight for Ed's Barbeque Barn at the corner. It was well past lunchtime and I was starving. Just as I reached for the door I spotted a familiar face walking toward me. "Mr. Alberts, what a surprise."

"Kevin, please. What are you doing here?"

I pointed to the building. "Lunch."

"Oh yeah, me too."

We stood in line and I did my best to keep up with my end of the chit chat. Sensing he'd ask to join me, I chose carry out instead. "Well, Kevin, it was nice to see you."

"Oh, you too. I was wondering if you heard about Sara, Brian's sister?"

"Yes."

"It's terrible. Mrs. Lewis is a real nice lady. Brian and Sara, they were good to her. I wish there was something I could do."

"Maybe you could spend a little time with Mrs. Lewis, so she's not all alone," I suggested.

"That's a great idea, Kim. Thanks. I guess I'll see ya soon."

"Yeah, well, gotta go. Bye."

The last thing I needed was Kevin hanging around. He was nice but I was pretty sure my interests wouldn't mesh with his, which I bet included smoking pot, eating pizza, and playing video games. Okay, eating pizza was pretty awesome, but that was it for me.

At home I grabbed a Diet Pepsi from the fridge and sat at the couch to eat lunch. Flipping through all the channels, I settled on an episode of *Finding Bigfoot* because it always made me laugh.

After lunch I went upstairs and went through the list Mrs. Lewis gave me. Some of the names on the list were also friends of Brian's. That wasn't so strange. What was strange was the other day Sara had called Brian's friends a bunch of losers. Kind of harsh to say about people considered to be close to you as well.

There were five names on the list I had not come across during my investigation into Brian's and Adam's murders. All were women. I left messages for two of them and set up appointments for Monday morning with the rest.

Sara's employer was a local home health agency. The name, We Care Nursing, seemed vaguely familiar. I couldn't figure out why. No one in my family had used them. Maybe they had one of those annoying commercials that were so bad you forgot the name of the product or the company. I called and the receptionist transferred me to the weekend supervisor. The supervisor told me to call back on Monday. The president of the company was the only one I could speak with. I thanked her and hung up, frustrated.

At the moment there wasn't much I could do. Brian and Adam were dead. I feared with Angie and Sara missing it was only a matter of time before their bodies showed up. This whole thing was connected but so far I couldn't find out how. All I had was a lawyer, mutual friends, and a couple of pictures.

The phone rang and, stupid me, I answered it without checking the caller ID.

"Kim, thank goodness, I've been trying to get ahold of you. I stopped by your office this afternoon. What the heck happened?"

"Lindsay, there was a fire. What did you need?"

"I was hoping you had learned something

helpful. I really need to get back to my life. This mess is so draining."

Yeah, I'd bet. I filled her in without telling her every detail. There were some things I just didn't feel like explaining. She was polite, for once, and didn't ask questions until I was done.

"Wow, you've actually learned quite a bit."

Not really, but I certainly wasn't going to bring that to her attention. "I've learned some but I'm not finished."

"All of this just proves it has nothing to do with me. I wouldn't be associated with these people. The police will have to leave me alone and find the real killer. Thank you, Kim."

"Yes, the real killer is still out there and…"

"That certainly isn't my problem. That's for the police to handle. Just send me a receipt and a check for the difference."

"Lindsay, this isn't over, not yet."

"It is for me. I have to go. We'll talk soon. Bye."

Lindsay was clueless. Even if there was proof she didn't kill Brian, she was still, somehow, connected. Brian was murdered in her apartment, an apartment that had been searched several times. Hell, for all anyone knew, the clues were still hidden inside her place.

Her apartment was just sitting there, empty. The cleaning company I had called wouldn't be available until Monday morning. The police tape was gone. There was no reason why I couldn't just go over and take a quick look around. I thought about it, for about a second, then went and got the key Lindsay had given me.

I hurried over before I could talk myself out of it. I went inside and made sure to lock the door behind me. It was daylight but I still felt my pulse race, and not in a good way. The last two times I'd been in here had not been pleasant experiences. It looked as bad as I remembered. Even worse now thanks to the addition of fingerprint dust everywhere.

Now all I had to figure out was where to start. Since the downstairs had been annihilated, I chose to start upstairs. It felt weird at first, searching through Lindsay's things. It was obvious whoever broke in never made it upstairs. The place was spotless and everything seemed to be in its place. This was good. Maybe whatever they had been looking for was still here. The problem was I probably wouldn't recognize what it was they wanted. Not unless it was a bloody knife, a loaded gun, drugs, or diamonds, something that screamed, *Look at me, I'm it*.

The last room I searched was Lindsay's bedroom. I pulled a photo box out from under her bed. Expecting to see pictures, I gasped when I found a bunch of sex toys instead. I put the lid back on and put it back under the bed. Even though I didn't touch anything inside the box I rushed into the bathroom and scrubbed my hands with french vanilla hand soap and water.

With the upstairs done, it was time to start the search downstairs. There weren't many hiding places that hadn't already been searched by the police and the thieves who broke in and left without stealing anything.

Fifteen minutes later and I had searched

everything but the kitchen. Odds were the only things I'd find in there were kitchen appliances and food, but it needed to be done. To be sure I didn't miss anything, I checked inside all the pots and pans, the canisters on the counter, and the refrigerator. Heck, I even checked the cookie jar. All that was left was the oven. Only an idiot would hide something of value inside an appliance with a broil setting but what the hell. I opened up the bottom drawer first and searched through several sauce pans, finding nothing, again. Finally I opened the door and my mouth dropped open. I knew there were people who stored pots and pans in their ovens but I was not one of them. I left a pan in mine once. The next day I preheated the oven and totally forgot about the pan. The smell of melted plastic was beyond awful. Between the mess and airing out my apartment in the middle of winter, it was a very painful way to learn a lesson.

The inside of the oven looked like it had never been used. I took the lid off the very last pot and found an SD card. Yes, I knew there was something in this place. Although with my luck the only thing on it would be pictures of Lindsay and her married boyfriend. Yuck. I took the card and closed the oven.

Thanks to my snooping I was covered in more black powder than a Civil War reenactment field. I was just grateful that I'd made it back inside my apartment without having been accosted by an evil monster with a microphone and a camera crew. I could imagine the phone calls from family and friends if I appeared on the evening news looking like a chimney sweep.

Not wanting to track the mess through my apartment, I kicked off my shoes and stripped out of my clothes just inside the door. After dumping the clothes into the washer, I rushed upstairs, eager to scrub off the grime and evidence of my illegal search. I tucked the SD card in a box of tampons. I saw a woman do that on a TV show and when her apartment was broken into they left the jewelry she had tucked inside the tampon box. Okay, so it was a TV show but it was worth a shot. By the time I came back downstairs from my second shower of the day I felt somewhat human again—a very hungry human. I started the washer and went into the kitchen.

I made a turkey sandwich with lettuce, tomatoes, mayonnaise, and two slices of bacon. I added a Vlasic dill pickle on the side and a handful, okay, two handfuls of sour cream and onion potato chips. To tie it all together I grabbed a can of Diet Coke.

Once again I ate dinner in front of the TV. I couldn't resist, an old episode of *NCIS* was on. After dinner I called and left a message for the geek hottie. I figured it was worth another six pack to find out if there was anything on the SD card that was important. In the kitchen I grabbed the trash bag then took it outside to the dumpsters, careful to make lots of noises as to avoid surprising the family of raccoons who made a habit of getting a free meal from our trash. They were cute, especially the babies, but they were mean as hell.

Back inside my apartment, I locked up and sat down and tried to push all thoughts of bodies, missing people, and reporters out of my head. I was successful for all of about three minutes, though really the last minute and a half I was thinking about ways to make a reporter disappear. Just when I had decided it would be perfectly fine to have the last donut for dessert both the doorbell and phone rang. I ignored the phone and ran to the door. "Hey, Shandra."

"Don't you hey me, Kim."

"Excuse me?"

"You are crazy. Do you have any idea how much legal trouble you would have been in if you had gotten caught? Do you?"

"Could you be a little more specific?" I asked as I made a rather long list of all the things that could have technically been considered illegal.

"You broke into an apartment and stole his things."

"Oh, that."

"What did you think I meant? No, never mind. I don't want to know."

"That's a wise decision. As for the other thing, nothing was stolen."

"Kim, you got rid of the pictures."

"Technically, I didn't. But, yes, the pictures should all be gone."

"You could lose your license."

"He's lucky I didn't take a baseball bat to his face."

Shandra, dressed in a white skirt and a pink patterned blouse and two-inch sandals, lunged at me. I tried to get away but didn't move fast enough. Shandra wrapped her arms around me so tight for a moment I feared she would squeeze the breath right out of me like one of those giant anacondas. I tapped her on the back harder and harder each time until she finally got the message and let go. It was funny how much she and Charmaine looked alike yet were so different. Charmaine was fun, laid back, and enjoyed having a good time, while Shandra was a serious-minded, focused, goal-oriented overachiever.

"Thank you."

"You're welcome," I said once I could speak again.

We talked for a few more minutes then said good night. She hugged me once more then she was out the door.

I checked the answering machine and swore. The voice on the machine was muffled but it was Sara and she was apologizing for her no-show stunt the other night. She said she'd be at Lakeview Cemetery in twenty minutes. She claimed to have information about Brian's murder and Angie's disappearance.

When I checked the caller ID it provided me with the useless information that she'd called from an unknown number. I grabbed my purse and headed out, ignoring that annoying voice in my head. Sometimes that bitch just needed to shut up. I arrived at the cemetery with a minute to spare. Parking near the entrance, I tried not to think too hard about how several generations of my family were buried behind those tall gates. Uncomfortable with the thought of playing music, I sat in silence. With the windows down a few inches there was a slight breeze that cooled off the still too warm air. I spent the next fifteen minutes checking my watch and trying to ignore the uncomfortable feeling that grabbed me and wouldn't let go. My heart began to race and the pounding in my ears was about to drive me mad, and not the good kind where you yelled at someone for being an ass. No, this was the kind where they put you in lockdown for forty-eight hours while they determined if you were a threat to yourself or others.

Telling myself that a cemetery was a sad, not scary, place did nothing to alleviate my increasing terror. Ghosts weren't something I had ever believed in but being in such close proximity to this many people who had passed on seemed like tempting the spirit world, and that was certainly not something I had any interest in being a part of. A gust of wind whipped through the metal gates, the clanking sound was like the dead pushing against the gates to be let free. With that thought, I started the car and took off as fast as I could without risking a three hundred dollar ticket and more unwanted points on my driver's license.

Back home, I parked in my spot, relieved I was no longer at the cemetery but pissed off that Sara had for the second time asked to meet with me and then bailed. I unlocked the back door and stepped inside. I had only taken three steps when I collided with something, or rather someone. One minute I was standing and the next I was landing on my butt. To be fair, the fall wasn't too bad with the extra cushion back there, but this had to stop.

I jumped up and ran outside after my rude

uninvited guest just in time to see a dark car peal out of the parking lot. It was too dark and my knowledge of car makes and models too limited to tell what kind of car it was. Back inside, I flipped on the lights and screamed. I rushed upstairs and into my home office. My office had, like the downstairs, been searched. It only took a couple of minutes to realize that nothing was stolen. My laptop and camera were still in their places. Next, I went into my bedroom; it too had been searched. I checked the box of tampons and was relieved to see the SD card still safely ensconced inside. As for jewelry, I had only a few pieces and they were also still in the box on my dresser.

With nothing stolen I debated if calling the police was necessary. Frustrated, I called the non-emergency number. Thanks to caller ID I didn't even have to identify myself. The operator said hello and asked what she could do for me. She promised to send an officer right away.

Over the next two hours I answered questions, filled out a report, and tried to ignore the looks of the crime scene techs who Officer Duncan had insisted come over. When everyone had left I spent the next hour cleaning my apartment to get rid of any and all traces of my intruder. With my home back in order I took a shower, put on a pair of Thumper pajamas, and crawled under the covers. When I began to toss and turn, I went and got my gun and, after checking the safety, slipped it under my pillow.

My phone rang and I froze. Good news never arrived between ten at night and eight in the morning. "Hello."

"I'm at your front door," Grant said.

"What's wrong now?" I asked.

"Nothing."

While on the phone I had gotten out of bed and made my way downstairs. I opened the door and Grant brushed past me. Heat inched its way across my body.

"You are frustrating," Grant said.

"Excuse me?"

"You're also stubborn, opinionated, relentless, and a royal pain in my ass."

"Well, if you came here looking to impress me with your vocabulary, you shouldn't have bothered. And so you know, you're pig-headed, obstinate, and a jerk," I said.

"You didn't let me finish." He pulled me against him and I felt his erection straining against his pants. "You're also kindhearted, generous, tenacious, and sexy as hell."

My pulse raced. "Grant…" I whispered.

"I can't stop thinking about you," he said as he slowly kissed a trail down my neck. "I promised myself I'd stay away from you until this case was over."

"I don't want to wait."

The words were barely past my lips when Grant picked me up and carried me to my bedroom. He gently placed me on the bed. I reached up and pulled him down on top of me.

"What the hell?"

He pulled his hand out from under the pillow, holding my gun.

"Kim, do you have any idea how dangerous that is?"

"Grant, put it in the drawer and help me with your belt."

Grant growled as my hand brushed against his erection. He opened the drawer and grinned. "Wow, another gun and a box of condoms. I'm not sure if I should be intrigued or concerned."

"How about enticed?" I slipped off my pajama top and tossed it across the room.

"Enticed, definitely enticed," he said.

"Good choice." I smiled.

CHAPTER TWELVE

Sunday

Grant had gotten a call at five and had to leave. I rolled over and went back to sleep until my alarm went off at seven. Normally I skipped exercising on Sundays but after the week I'd had it wouldn't hurt to put in the effort. I closed my eyes while I decided what to do. The next time I opened my eyes it was nine o'clock and I was starving. After last night's workout I wasn't surprised. Grant had not only taken care of my sexual drought, numerous times, but I was having feelings I wasn't sure I'd ever be ready to have again. For now, I had other things to focus on.

Out of donuts, I made a cheese and mushroom omelet, which I gulped down with the help of several cups of coffee while I read the best part of the newspaper—the comics. I cleaned up the kitchen, ran upstairs, and got dressed. Motivated, I took the SD card from the tampon box and headed over to my *favorite* geek without bothering to call first. I knew from past experience Ryan spent Sunday mornings, if weather permitted, laying out by his parents' pool. Sure enough, that was where I found him when I got there. I explained what I needed and promised to bring him a case of beer the following day if he could just do me this favor. Reluctant to leave the poolside, he finally agreed.

Twenty minutes later I was back home, sitting on my couch, looking at all of the pictures that had been on the card. There were only ten pictures, all of which looked to have been taken at the same time. Two of the pictures were like the crumpled ones I'd found at Angie's and Sara's. This was the tie to Brian's and Adam's murders and Angie's disappearance. I stared at the pictures until my eyes ached but for the life of me I couldn't see what was worth murdering someone over. Defeated, I left a message on Grant's voicemail asking him to call me. I put the pictures and the card in the cabinet above the refrigerator. I had to stand on a chair to reach it but I felt the things would be safe there. I spent the rest of the day running errands, reading, doing absolutely anything to try to keep my mind off of the pictures and Grant's impending phone call.

When it was time to get ready for my mom's birthday party, I took a shower, dried off, and even attempted to style my hair. Finished with the makeup, I added a few drops of perfume. I slipped on the new dress and stepped in front of the full length mirror. Not bad. The new shoes looked great. I just hoped my feet would survive the evening in the two-inch heels.

The new purse was great except it was too small to hold my gun. Figuring it was better if I didn't attend a family function armed, I put my favorite Glock in the bedside drawer before locking up. I chose not to return Lindsay's call. She would be tomorrow's problem. I wasn't sure how I was ever going to be able to look her in the eye again after finding her box of sex toys. I was, however, quite impressed with her collection. It put my own to shame.

For my mom's fiftieth birthday, my dad had rented a room at one of the banquet halls. It was the only place big enough to hold our family. My mom was the youngest of five and my dad was the oldest of six. I had twenty-five cousins, thirteen female and twelve male. Add in the aunts, uncles, spouses, kids, and family friends and that required a heck of a lot of space.

I parked in the lot behind the building like everyone else. My dad was to bring my mom through the front entrance so she wouldn't recognize any of our cars. I walked in the door fifteen minutes early. Evidently that wasn't good enough. As soon as Brenna spotted me, she spent the next five minutes lecturing me about punctuality. At least I thought that was what she was harping about. It was hard to concentrate with that many people milling around.

"Kim…Kim?"

"Huh?"

"Have you listened to a word I said?" Brenna asked.

"Yeah, sure. Look, I need to go find Brandon."

"He's not here yet."

"What? He's not here and you're lecturing me? What is wrong with you?"

"I do not lecture."

"Hah, could have fooled me," I muttered.

"What?"

"Nothing. You look nice."

"Thank you." She looked me up and down as if searching for something to criticize. "So do you," she finally said.

I took off to look around before she could change her mind. The room was set up a lot like my wedding reception. Lots of round tables with green, my mom's favorite color, table cloths. I sincerely hoped this ended better than my reception. My new husband got so drunk he got into a fight with his brother in the parking lot. Later at the hotel, he passed out before we could do anything. Our first time as husband and wife was about noon the next day after he had recovered from his hangover and, to be honest, it hadn't been all that great. It hadn't helped that he still smelled like cigarettes, sweat, and alcohol.

The room was filled with people I loved here to celebrate my mom's birthday. It was wonderful, but it made me a bit sad none of my grandparents had lived long enough to see this. They would have loved to see fifteen kids running around the room being chased by their parents. Many families would have been shocked at kids being invited to a fancy dinner but not my family. Kids were to be celebrated, not tucked away somewhere, hidden from view.

At the door, Brenna was waving her hands in the air. No one seemed to pay any attention. I made my way, through the crowd, over to her side. "What's up?"

"Brandon's here, finally, and he said Dad just pulled up. We need to get everyone's attention."

"No problem." I turned around and shouted, "Shut up, everybody, they're here!"

All conversation stopped. A few chuckled at my rude command, but as mortified as my sister appeared at my behavior, she couldn't dispute the fact it worked. My brothers, sisters-in-law, nieces, nephews, and brother-in-law, appeared around Brenna and me. We would be the first to greet my parents.

They walked in and everyone shouted, "Surprise!" The shock on my mom's face meant we had actually pulled off the surprise. They looked so good together. My dad was in a black suit and gray tie while my mother had chosen a little black dress that flattered her figure. For accessories she had added her mother's pearl necklace and a pearl bracelet my dad had given her for their anniversary. She looked amazing. They both did.

We all rushed forward and took our turns hugging the birthday girl. Not long after they arrived everyone was seated for dinner. Michael, Brandon, and I were seated at our parents' table. Our married siblings sat with their spouses and kids at tables on either side of us. Dinner included our favorite Italian dishes and a few Irish ones thrown in for my dad's side of the family.

After dinner they began playing music and

everyone was encouraged to get out on the dance floor. Saving me from that embarrassment were my three best friends, who joined me at my table. Michael and Brandon had disappeared in search of women or alcohol, I wasn't sure which, not that it mattered. My parents were dancing and having a good time. Charmaine, Shandra, and Melissa spent the next half hour talking about nothing important. It was wonderful. Family and friends stopped by to say hello. Mercifully no one mentioned the case or my lack of a current boyfriend. In my family most women were married with children before they were thirty. As I was twenty-eight, I was coming up on an unofficial deadline.

I needed a bathroom break and my friends were eager to dance. I promised I'd catch up with them and headed for the back of the room where the women's restrooms were. A few minutes later I was out and looking around when someone tapped me on the shoulder, I turned and sighed. "Zack, hi."

"Kim, you look great," he said, his eyes roaming over me before settling on my face.

"Thanks, you're looking good yourself."

"I do, don't I?" He laughed. "Nice party. Your dad did a good job."

"Yes, he did. Well, Dad and Brenna."

"Not you?"

"Did you really think Brenna would trust me with something as important as tablecloths or seating arrangements?

"I think you could have handled it. Are you here with anyone?"

"Yeah, my whole family."

"You know what I meant."

"I'm not crazy enough to subject a date to this much of my family all at once."

Zack laughed. "Your family is awesome. You're lucky."

"Yeah, I know. So what about you? Bring anyone?"

"Yes, sort of." He pointed to a skinny blonde laughing at something my Aunt Josephine said.

"How nice."

"It's business. My dad is considering bringing her dad's law firm into ours. So I agreed to bring her with me tonight."

"That's great." She was the exact type Uncle Charlie would expect Zack to go for. She was beautiful, blonde, wealthy, and probably fertile enough to provide plenty of Wellington grandchildren. Throw in a possible merger as a bonus. Super.

"Dance with me."

"Zack, shouldn't you be dancing with that skinny, over-mammaried, bleach blonde you brought?"

"Jealous?"

"Ugh, no."

"Good." Zack's hand closed on my wrist and I found myself being gently escorted onto the dance floor.

"This isn't a good idea," I muttered.

"Why not?"

"Because."

"That's it, because?"

"You know why."

"You mean because every time we're close, we want to rip each other's clothes off?"

I didn't even try to deny it. We both knew it was true. The combination of our bodies swaying in motion to the music and his words caused a reaction in me I tried desperately to ignore. There was, however, no way to ignore Zack's reaction as it was hard and pressed up against me. "Oh jeez, Zack, you're going to have to do something about that."

"Have any suggestions?"

"Sorry, but you'll have to take care of that yourself."

"Are you sure? I bet we could find someplace private."

"I bet."

"You know you want to," he whispered in my ear.

I had no choice. Zack must die. What the hell was he doing getting me hot and bothered at my mother's birthday party? It was time to make him pay.

"Oh look, Maria just walked in and she's headed this way." I took a step back and I saw real fear in his eyes as he frantically scanned the room.

"Got ya."

"Kim, that wasn't funny."

"Yeah, it was." I giggled.

He pulled me back against him and I knew he had already started plotting his revenge. It just wasn't fair how good it felt to be in his arms. Fortunately, the song ended. I stepped back from Zack. He pulled me back against him.

"Hey, you can't leave me like this."

"I had nothing to do with that," I said, glancing down.

He leaned forward and whispered in my ear, "You had everything to do with this." His hand pressed against my back. "It's been too long." He groaned.

The last time we'd been together was six months ago. It was also the last time I'd had sex until Grant and I had been together.

"Kim," he whispered.

My nipples hardened. The traitors. Grant and I weren't in a relationship but I wasn't the type to have sex with one guy and then jump into bed with another a few days later. "Uh-oh, your dad's headed this way."

"Funny. I'm not falling for that again."

"I'm not kidding."

"You better be. The last thing I want is to be distracted from what I want to do to you. So let's find a place to be alone. Now."

"Zack…"

"Mind if I cut in?"

"Shit," Zack whispered. "Dad, why aren't you dancing with Mom?" We had stopped dancing but Zack had not let go of me.

"As much as I love your mother my feet needed a break before they actually were broken."

"Ouch," I said.

"Yes, ouch indeed. So would you humor an old man?"

"Of course." I smiled and pried Zack's hand from my waist.

"Wonderful. Zack, why don't you ask your date

to dance? If she sits there for long, there'll be a line of men eager to ask her for the privilege."

"Let them," Zack muttered.

"What?"

"Nothing, Dad. Kim, I'll see you later." He turned and walked toward his date while his dad began to spin me around on the dance floor.

"Wow, Uncle Charlie, I forgot what a great dancer you were."

"Where do you think that son of mine got his skills?" He smiled.

"So not from his mom?"

"Sadly, no. She's perfect in every way but for this one simple flaw. Don't you ever tell her I said that."

"Yes, sir." I laughed.

"So, Kim, your father and I were talking."

"Oh boy, that can't be good."

"Now, now, none of that. It seems you've gotten into a bit of trouble."

"I'm okay."

"I'm glad, but I must say I was disappointed you spoke to that detective without representation."

"I was fine. It wasn't that bad."

"Kim..."

"Uncle Charlie, I couldn't have gotten through that mess six months ago without you. I'm trying to save my favors for when I really need them. I'd never be able to pay you for what you did for me."

"I still can't believe you expected me to charge you. You're my best friend's daughter and my goddaughter. Besides, do you know the hell I'd pay from my wife?" He chuckled.

"Yeah, well, still. Don't worry, if it makes you feel any better, I'm sure I'll need your help again." I laughed.

"Oh, Kim, I'm not sure how to respond to that."

"How about we just finish dancing?"

"That sounds good."

The music ended. I hugged Uncle Charlie and headed back to my table. Fifteen minutes later, the birthday cake was brought out. Everyone sang and my mom blew out the candles. The guests returned to their tables and the servers began delivering pieces of cake. After the cake was gone the people began to say their goodbyes. I stayed with my family until the guests were gone.

"So, Mom, were you really surprised?" Brandon asked.

"Oh yes, definitely surprised. This was a wonderful evening. I can't think of a better way to spend my birthday than to be with my loved ones. Thank you all so much."

I hadn't actually done anything but show up, but I did have the perfect gift—in my car. "I'll be right back."

I grabbed my purse and exited through the back door to darkness. It was ten o'clock and the moon was hiding behind some clouds. Someone had forgotten to turn on the parking lot lights. Keys in hand, I walked past a white SUV and tripped. Falling forward, my hands spread out to protect me from the fall. My already damaged hands landed on the gravel lot. "Ouch! Damn it!"

I tried to push myself up but two sets of hands grabbed me. My foot shot out and connected with one of the person's knees. The cracking sounded like logs burning in the fireplace. A deep voice cried out. Before I could take advantage of the situation I was pulled up and shoved into the SUV. I tried to scream but the person who had climbed into the back with me slapped tape over my mouth and a cloth bag over my head. There wasn't a lot of space in the backseat but I tried to kick and scratch my way out of the car. For my effort my wrists and ankles were wrapped in tape. Just my luck I was trussed up like a Thanksgiving turkey. The guy must have figured out sitting next to a person with a bag on their head just might attract some unwanted attention because I was shoved to the floor, then the car moved—fast. Whoever was driving seemed to be in a rush to get to wherever they were taking me. It seemed I had found the mysterious SUV.

There was no point in struggling yet. So I took a deep breath to calm down and save my strength. I listened for clues to where I was being taken. My two kidnappers were quiet. It seemed they weren't into nervous chatter about having just kidnapped someone. Maybe this wasn't their first time. I really didn't want to think about what that meant.

To be fair, this wasn't my first kidnapping experience either. Now was not the time to dwell on what happened before. I needed to survive this one. We'd been driving for about twenty minutes when we went over two sets of railroad tracks. At least now I had an idea of where we were headed. The only tracks left were in the north end of Lakeview. There were several dozen warehouses and factories at this end of town that backed up to the south side of Dayton. This area wasn't an especially pleasant part of town. I wouldn't feel safe walking down these streets in broad daylight wearing a bulletproof vest, carrying a loaded rifle, with a pair of pit bulls at my side.

We turned to the left, then to the right, before driving over something with a metallic sound. The car stopped and suddenly hands were pulling me out. They carried me like a giant duffel bag for a bit before dumping me on the floor. The sound of their footsteps got softer then stopped, followed by the sound of what I assumed was a metal door clanging shut. That sound was followed by silence.

I wasn't sure how long I waited but when no one bothered me, I leaned over and shook my head until I got the bag off. After a look around I considered, briefly, putting the bag back on. One lone light bulb hung down from the center of the room, an old wooden chair sat below it. I was dumped on a concrete floor in a room where a third of the drop ceiling tiles had brown stains or were missing entirely. Paint peeled from the walls. A filthy sleeping bag and several blankets lay crumpled on the floor under the lone window.

My arms were behind my back and taped together at the wrist. I wriggled around on the floor until I was able to get my arms in front of me. I sat back up and concentrated on the tape across my mouth. The last time I'd managed to take a layer of skin off my lips. Having learned my lesson the hard way, I slowly peeled off the tape, saving my skin in the process.

My kidnappers had managed to leave me with

my purse—the strap was still on my arm. I'd have to remember to thank them, if I got out of this place. I dumped out the contents and searched for something useful. All I found was a wallet, a tube of lipstick, my keys, and a hairbrush. I leaned against the wall, using the largest key to saw away at the duct tape. I had no idea how long it took, ten minutes or ten hours, but eventually, just as I was about to give up, the tape finally gave way.

With my hands and mouth free I got to work on freeing my ankles. The tape had adhered to my pantyhose, which could be easily replaced at the nearest Wal-Mart. The same could not be said for my skin.

Finally I was free from my restraints. My hands ached but I was free—sort of. I sat there and waited. When no one came bursting through the door to tape me back up, I grabbed my purse and stuffed everything back inside. I stood up and made my way over to the window, which, to my surprise, wasn't even locked. Silently thanking my stupid kidnappers I pushed the window open, stuck my head out, and looked down—way down. It seemed my kidnappers weren't as stupid as I'd thought. With the moon no longer hiding behind the clouds it provided an unobstructed view of the outside. The ground, and my only escape, was three stories below. No problem for the Man of Steel, but I was a mere mortal human, emphasis on the mortal.

A jump from this height would not only hurt like hell but would most likely be fatal. I really didn't want to end my life in the filled to overflowing dumpster located not so conveniently below the window. I leaned out the window, looking for anything I could use to climb down. Finding nothing, I stepped away from the window. A quick look around the room and I zeroed in on the blankets. If I could tie them together and find something to tie them off to maybe I could climb down and get the hell out of here.

By this time my family would have surely noticed my absence and realized my car was still in the lot. There were laws regarding filing a missing person's report, but considering the situation, I was pretty sure my dad and the department would choose to ignore some silly regulations. They were probably already looking for me. Too bad they had no way of knowing where I was and would never get to me in time. Any rescue would have to be a do-it-yourself.

I walked over and picked up the blankets and sleeping bag. The smell of mold, urine, and God only knew what else made my eyes water. A closer look revealed spots of what appeared to be dried blood. That clinched it. Without a weapon I'd end up like the room's previous occupant. I unzipped the sleeping bag and began to tie it and the sheets together. With that done I tied one end of my makeshift rope to the chair and wedged it under the window. I looked around below to make sure no one was hanging around outside. If they were, my chance to escape would be screwed.

This had to be one of the dumbest ideas anyone had ever had. I had no idea if the chair and the blankets would hold my weight. If they didn't, I'd have one hell of a free fall. Though it wasn't the falling but the landing I was more concerned with. Even if everything worked out, I still had half a floor to drop since the blankets ended far above the dumpster.

My plan, if you could call it that, was to climb down and aim for the dumpster. On the plus side, with all the trash piled high, my landing, if I made it, should assure only minor injuries. On the down side, well, there were several, but the worst was if I missed the giant pile of trash, there was a good chance any injuries would likely be merely fatal.

My only other option was to stay put and try to talk my way out of here. I had about as much chance of that happening as one of the Kardashian sisters had of winning an Oscar, an Emmy, and a Tony award. I had no idea why no one had checked on me but I knew it was only a matter of time before someone did. It was now or never.

I slipped the purse strap over my shoulder. After a quick look below I tossed the blankets out the window. Just as I was about to climb out I flashed back to my sixth grade gym teacher, Mr. Clendenin, ordering me to climb the rope. I was so skinny I had no upper body strength at all. My nickname wasn't Toothpick for nothing. After a dozen attempts that year, the highest I ever made it off the ground was six feet. Not a huge accomplishment considering I was five feet six. Of course all but one of the boys in the class made it to the top. Even several of the girls had succeeded, but my friends and I had just thought they were freaks. After all, who needed rope climbing skills? Apparently I did.

Trying to block out negative thoughts, I took a

deep breath, grabbed the blanket, and put one leg over the window sill. Of course my kidnappers chose that moment to come in and check on me. The door opened and two men wearing ski masks walked in. It was hard to know who was more surprised, them or me.

"Hey, get back in here!" the taller of the two shouted as he rushed toward me.

Yeah, like that was going to happen. I kicked my other leg over and was hanging onto my rope of blankets just below the window. Some pretty colorful swearing was coming from inside. I tried to take one hand off to move down but I was so scared I couldn't let go. So there I was, hanging three stories above the ground with the assholes who had taken me leaning out the window, staring down at me. The bigger of the two leaned down and tried to grab my hands. There was no way in hell I was letting this idiot pull me back inside. If they got me back I was as good as dead. That was all the incentive I needed. I let go of the rope with my left hand and began to lower myself down.

Since grabbing for me hadn't worked, they grabbed the blanket and tried to pull me up, grunting while they pulled. I wasn't that freaking heavy. These two had to be real losers. I had made it down a few more feet when the blanket began to tear. I climbed down five or so more feet when there was a terrible ripping sound. The idiots pulled and fell backward through the window while I experienced free fall for the first, and quite possibly the last, time in my life.

The screaming was so loud I didn't realize at

first it was coming from me. I landed in the dumpster with a thud. My heart pounded so loudly I couldn't hear anything else. I thanked God for my relatively safe landing before the realization struck that not only was I still not on the ground, but I was now stuck in the dumpster and had landed in something sticky. It was at that moment the smell of decay slapped me across the face and invaded my nose. It was just my luck to end up where something had crawled in and died. If I didn't get out of here and away from the lunatics upstairs fast, this would most likely be my final resting place. I sat up and struggled to get to my feet, a difficult enough task in high heels when the ground wasn't constantly shifting underneath.

I grabbed a box to stop from falling face first into the sticky goo. Steadier, I took two steps toward the nearest side of the dumpster and sunk down to my waist. I pushed several boxes out of the way and froze. After days of searching and coming up with nothing, I had finally found Angie. I stumbled backward and hit my hand on a piece of metal. Thankfully for Angie, her eyes were shut. Unfortunately for me, mine were not. She was dressed in the same outfit I'd seen her in at the bar, only now it was covered in blood. So was the side of her face. Tears streamed down my face. No one deserved to be thrown out like garbage. She deserved better than this. Her loved ones deserved closure. I promised myself they would have it.

Exposed to the heat and God only knew what else, Angie's body had begun the decaying process. The trash shifted and so did Angie. A group of flies

259

flew out and around me. I clapped my hand over my mouth to keep the vomit and screams from escaping and to prevent any flies from getting inside. With the vomit temporarily under control, I scrambled backward and twisted my ankle in the process.

Just great. I had to get as far away from here as quickly as possible and running was now out of the question. The best I could do in heels and a sore ankle was hobble, but it would have to be enough. I grabbed onto the edge of the dumpster and jumped down. The pain in my ankle brought fresh tears to my eyes. I looked around for a place to hide. To my right was the entrance we must have driven through, only now it was blocked by a six-foot-high gate. Climbing that wasn't an option. To the left was the end of the building. Since this seemed like the best option I slipped off my shoes and took off as fast as a sore ankle let me. I had just made it into the shadows when behind me I could see two small beams of lights swinging back and forth.

Just great, the idiots had made it outside. I plastered myself to the side of the building and kept heading for the back as quietly as I could manage. Ignoring the creative cussing going on behind me, I got to the back of the building and froze. The land sloped down, way down. In the dark I couldn't tell how deep it was. Not that it mattered. I had to keep moving. I made my way over to the edge and took one too many steps and found myself on my backside, sliding down into what for all I knew was a bottomless pit or a gateway to Hell. Eventually the sliding stopped and the splashing began, as did the flailing and sputtering. The water was freaking cold and the smell was only slightly less nauseating than the dumpster.

After several attempts I finally made it to my feet. Off in the distance I could hear Frick and Frack yelling and slamming things in their search of the dumpster. The water was just above my knees. I tried to climb up the side but it was too steep and way too slippery. Slogging through it would make the going slow but I didn't exactly have a lot of choices. I tried to ignore the noises of the creatures that scurried around, grateful that Ohio didn't have any alligators, sharks, or anacondas I needed to worry about. I hobbled along, trying to put as much distance between me and the warehouse with the ski mask twins.

The uneven ground and the unexpected rise in water level made travel slow going. At its deepest the water rose to my armpits. As long as it didn't get any higher I should be okay. With each step my ankle throbbed. I was convinced there had to be a broken bone or two in there somewhere. Despite it being summer, the water was so cold I began to shiver. Though my ankle begged for rest, the best thing was to keep moving and hope all the activity warmed up my body from freezing to merely cold as hell. Besides, the faster I went the closer I got to help.

As my body moved along, my mind couldn't stop going over and over the image of Angie in the dumpster. She needed to be cleaned up before her family saw her. I knew Doc Gardner would make sure of it. I had liked her for the few minutes we'd talked. I had believed her when she said she was clean. Maybe she was, but I couldn't imagine why else she, Brian, and Adam had been killed. To be honest, there could have been a million and one reasons. None of this made any sense. What was up with the pictures? What, then, did the killers, who I assumed were my kidnappers, want with me? Did they think I had them? So what if I did? I hadn't noticed anything worth killing people over.

Glancing over my shoulder, I spotted beams of light off in the distance. Evidently they hadn't given up looking for me. I quickened my pace, wincing in pain with each step. If I stayed in the water for much longer, I wouldn't have to worry about the kidnappers finding me. I'd be frozen stiff in a block of ice like an episode of *Scooby-Doo*. The moon that had thankfully been hiding behind clouds that threatened rain made judging the distance I'd traveled impossible. While the darkness helped hide me from my captors it also made the going more difficult.

The going was slow thanks to an injured ankle, freezing water, and lots of mud. A sloth could have passed me, but as long as I stayed ahead of the idiots following me, it would have to do. After what felt like days I made it to a point where the sides weren't so steep. I did a combination of climbing and crawling to make my way up the side and out of the water. Thankful to be on dry land, I stuffed my feet into my shoes then walked to the back of a building and collapsed, hiding myself between the building and a parked delivery truck. I had spent so much time in the water that walking on dry land felt awkward. I leaned against the truck and tried to catch my breath. Though it was tempting, I couldn't rest for long. Getting far away from here and getting help was a priority. Falling asleep and letting the ski mask twins find me would not be an ideal situation.

I stood up and had to decide between returning to the water and going closer to the street. At the moment neither felt safe, but just the thought of returning to the water was enough to get me up off the ground and heading for the street. I limped along, leaning against the side of the building for support. My progress was slow but I made it to the front of the building. Luckily the owners of this place hadn't found it necessary to wrap it with a six-foot fence. There was also a line of hedges along the edge of the curb which I used to shield me from prying eyes on the street. Another advantage was no more slipping in mud and my body temperature was working its way back to normal—I hoped.

This end of town was usually deserted at night. To be fair, it was pretty deserted during the day too. Drug dealers, hookers, and gang members called this part of the city home. Most of the businesses here had gone out of business, leaving behind large, empty buildings. Once again I was desperate to sit down and rest. If I did, odds were I'd fall asleep, which sounded pretty good. Instead of giving into the temptation I kept going.

I would have danced my own little happy dance, if I could have, when finally Route 48 was in sight. If I followed it, I would eventually make it home. Running through the center of Lakeview would mean patrol cars and possibly a nice safe ride home. My immediate problem was I had to cross the street.

My kidnappers could be lying in wait, ready to catch me when I dared step foot into the street. It was a risk I had to take. I slowly slid out from behind the hedges, half expecting someone to jump out and grab me. When that didn't happen I took a deep breath and walked across the street. By this time both feet ached. I swore if I ever got out of this I'd never wear heels again, ever. Okay, maybe not never, but for a week at least, pinky promise.

The lack of sound was quite eerie. It kind of reminded me of the horror movies when it got real quiet before the scary music started. These weren't really the uplifting thoughts I needed right then. I was so happy when I made it to the other side of the street. It really was a small accomplishment, but, at the moment, it felt huge. Of course my bladder chose that moment to remind me who was boss. I looked around, desperate for a porta-potty. With none in sight I did a quick look around before squatting behind a large bush. It reminded me of one night in high school my friends and I had gotten two cases of beer and had gotten plastered. We were at a party near the University of Dayton. All of us had to pee but every one of the bathrooms was full. Desperate, we ran outside and hid behind some bushes in the backyard. Since my idea of camping had always been a hotel with room service, that had been, until now, the only time I had ever gone to the bathroom outside.

Every summer my dad would take my brothers camping. They'd spend a week hiking, fishing, and hunting while living in tents and cooking whatever they caught that day over a campfire. God bless him because each time he always asked Mom and us girls to go and each year we turned him down. Just the thought of a week without electricity and sleeping outdoors with bugs was enough to incite nightmares.

The rain weathermen had promised had yet to arrive for whatever reason and I was just grateful. Fifteen minutes of walking and my ankle needed another break and so did I. Off to the right there was a large pine tree surrounded by three-foot-tall bushes. It was the perfect place to sit and rest. The uneven ground took far longer to traverse than it should have but I made it. I squeezed between two of the bushes. A beam of light hit me right between the eyes. I froze, convinced they'd found me.

"Hey, git outta my house!"

I stumbled backward. "Jeez, what is wrong with you?"

"Me? You be the one trespassing, missy."

"Sorry, I didn't know this tree was taken."

"Don't sass your elders. Didn't anybody ever teach you nothin'?"

I swallowed a laugh. The curmudgeonly man reminded me of my grandfather on my dad's side. All grump on the outside with a soft, tender center on the inside. He even had a hint of the brogue.

"You're right. I should have knocked first." I smirked. "Would you mind pointing that light somewhere else?"

"Ha, young ones, smart mouths the lot a ya," he said, pointing the flashlight to the side.

I laughed. Only a man in what appeared to be his eighties would consider me in my late twenties and holding as a young one. I could be off though on the estimate of his age. It was hard to tell with the scraggly gray beard and gray hair—what was left of it anyway. "So just camping out to see the stars?"

"No, I'm not camping. This is my home and you're sittin' in my bedroom."

"Oh, sorry."

"You're workin' a bit late. Most of the workin' girls in this part call it quits by two."

"I'm not a hooker!"

"Oh, sorry, I forgot you call yourselves escorts now, don't ya?"

"I'm not an escort. I just have had a really bad night."

"Well, that's good, 'cause you wouldn't be makin' much lookin' like that."

"Thanks. So this is your home?" I asked, eager to get off the subject of my not looking like a hooker.

"Yep, and there's not a better one to be found. I've got a view of the stars, when the clouds aren't hoverin'. There's nothin' better than fallin' asleep lookin' at the stars."

"What about bad weather or animals?"

"I've got a tent for when it gets wet or cold, lots of blankets to keep me warm."

"What about squirrels and bugs? Don't they bother you?"

"Nope. Besides, the only wildlife around here are those no good gang bongers."

"Bangers."

"Bangers, bongers, whatever."

"Don't they bother you?"

"I'm just an old man. I leave them alone, and they leave me alone."

"How do you manage that?"

"Well, those fools don't know how to find me." He chuckled.

I reached into my purse and pulled my now wet twenty dollar bill from it. I held the money out to him. "Well, I've gotta get going, but thanks for the hospitality."

"Young lady, I've got everything I need right here. My social security buys me two square meals a day and a pint of whiskey each week. I spend my days in the library, surrounded by books, and my nights under the stars. I've also got my health. What more could I be wantin'?"

I understood his love of books and spending days in the library but I couldn't imagine my life without TV and computers, plus walls and air conditioning. I was also pretty fond of my hair dryer and coffeemaker. "Well, thanks again."

"I'd like to say it was a pleasure but, dear girl, you did interrupt my beauty sleep." He chuckled.

"Sorry, but it didn't appear you needed any more." I winked and waved goodbye, his laughter trailing after me.

The sidewalk would have made traveling easier and faster but then even the two idiots looking for me could find me. About a block away a lone working street light shone. Civilization was getting closer, which meant people inside. Those people would have phones and I could call for help. Lakeview was the type of town where decent people were in bed asleep by now. Only those up to no good would be out and about at this hour, whatever hour it was. If I went up and knocked on someone's door, I was likely to have a gun pointed at my face.

As eager as I was to get to what most people would consider civilization, I wasn't eager to make myself an easy target. Paranoia had finally set in. The closer I got to the light the more I expected someone to jump out of the shadows and grab me. It was weird that not a single car had driven down what was usually a busy road. To take my mind off scary thoughts I tried to think about how good it would feel to get home. Being in my own bed would feel wonderful.

Eventually an occasional car zipped past. As desperate as I was to get out of there I wasn't about to get into a car with a complete stranger, so hitchhiking was out of the question. When my feet couldn't take it any longer, I sat down and leaned against a telephone pole.

"Hey, are you okay?"

"Huh? What?" I opened my eyes, confused.

"Can you stand up?"

What was this guy talking about? I was standing. Wasn't I? I opened my eyes and found myself staring up into a face that seemed vaguely familiar.

"Ma'am?"

Oh my God. He may have come to my rescue but how dare he call me ma'am. I'd have to shoot him. Of course it'd have to wait until he got me the hell out of here and, of course, he'd have to wait around while I got my gun, since I didn't happen to have it with me.

"I think so." I finally answered his question.

"Here, let me help you up."

He grabbed my hands and gently pulled me up. I kept most of my weight off the injured ankle. We stood a few inches apart. His voice had sounded like one I'd heard recently. Looking at him up close I suddenly realized why. "Kevin!"

"Yes. Miss Murphy, is that you?"

"It's me all right. What are you doing here?"

"I was headed home when I spotted someone, well, you, leaning against the pole. I pulled over to see if they, I mean, you, needed help."

"I'm so happy you did. Could I use your cell phone? I need to call the police."

"Sorry, my battery crapped out a couple hours ago."

"Oh."

"If you want, I can give you a lift."

I considered my options. I could stay where I was and pray help showed up before the idiots who'd kidnapped me or I could get in the car with a virtual stranger. Neither option sounded great but only one of them would get me home fast. "Thank you."

"No problem. Here, let's get you inside."

Kevin moved to my side and had me lean on him for support. His car, a blue Toyota Corolla, was parked at the curb, running with its lights on. He helped me in, closed the door, and ran around to the driver's side. Once seated behind the steering wheel, he asked me where to. I gave him the first turn he had to make and leaned back against the headrest. Kevin's car was warm and it smelled like Heaven—pizza and garlic. I closed my eyes and inhaled the familiar scent like a dog sniffing the local fire hydrant. I woke to the sound of arguing. I chanced a quick look around. I was still in Kevin's car but me and the car were now inside a garage.

"Are you crazy? I told you not to bring her here." I heard a woman's voice say.

"Well, what else was I supposed to do? She was just sitting on the ground. I thought it was a sign," Kevin said.

"A sign? What the hell are you talking about?"

"Like God telling me it was okay to get her and bring her here to you."

"What the hell am I going to do with her? If she wakes up, she could have us arrested for kidnapping," the woman said.

"No way, I didn't kidnap her. I think something bad happened to her, but I swear it wasn't me."

Oh no. What the heck was going on? It sounded like my *hero* had just kidnapped me. How the freak had I managed to get kidnapped not once but twice in a matter of hours? If my dad found out about this he'd have me married off and having babies like my sister. I shuddered. As much as I adored my nieces and nephews I wasn't ready to be anyone's mom. Besides, I'd tried the wife thing and that hadn't exactly been a rousing success. After tonight, I had to admit my dad's plan held some merit, at least more than it had last week or even this morning.

"Bringing her here was a bad idea. What if someone saw you with her?"

"I'm not an idiot. No one saw us and I made sure I wasn't being followed."

"Good. Now you can take her back to wherever

the hell it is you found her."

"I can't take her back there. She could get hurt or worse."

Well, at least someone was concerned for my safety.

The woman he was arguing with sighed. "Did you honestly think she'd help us after you kidnapped her?"

"Stop saying that. I helped her, that's all. I'm sure she'll help us now. She owes us, well, me, anyway."

"She sure as hell wasn't willing to help before."

"That's because she couldn't then, but she can now. You'll see."

"She'd better."

"She will. So, are you going to help me get her inside or not?"

"Fine, but if she pukes all over my carpet, you'll be cleaning it up."

"Okay."

Just great. What the heck was I supposed to do? I closed my eyes and tilted my head to the side just in time for Kevin to open the passenger side car door. I was impressed when he scooped me up and carried me out of the garage and down a long hall. I wasn't really heavy, it was just Kevin didn't strike me as the type with a lot of upper body strength or any body strength at all. After a few turns he placed me down on a bed. I held my breath while he placed a blanket over me. A few seconds later I heard the door shut behind him.

As far as kidnappings went I had to admit I much preferred Kevin's method. It didn't make any sense.

Why did he kidnap me and then tuck me into bed? That thought led to some really creepy ones I just didn't have the energy to think about. Besides, I wasn't really getting the creepy feeling here, but then what the hell did I know? Plus my brain wasn't exactly functioning at a hundred percent. I stayed still for a few minutes in case Kevin or his lady friend decided to check on me. When neither one appeared, I eased up and looked around. It seemed I'd been relegated to someone's guest room. The queen-size bed was way too soft and fluffy for my taste and someone had placed half a dozen pillows on it. The furnishings were upscale. Just because I couldn't afford it didn't mean I didn't recognize it when I saw it.

My search for a phone turned up empty. What the heck kind of person had a guest room without a phone? Maybe Kevin and his friend weren't as hopeless at this kidnapping thing as I'd thought. Though I couldn't figure out how they could have planned Kevin's finding me on the side of the road. The closet was empty except for a bunch of fancy cloth covered hangers—not exactly an ideal weapon. Unless, of course, I hoped they would laugh themselves to death. The dresser drawers weren't of any help either. In the bathroom I had my choice of weapons: a toothbrush still in the package, a strawberry-shaped soap, or an unopened condom, which wasn't exactly the type of protection I was in need of at the moment.

As for exits, the window in the bathroom was way too small. Back in the bedroom, there were two big enough for me to climb out of. The one on the right was directly behind a side table with a lamp. I was a bit of a klutz under the best of circumstances, and this was not the best, but not exactly the worst either, but it didn't seem prudent to try to move furniture around. The other one was free of any obstacles. I pushed aside the flowery curtains and flipped the latch. I held my breath and slid open the window. God, fate, or karma chose that moment for the bedroom door to open. I spun around and grabbed a vase.

"Put her down!"

"Huh?"

"My grandmother, you're holding her urn."

Sometimes it didn't pay to ask questions. I placed the urn back down, careful not to spill any of Grandma on me.

"Thank you."

"Uh, sure."

"Well, you may as well come into the living room, but please stay off the furniture. You reek." She turned around without waiting for me to follow.

I sniffed and winced. Until then I hadn't noticed but all that time in the water had left a disgusting odor. If I was lucky, it would only take a couple of hours of scrubbing to feel clean again. Unfortunately there would be no saving the dress or the shoes. Oh well, maybe I could think of it as an excuse to go shopping. Eager to get this night over with I closed the window and traipsed through the house, looking for the living room. When I spotted Kevin I figured I'd found it. He was not alone.

"Mrs. Hardin, I guess I should thank you for your hospitality."

"Don't thank me, I had nothing to do with this." She turned and looked at Kevin seated on the couch next to her.

"Sorry, Miss Murphy. When you fell asleep I thought I should bring you here."

"Why?"

"You know, so you could rest before you helped us."

"Help you?

"Yeah, well, us." He pointed unnecessarily at Mrs. Hardin before pointing to himself.

"Kevin, this is ridiculous. She's in no shape to help anyone. Besides, she already turned me down."

"There were extenuating circumstances."

"Of course there were. You conveniently forgot to mention you were friends with my husband's latest little slut."

"Huh?"

"Lindsay Pembrook."

"Oh, well, she's just a neighbor. I don't know anything about whatever."

"Yeah, right. I've gotta say, I figured you'd be a better liar than that."

I thought it funny she was concerned about the woman her husband was sleeping with while she was dressed in a gray silk robe, snuggled up on the couch against Kevin, who looked mighty comfortable there. "So, I guess you and Kevin are just friends?"

"Now, Miss Murphy, this isn't what it looks like. We're in love."

"Congratulations. Does Mr. Hardin know?"

"No, and we'd like to keep it that way, for now

anyway."

"I'm sure you do."

"I told you, Kevin, she wouldn't understand. Just get her out of here." Mrs. Hardin moved as if to stand up. Kevin grabbed her hand and pulled her back against him.

"You didn't give her a chance last time. I mean, you lied to her. I'm sure if you tell her the truth, she'll help us."

He may have been sure, but I certainly wasn't.

"Fine." She sighed and turned toward me. "When I came to your office I lied about needing proof my cheating scumbag of a husband has been busy banging his little bleach blonde bitch."

I had to fight the urge to warn her about the whole pot and kettle saying, but I figured she probably wouldn't understand.

"Lizzie, come on, start at the beginning."

Oh, yes, please, Lizzie, please do. It wasn't as if I didn't have anything better to do in the middle of the freaking night than listen to your self-absorbed ramblings.

"A few months ago, I found out about my husband's, uh, infidelities. I wanted to hurt him. One afternoon I was at Evan's office and met Kevin in the waiting area. We got to talking and, well, one thing led to another." She stopped talking and turned toward Kevin. Their eyes met and both wore the same silly smiles on their faces.

Oh, gross. "And?" I prompted.

"We fell in love, Miss Murphy. We didn't mean to, it just happened."

"Congratulations. Now what does any of that

have to do with me?"

"Go on, Lizzie, tell her."

"Well, my husband has been married before, twice actually. So when we got married he insisted I sign a prenup."

"So you tried to hire me because you wanted proof of his cheating," I said.

"Yes, but that was only part of it." She turned and looked at Kevin.

"Brian had pictures of us. He threatened to give the pictures to Mr. Hardin if we didn't help him with a problem," Kevin said.

"Your friend was blackmailing you?" I asked.

"No, I mean, yeah, sort of, but he didn't want to. He just didn't have any other choice."

I couldn't believe Lizzie and Kevin had just given me a large motive for Brian's murder. Though I couldn't see how any of the others fit into this.

"Look, Miss Murphy, I know what you're thinkin' and I swear we didn't mean to do it."

I so did not want to hear a confession right now. Though I had no one to blame but myself for getting into this mess, all I wanted was a shower, my bed, and the cops to arrest Brian's, Adam's, and Angie's killer or killers. Was that really too much to ask for?

"Wait a minute. Did you say something about needing my help?" I asked, hoping to put off the confession until I was safely surrounded by, oh, I didn't know, an entire SWAT team maybe.

"Oh, well, we were hoping you could help us find the pictures."

"What makes you think I could find them?"

"Because you had one on your desk when I was in your office," Lizzie said.

"What? Wait a minute, the picture of the party?"

"Yes, Kevin and I were in the background. Brian took a bunch of pictures that night. He didn't even know about us until he printed the pictures off his computer and looked at them."

"Yeah, they were partying at a hotel and some old buddies were in town. Lizzie and I were having our own party. I didn't know which hotel the guys were staying at, so we got out of there as fast as we could."

"It just wasn't fast enough," said Lizzie.

"Please, Miss Murphy, we've looked everywhere for those pictures. Where did you find the picture?"

I considered my answer carefully. Since it didn't matter now I figured it was safe to answer the question truthfully—sort of.

"At Angie's apartment." I tried unsuccessfully to block out the image of Angie that slammed back into my brain. I had to get out of here and call the police.

"Why didn't I think of that?" Kevin asked.

"Well, they were broken up. Why would he hide something at his ex-girlfriend's place?"

"Yeah, I guess you're right." He smiled.

"You know, as much as I've enjoyed this, I'm exhausted. Why don't the two of you meet me in my office later tomorrow or today or whatever?"

"Fine," Lizzie said before turning toward Kevin. "Take her home and then hurry back."

"Oh, I don't want to be a bother, I'll just..." I stopped talking because I wasn't quite sure how to end that sentence.

"It's no problem, really. It's the least I can do for all the trouble I've caused."

"Trouble? What trouble?" I asked, forgetting I wasn't really in the mood for answers.

"Well, you see, it's kind of my fault you got hurt." Kevin stared at the floor.

"Your fault? You hit me in the back of the head?"

"No, I'd never do that."

"Then what the hell are you talking about?"

"I…it's just. Oh hell, I'm the one who searched Lindsay's apartment after Brian was killed."

"I'm going to need more than that."

"I was looking for the pictures and I was so scared about the cops showing up I left without locking the door. I was halfway home when I realized it. I turned around and went back. That's when…"

"When what?"

"When I…found you on the patio."

"What?"

"Yeah, you were out cold. I didn't want to just leave you outside like that, so I carried you inside Lindsay's apartment."

"You left me there? What about calling 9-1-1 for help? What if the person who attacked me came back?"

"They didn't. I stayed with you until you woke up then I got in my car. When the first cop car showed up, I left. I figured you'd be okay then."

I stared at Kevin, unsure of what to say. He had brought me inside, but instead of calling for help, he just watched over me. Of course there was nothing creepy about that or anything. Yeah right. I was at a complete loss. Between the alcohol, two kidnappings, finding Angie's body, and my long escape, it was all just too much. All I wanted was to crawl into bed and when I woke up in, say, a day or two, the murders would be solved, the reporters would have kindly dropped off a cliff, and these two would never darken my door or life again.

"You know, you should be thanking him."

I turned to look at Lizzie. She was staring at Kevin like he'd just pulled a family from a burning building. Yeah, the man was a real hero. "Thanks. Look, I need to use a phone."

"It's four o'clock in the morning. Don't you think you should wait a while before you start callin' people?"

"I need to call the police."

"The police? No way are you calling the cops from my phone. Kevin, take her home now!"

"Okay, okay."

I followed Kevin into the garage, grateful to be leaving. Once inside his car, the pizza smell wrapped around me like a giant blanket. After giving Kevin directions he probably didn't need, I couldn't stay quiet. There were so many unanswered questions. "Why did you search Lindsay's apartment?"

"Well, you know, since Brian was killed there, I figured he may have gone there to give her the pictures."

"Okay, but why did you try to search for them after the police sealed the door?"

"I didn't know about that. Not until I got to Mrs. Kanisky's apartment."

What the hell? Little warning bells were going off in my head but the words were out of my mouth before I could stop them. "How did you know Mrs. Kanisky?"

"I didn't. Brian did, sort of."

"How?"

"It's really not important."

"She was a nice old lady. What did she have to do with Brian?"

"Nothing, just drop it," Kevin snapped. His hands gripped the steering wheel so tightly it looked as if someone had super glued them to the wheel.

Whatever Kevin, Brian, and the others were up to somehow involved my former elderly neighbor. Mrs. Kanisky's death had been attributed to old age and several medical problems but I'd always felt something just wasn't right about her passing. I'd chalked it up to my sadness over her death. She had waved bye to me as I got into my car that morning. That evening when I returned home, one of the neighbors told me she had died during the day. Had their actions somehow caused her death? I didn't know how they could have, but I knew if Kevin and Lizzie were involved, I'd make sure they spent some quality time in the prisons of the court's choosing.

I looked at Kevin and wondered if that was the face of a killer. He had seemed so nice, even helpful, but was that just an act? Didn't the neighbors of serial killers always describe them as friendly? "Stop the car."

"What?"

"Stop the car. I'm gonna be sick."

"Hold on." Kevin pulled the car to the curb. I jumped out, bent at the waist, and pretended to have the dry heaves, though it didn't take a whole lot of acting skills at that point.

"Jeez, Miss Murphy, are you okay?"

Unable to speak, I nodded my head.

"Wow, you don't look so good."

"Thanks, just what I needed to hear."

"What?"

"Nothing."

"If you're feelin' better, let's get in the car. I promise I'll tell you everything."

I stood back up and froze. Behind Kevin two men in ski masks, guns in their hands, were heading toward us. "Shit!"

"Are you feelin' sick again?"

He had no idea. "Kevin, why don't you take off? It's not too far, I can walk from here."

"No way am I leavin' you on the side of the road."

Ironically, that was exactly where he had found me a few hours before, but at the other end of town. If only he'd left me there, he wouldn't be about to pay for it now. One of the gunmen grabbed Kevin while the other stepped around them and closed his free hand around my arm.

"What the hell?" Kevin struggled with the man holding onto him.

"Kevin, don't!" I had images of the gun going off in the struggle. If we were lucky, it would hit one of our attackers. I didn't figure Kevin or I had that kind of good luck.

"Listen to her, Kevin. It seems she's the smart one."

I'd have thanked him for the compliment if not for the fact that they were leading us to an old van with blackened windows.

"Let's go. Our boss would like to talk to you, Kimberly Murphy."

"It's Kim." What the hell was I doing correcting him? I really must have lost my mind.

"Look, guys, since I'm the one your boss is so eager to talk to, why don't we just leave Kevin here and the three of us can go?"

"A threesome, huh?" the one holding me asked. "Tempting, very tempting," he said, pulling me up against him.

The one holding onto Kevin chuckled. "Maybe later, sweet cheeks, after the boss is through with you. Afraid we're going to have to take your friend here."

Kevin and I were shoved into the back of the van. I wondered if my own face mirrored Kevin's panic-filled one. While one of our ski-masked kidnappers got in back with us, the other got behind the wheel of the van. The driver, before pulling away from the curb, yanked off his ski mask and tossed it onto the passenger seat. He probably figured it wasn't wise to draw attention to himself by driving in the summer with a ski mask on. Both of our kidnappers were wearing identical outfits of black pants and black long-sleeved shirts. They reminded me of a couple who had the poor taste to dress alike, minus the matching ski masks, of course.

Beside me, Kevin whimpered. Our companion in the back chuckled. So, okay, Kevin was scared. Who wouldn't be after two guys pointed guns at you and shoved you into a van? Being kidnapped was scary as hell. I should know, since it was quickly becoming a regular occurrence for me. The only reason I wasn't sitting in the corner babbling incoherently to myself was I had had my fill of scary for one night. The fact that I'd escaped from these idiots once gave me a bit of encouragement that my luck hadn't run out yet. Not so lucky was the fact that who other than me could have managed to get kidnapped three times in under eight hours. It must be a gift, the kind you were desperate to return the day after Christmas.

Kevin didn't look so good. His face was pale and he was sweating—a lot. "Hey, you okay?"

It was a stupid question but it was the best I could come up with at the moment. Kevin didn't answer me at first, but eventually he nodded his head. I scooted closer to him. "Take slow, deep breaths."

He did and seemed to calm down a bit. That was good because the last thing we needed was Kevin freaking out. Our masked and unmasked companions were likely to be way too eager with the trigger fingers, especially since I'd escaped their little party earlier. They were sure to be on their guard for any antics from me. If not, all the better for me and Kevin.

"Sorry, not much of a view back here," my ski mask-wearing buddy said. All of the windows in the back of the van had been blacked out.

"That's okay, it's too dark to see much anyway. Now, if there was something we could do to make the floor more comfortable, that would be nice."

He laughed. "Maybe next time we'll use a limo."

"Sounds great," I replied, as long as it wasn't me and it wasn't the inside of the trunk.

I looked back at Kevin to see how he was doing. The labored breathing had stopped but his eyes were glued to the gun still pointed in our direction. I assumed we were traveling in the general direction of where they'd taken me the first time. Could they really be taking me back there? The question had just popped into my head and now we were once again crossing over train tracks. Now my own heart began to race. Kevin and I were being taken back to where Angie's body had been dumped like any other garbage. No one deserved that. Well, except pedophiles and rapists. They deserved that and oh so much worse. Kevin had returned to whimpering. I'd have joined him if I thought it would do any good.

When we stopped at what I assumed was a red light, the driver glanced back at us. He chuckled at Kevin's obvious fear. Looking at me, he licked his lips and winked.

"Get moving. The light's green."

Our driver turned around and once again we were on the move. Before long we stopped once again. Only this time our driver put the van in park and turned off the engine. He got out and a few seconds later the back doors opened. Kevin, experiencing a moment of either bravery or stupidity, rushed forward, knocking Mr. No Mask backward. Kevin turned toward me, his eyes large and round like two DVDs. He was as surprised as I that it had worked.

"Come on, let's go."

Kevin grabbed my hand. In his excitement he must have forgotten about Mr. Ski Mask sitting in the back with us. I turned to look and found myself staring at a large, shiny gun. I looked back at Kevin, and he had his own problems. Mr. No Mask had gotten back up and was also pointing a gun, at Kevin's head.

"Move it, asshole, and don't try to play hero again."

Kevin scooted toward the back of the van. When he got to the edge Mr. No Mask grabbed him and yanked him out, tossing him onto the ground. Kevin struggled to his feet just in time to collide with Mr. No Mask's fist. I shouted for him to stop but he ignored me and landed several more punches to Kevin's head and stomach. The last punch sent Kevin sprawling to the ground.

I crawled out of the van and leaned down next to Kevin. He was still breathing but his face looked like someone had mistaken it for a piñata. Except instead of sugar-coated treats trickling out, a steady stream of blood dripped from his nose. Mr. No Mask pulled his foot back as if to kick Kevin.

"Enough! Get them inside."

I couldn't see the person who belonged to the voice but it was obvious this was someone in charge. Mr. No Mask half dragged, half carried Kevin while Mr. Ski Mask grabbed my arm and escorted me inside. Having learned a lesson from their previous attempt to keep me here, they stuck us in a small room with a window the size of my head on the first floor. Neither Kevin nor I had been bound, which should have been good news, but it wasn't. They hadn't bound us because a quick look around the small room revealed nothing, absolutely nothing. The room was as empty as Brandon's refrigerator, if you ignored the beer and the science experiment in the back.

This sucked. They had even kept my purse this time, not that I had anything useful in it, but I'd only used it twice. Maybe now wasn't the right time to focus on the loss of my purse but it at least took my mind off the very real possible loss of me. Which I was pretty sure was the only outcome possible. The worst part, well, one of them, was I'd inadvertently gotten Kevin dragged into this mess. His murder would weigh heavily on my conscious, if only for a short time. I figured these lunatics wouldn't take long to kill me after getting whatever it was they wanted from me. Angie's death felt like it was my fault as well. I couldn't figure what all this mess was about. I just hoped before the end they had the decency to explain it to me. No sense in leaving a lady in limbo for all of eternity.

The thought of eternity was terrifying. I was a good, somewhat of a good, person, but I didn't have any guarantees which way my soul was headed. Was my eternal resting place one giant party or someplace that required a sunscreen with an SPF of about a million?

Kevin whimpered, drawing me out of my

depressing thoughts. I knelt down beside him. His whole body jerked when I placed my hand on his arm. "It's okay, Kevin, they're gone." What I didn't say was *for now*. I was sure if he hadn't already, he would soon figure it out. There was no need for me to point it out.

"Are you sure?" He lowered his hands, revealing his beaten, terrified face.

"Yeah. Do you think you can sit up?"

"I think so."

I stood up and took several steps back to give him some room but to be close enough in case he needed help. Kevin pushed up and leaned back against the wall.

"I've felt better, that's for sure."

"Sorry."

"What do these guys want?"

"I have no idea, but they sure as hell are determined."

At his questioning look I filled him in on my previous kidnapping, careful to leave out the part about finding Angie's lifeless body in the dumpster.

"Jeez, Miss Murphy, that's crazy."

I had to agree. This whole thing was crazy. "Yeah, I just wish I knew what they wanted."

"So if they want you, what am I doing here?"

Kevin was collateral damage, a witness that would need to be dealt with. "Wrong place wrong time, I guess."

"Story of my life."

"Me too. Don't worry, we'll get out of here." I tried to sound more positive than I felt.

"You think so?" he asked, sounding so hopeful.

"Absolutely," I lied.

Kevin's smile morphed into a wince as blood seeped from his bottom lip.

"How do you feel?"

"Like I got hit by a semi."

"Well, you kinda look like it too." I smiled.

"Good to know." His laughter turned into a round of coughs.

I held his hand while his body shook in time with each cough. Eventually the coughing stopped, as did the shaking.

"Thanks."

"No problem. I always help my co-kidnapees."

"I don't think that's really a word. Is it?"

"It is now."

I smiled and let go of Kevin's hand. Desperate and determined to find a way out of this, I stood up and walked around the room. It was possible, though unlikely, our captors had left something behind. It took less than a minute to discover that, sadly, they had not been quite so stupid this time. With nothing left to do I sat back down next to Kevin and leaned against the wall.

"So, how was your day?" I was rewarded with a smile.

"I've had better. How about you?"

"I hate to admit it but, sadly, I've had worse."

"Worse than this?" he asked, his eyes wide open in what I assumed was disbelief.

"Yeah, I'm just sorry you got dragged into this."

"Me too, I mean…"

"It's okay. You should blame me."

"Miss Murphy, what do you think they want

with us?"

"I don't know, but I wish to hell I did." I laid my head back against the wall and closed my eyes. "I wish I knew."

CHAPTER THIRTEEN

Monday

I opened my eyes and wiped the drool from my chin. To my left, Kevin slept curled up into a ball. The steady rise and fall of his chest was the only reassurance I was likely to receive anytime soon. A thin line of light peaked from underneath the metal door. It made me wonder if the man with the deep voice was on the other side. Was he the one in charge? Had they just dumped us here and left? Not very likely, especially after all the trouble they had gone through to bring me back here. Was there someone guarding the door in case we attempted to get out?

None of this made any sense. If they had somehow seen me as a threat, wouldn't they have eliminated us by now? Why just keep us here? I knew one thing. I had too many questions and absolutely zero answers. Frustrated, I stood up, relieved when my sore ankle didn't buckle under my weight. Sometime in the night I had kicked off my shoes. My pantyhose were shredded. Looking back to make sure Kevin was still asleep, I took them off and stuffed them into my bra. As far as weapons went, they were pretty pathetic, but they were all I had. While I was thrilled our kidnappers hadn't killed us in our sleep, I couldn't help but wonder what they were waiting for.

A little voice in my head was urging me to stop pacing, sit down, and save my energy. While another voice was busy telling that one to shut up and look for a way to get the hell out of this mess. With a headache, the last thing I needed was dueling voices in my head. It just figured I'd spend what was sure to be my last few minutes or hours on Earth going insane. Which I guessed would have been okay as long as I wasn't sane enough to figure that out.

The pacing back and forth accomplished absolutely nothing except for making me irritated as hell. I felt like a caged animal. If I ever got out of here, I'd have a lot more sympathy for zoo animals, though at least they had nice little exhibits similar to their natural habitats. Plus, besides living rent free, they also had food delivered daily and had free medical care. So maybe being on display at a zoo wasn't half bad.

I sat back down, careful not to disturb Kevin. Patience, according to my parents, was a virtue. Evidently it was one I had not received. If our *hosts'* intent was to do nothing but wait for us to slowly unravel, I feared they were about to get quite a show.

"How long was I asleep?"

291

My body jerked at both the voice and the hand on my shoulder. Embarrassed, I used the sleeve of my dress and swiped at the sudden stream of tears. "It must be morning. There's some light coming through the window."

"I bet Lizzie's worried I never came back."

"The police have found your car by now. I'm sure they're looking for us."

"Good."

"I'm thirsty," he said. His stomach growled. "Hungry too." He smiled.

"Me too. Do you think they'll bring us a menu so we can order room service?"

"It would be nice."

The door opened, letting in our kidnappers, ending our conversation. Our *friend*, Mr. Ski Mask, entered along with his jerky partner, Mr. No Mask. They walked in and stopped at the center of the room. They had left the door open. I looked away, trying not to draw their attention any more than possible. "Great, you're here. We were just discussing what we'd like for breakfast."

Mr. Ski Mask chuckled while his buddy glared at us.

"Oh, and a shower and a change of clothes would be great too."

Before either could respond, a gentleman in a dark blue suit, striped tie, and expensive-looking shoes entered the room. His dark hair was graying at the temples and as he walked toward us he exuded an air of authority.

Just great. Though I had limited fighting skills I kicked ass in self-preservation, but now, with this guy's arrival, our odds of getting the hell out of here had just been flushed down the toilet.

"Kimberly Murphy, I'm terribly sorry we had to meet like this."

"You'll have to excuse us for not getting up."

He chuckled. "Of course, I'm just pleased you're still here."

"Well, unfortunately, your employees learned from our previous encounter."

"I'm afraid your early departure was a bit inconvenient."

"It was a bit inconvenient for me as well." I looked pointedly at my ankle.

"I'm terribly sorry about your injury. If you had stayed, this whole thing could have been wrapped up and one of my associates would have taken you home."

What he meant was one of his goons would have taken care of me, just like they did Angie. This guy dressed and talked like a businessman, but he was a killer, or, at the very least, employed killers. It was doubtful this guy got his hands dirty unless he had no other choice. "You didn't have to go to all this trouble. You could have called."

"True, but sometimes a more personal touch is necessary."

I bit the inside of my cheek. I had a huge problem with the touching part. My family and half the Lakeview Police Department were looking for me. I just had to stall until they could find me. I faked a yawn and rubbed my eyes.

"Sorry we're keeping you from your beauty sleep. Not that you need it." Mr. Suit smiled.

Oh jeez. Did this guy really think I'd be flattered by his lame compliment? I yawned again and leaned my back against the wall, ignoring Kevin's glare. "I certainly could use a couple more hours of sleep, or, at the very least, a pot of coffee."

Mr. Suit turned toward Mr. No Mask. "Go get our guests some coffee."

"Ooh, I'll take two creams and two sugars." I smiled.

Mr. Suit chuckled before asking Kevin, "What about you?"

"Black. Thanks."

Mr. No Mask glared at me before turning around and stalking off without a word. Unfortunately he remembered to close the door behind him.

"So, what should we talk about while we wait for our coffee?"

I had an idea about what he wanted to discuss but I had zero interest in that conversation. "The Reds won," I said.

"Hardly impressive, considering they lost the previous three," said Mr. Suit.

"Huh, you must be a Cleveland fan."

"Not at all, I'm just a realist. So, no love for the Browns?" he asked.

"Hell no."

"Something else we have in common."

I hadn't realized we had a first, but I certainly wasn't going to ask.

Oh hell. "What else is there?" I hated myself but I had to know.

"You certainly are a curious one."

"Yeah, like a cat." I really should have learned to

shut my mouth.

"Don't fret. I can assure you that you won't end up like that unfortunate creature. Besides, I have a feeling you're quite clever. Both of my feline friends are as well."

A cat lover? Well, he couldn't be all bad, then, for a kidnapping, psychopathic killer. "So we both like cats and hate the Browns. What else do we have in common?"

Before Mr. Suit could answer, Mr. No Mask returned. Wordlessly he passed around coffee to each of us. With a cup of his own, he positioned himself next to Mr. Ski Mask.

Before I could stop him, Kevin took a sip from his cup. "How do I know you didn't put something in this?"

Mr. Suit sighed. "Miss Murphy, if I'd wanted to harm you, that could have been easily arranged. I wouldn't waste my time with poison."

Next to me, Kevin sputtered and coughed. I patted him on the back. "Kevin…"

"Oh for God's sake." Mr. Suit walked over, took the cup from my hands and drank. "Yuck."

I gasped.

"Relax." He handed me the cup. "I take mine black. You must have one heck of a sweet tooth."

I took the cup from his hand and once again hesitated.

"Now what?" asked Mr. Suit.

"You don't have any diseases or a cold?"

Mr. Suit laughed. "No diseases and no colds, I swear." He put his hand over his heart.

He could be lying, but at this point it didn't

really matter. If I had to go out, there were worse ways to die than by coffee. I inhaled the scent and couldn't wait any longer. I gulped down half the cup and sighed.

"Well?" asked Mr. Suit.

"Heaven in a cup."

A lifetime of Catholic church had me wincing and adding a silent prayer of forgiveness for what my grandparents would have considered blasphemy.

"Now that we're all caffeinated I think we should talk."

"We have been talking," I pointed out.

"Yes, well, as pleasant as this has been I'm afraid we have business to discuss."

"Business? You want to hire me?"

"I may have need of your services in the future."

Mr. No Mask chuckled. One quick glance from Mr. Suit silenced the laughter.

"For now I have a little problem that needs to be handled."

Though there was nothing menacing in the words per se, I wasn't thrilled to find out what he wanted. Plus, not for a minute did I believe we would be having any future dealings, especially if Kevin and I didn't have a future of any kind. Though if he could pretend we were all walking out of here, so could I.

"Now, Miss Murphy, I'm missing something rather valuable and I was hoping you could tell me where to find it."

Of all the things he could have said that wasn't one I'd expected. "What are you missing?"

"Someone stole a small, black bag from one of

my employees."

"What was in the bag?" I swore I couldn't help myself. Sign me up for Nosy Addicts Are Us.

"A list of my clients and some medications."

It figured drugs was the connection between them. Kevin, the poor guy, had been right. Too bad his reward for being right was an untimely death. "Yeah, well, I would love to help you but I have no idea where they are or even where to begin looking."

"That's unfortunate. You see, Brian took the list and the medications and he hid them. Sadly, he died before he could tell my associates and me where they were. That list could get my clients into quite a bit of trouble. Now you see my dilemma."

"Yeah."

"So do you have any idea where we should look?"

"I guess I'd start with Brian's car or his…"

"His what?"

"His home," I said, afraid of what would happen to Brian's mother and sister if they came home while Mr. Suit's goons were there.

"Yes, we've already searched his car and his sister was kind enough to let us search their mother's home."

"His sister?" Oh God, was she in one of the other rooms, or was she like Angie, in a dumpster somewhere?

"Yes, she was rather cooperative at first."

No, no, no. People who ended up in this guy's way had a habit of ending up dead. It was bad luck for Kevin and me.

"It's the least she could do after causing all this mess," Mr. No Mask said.

"Causing it?"

"Yes, I'm afraid Sara couldn't keep her mouth shut about our little business venture."

"She worked, I mean, works, for you? I thought she was a nurse."

"A home health nurse actually. We had a profitable arrangement but now that's over."

Over as in he dumped her off a cliff? That was silly, we didn't have any cliffs in Lakeview. I leaned back against the wall and closed my eyes. An unwanted image of Sara in her scrubs surrounded by a pool of blood refused to go away. I blinked several times and looked up at Mr. Suit.

"You're shivering. Are you cold?"

"No, I mean yes. I'm fine." Maybe I'd have believed his concern for me was genuine if he didn't have a body in his dumpster, and I was only ninety-nine percent sure he and his colleagues had killed Brian and Adam. Plus, Brian's sister was missing and most likely dead. These guys had bodies piling up all over town.

"It would be very bad for me and my clients if the police got ahold of that," he said, staring me in the eyes.

Oh crap. He knew. Somehow he had figured out my connection to the police. "As far as I know, the police don't have what you're looking for."

"Excellent." He clapped his hands and smiled. "I really need to find my bag. Now."

"Look, I really don't know anything else."

"I understand." Mr. Suit turned and looked at

Mr. No Mask. He nodded his head before turning back to me.

Mr. No Mask tossed his coffee cup across the room and walked over to us. I braced myself but gasped when he grabbed Kevin and yanked him up by the arm. Kevin shouted and tried to break free but he was out-muscled and outmatched. Meanwhile, Mr. Suit pulled a gun from his pocket and pointed it in Kevin's general direction.

"Wait. Don't!" A completely stupid idea popped into my head but I didn't have anything to lose at this point. "Lindsay's apartment."

"Sorry, but that has already been searched." He gestured to Mr. No Mask.

"Not completely. Did you check the oven?" I asked.

All four heads turned and looked at me, wearing identical confused expressions.

"Well, did you?" I asked.

Mr. Suit looked at his employees. Both shook their heads *no*.

"So, why, Miss Murphy, do you think what I'm looking for is in the oven?"

"I'm assuming Sara was Mrs. Kanisky's nurse. Right?"

"Yes."

"Well, Mrs. Kanisky didn't use her oven for at least six months before she died."

"I'm missing the point."

"You've obviously not met Lindsay."

"I can't say I've had the pleasure," Mr. Suit replied.

"Trust me, there's no pleasure."

"If you have a point, please make it."

"Oh, right, well, anyway, if Lindsay wants food, she orders it. She probably has more restaurants on speed dial than all four of my brothers combined."

"So you think Sara or Brian hid my things in Lindsay's oven?"

"Yes. It makes perfect sense."

"Boss, maybe we should check it out," Mr. Ski Mask said. Once again his voice sounded familiar. I couldn't figure out where I'd heard it before.

"It sounds pretty stupid to me," said Mr. No Mask.

"That's 'cause you're stupid," Mr. Ski Mask said.

"Don't call me stupid."

"Then don't be stupid."

"Quiet!" shouted Mr. Suit. "I believe Miss Murphy may be on to something."

"Oh, this is bullshit," said Mr. No Mask.

"It may be but we need to find out. Tie her up then go see if she's right."

"What do you want me to do about him?"

"I think we're done."

"No! Leave him alone. I swear it's got to be there. I've checked everywhere else. I even found the memory card for a camera. It has pictures of you in the background."

"See, I told you she could be reasonable," said Kevin.

The demon duo released him and Mr. Suit's gun was no longer pointed at Kevin. Actually it was pointed a bit toward me now. "Kevin?"

"I'm sorry, Miss Murphy, but we had to find out

what you knew."

"I don't understand. You're with them?"

"Afraid so."

"Brian and Adam were your friends."

"Yes, well, I discovered money was more important to me."

"So you killed Brian over some pictures?"

"Not the pictures. I didn't give a damn if Lizzie's husband got ahold of those, but I do need my list back, and the drugs."

"Brian took them."

"Yes, he thought he could blackmail me to get Sara out of the business. Sadly, he refused to tell me where my property was."

"What about Adam?"

"Adam couldn't keep his mouth shut."

I kept my mouth shut about Angie, though at this point it didn't really matter. They had no intention of ever letting me out of here alive.

"Tie her up and watch her this time. I don't feel like going out looking for her again," Kevin said.

Mr. Ski Mask was in front of me in four long strides.

"Don't even think about it."

He chuckled and grabbed for me. In no mood to be manhandled again and desperate to get the hell out of here for good, I kicked him in the nuts, and not the kind you sprinkled on top of a sundae. Mr. Ski Mask growled and bent over at the waist. Mr. Suit and Kevin winced in what I assumed was sympathy.

Mr. No Mask laughed. "What a dumbass," he said as he walked over and grabbed my arm, careful to keep his crotch out of range of my feet. I rewarded his cleverness by sinking my teeth into his hand. He let go and shoved me backward.

"Ouch! You dumb bitch, you're gonna pay for that."

Mr. Ski Mask stood up and pulled a gun from somewhere.

"You're pointing that thing in the wrong direction, you idiot!" Kevin yelled.

I seemed to be the only one to notice Mr. Suit slip out the door. Good, my odds had just improved by one.

"All of you get down on your knees, hands locked behind your heads."

"What the…" asked Mr. No Mask.

"Get on the floor. Now!"

"What the hell do you think you're doing?" Kevin asked.

"No way." The words were barely out of his mouth when Mr. No Mask lunged for my supposed would-be savior.

Kevin and I stood on opposite sides of the two as they struggled. The gun went off and each of us jumped. By some strange miracle the bullet managed to miss us all. In the chaos the gun slid across the floor. Mr. Ski Mask was the first to recover. He dove for the gun, grabbed it, and then pointed it at Mr. No Mask's head. Seeing how things were playing out, Kevin turned and headed for the door. I took off after him. Running in heels with a sore ankle wasn't easy but I was highly motivated. Adrenaline, or maybe endorphins, had me moving faster than I thought possible for someone who hated every second on the treadmill.

Kevin stopped and turned around. With the thunderous noise my running caused I hadn't held much hope of sneaking up on him. I hadn't expected his sudden halt in motion but took advantage of it. I lunged at him. His eyes grew wide like a kid's on Christmas morning. Kevin, though, wouldn't be receiving any presents today. Killing a few innocent people had put him on the naughty list—permanently. I landed on him and we both tumbled to the floor. My elbow bounced off the cement. I yelped in pain. Kevin took advantage of my loss of concentration and shoved me off him. He tried to crawl away from me but didn't get far. Not with me on his back, hanging on for dear life. Kevin flopped around, trying to shake me off. It felt like I was on one of those bucking bronco rides. I grabbed onto his shirt and held on. I had him. The problem was I had no way to keep him. As if sensing my dilemma, Kevin tensed up and flipped over, sending me flying backward with strips of his shirt in my hands.

Before I could stop sliding across the floor, Kevin was on top of me, pinning my arms to my sides. I closed my eyes. This was going to hurt but I was running low on options. I took as deep of a breath as I could with a full-grown man sitting on me and slammed my forehead into his.

"God, you crazy bitch." Kevin leaned up, his hands on his forehead.

If he was in as much pain as I was, he had to be seeing spots or stars or whatever the hell those little bright thingies were in front of my eyes. At least I'd learned a lesson. If I ever did this again, I'd have to remember not to open my eyes so soon afterward. Of course this handy lesson would only be useful if I got the hell out of here in one piece.

Kevin shook his head and reached into his shirt pocket, pulling out a pocket knife. I could feel my eyes grow wide in shock and fear. I flailed my arms around, punching him in the chest and shoulders. Finally, my fist connected with his hand and the open switchblade. I knocked it out of his hand, slicing mine in the process.

"Damn it."

Kevin wrapped his hands around my neck and began to squeeze. I grabbed his hands and tried unsuccessfully to tear his from my throat. The blood was making it difficult to hold on. Desperate to breathe, I brought my knee up. The first attempt was a miss but the second was a direct hit right between his legs. Kevin let go and rolled off me, howling in pain. I suffered through a coughing fit, grateful to breathe again. Kevin cupped his balls and moaned. A gunshot from the next room propelled us both into action. We lunged for each other. Kevin came up with a handful of my hair and pulled. I screamed out in pain. My hand brushed against something on the floor. I grabbed it and slammed it into Kevin's face. Kevin let out an unhuman sound of pain and let go of my hair. I looked up and realized I had shoved the heel of my shoe into his right eye. I sat frozen, listening to his screams of agony. Kevin leaned over me. I closed my eyes.

Bang. Bang. I opened my eyes and watched

Kevin fall backward. I tried not to focus on the two holes in his head.

"Are you okay?"

Standing a short distance behind me was Mr. Ski Mask himself, without the mask. He looked familiar, with short black hair, dark eyes, and a Glock in his hand. At least we had similar tastes in guns.

"I think so. I'm better than him anyway." I pointed toward Kevin.

"Good. Don't move. I've got to call this in. Shit, you're bleeding." He tore off his shirt and handed it to me. I wrapped it around my hand to stop the bleeding.

"Have we...do I know you? You're a cop."

"We've never been introduced. I've seen you a few times at the station. Of course there's also a picture of you in the chief's office. I'm Glenn Clarkson."

"I'd say it was nice to meet you but that might be a stretch."

"I bet."

"What about your friend?" I pointed to the room we'd come out of.

"The only place he's going is the morgue. Like this one." He pointed at Kevin but I averted my eyes. I wasn't sure how much gore I could handle just then.

Mr. Ski Mask, or rather Officer Clarkson, made his call. I sat facing away from Kevin and concentrated on my breathing. Never a fan of blood, I slowly removed the shirt and was relieved to see the river of blood had slowed to a mere trickle.

"Sorry I kicked you in the nuts," I told him after he got off the phone.

"Thanks. I was wishing I'd worn a cup. You do have great aim."

"You should see me with a gun."

He winced. "I think I'll pass."

I laughed. "I meant on a gun range."

"Oh, thank God. How's the bleeding?" He leaned over and looked, careful not to touch me.

"A lot better. Thanks."

I was working up the courage to ask him what he'd been working on, but, before I could ask, we were bombarded with sirens blaring and lights flashing. Yeah, the cavalry had arrived. I turned toward the door in time to see my dad, Michael, Brandon, and a cousin charge inside the room. My dad was the first to get to me. He went to reach for me but stopped. This place was a crime scene and I was wearing evidence.

"Thank God you're all right. Your mother was up all night worried about you. Your aunts were finally able to get her to rest."

"I found Angie."

"Who?" asked my dad.

"Where?" Brandon asked.

"She's in the dumpster out back."

"Don't worry, we'll take care of it," Officer Clarkson said.

"Her. You mean take care of her."

"Right. Sorry."

"What the hell happened?" Michael demanded.

"Long story. I don't think I'm up for telling it more than once."

"No offense, Kim, but you smell."

"Thanks, Brandon."

I could always count on him and his dopey smile and his enormous heart. I saw a look pass between my dad and Michael; some kind of nonverbal communication was going on between the two and there was no doubt in my mind it was about me.

"Kim, why don't we wait outside? The ambulance should be here soon."

"I don't need an ambulance."

All four men looked pointedly at my bloodstained hand. "Whatever. I need some air."

I wasn't even the slightest bit ashamed that I was eager to get as far away from the dead bodies as possible. I followed after Michael and Brandon but not before hearing my father demand Officer Clarkson tell him what the hell had happened. My brothers kindly chose to take me away from the flashing lights. They did, however, argue over whose car I would wait in since both had driven their personal cars. Under other circumstances I would have been offended but my ability to smell had begun to return. Brandon lost. He got a trash bag out of the glove compartment and covered the seat. I sat pretending not to have seen the worried expressions on their faces. I began to shake. Brandon turned up the heat. I smiled my thanks, grateful they hadn't bombarded me with questions they were surely dying to ask.

It wasn't long before several other vehicles arrived, one of which was an ambulance.

"It's about time. What the hell took them so long?"

"Relax, Michael, they're here now."

"You relax."

"Guys, please."

The passenger side door opened and I found myself face to face with my cousin Marco. "Go away."

"It's nice to see you too, sunshine."

"Sorry."

"That's better. Now get out of the car and come over to the ambulance."

"No."

"Am I going to have to carry you?"

"Try it and you'll never give your mother grandkids."

He hissed. "Dear God, you better not let my mom hear that."

"Yeah, Aunt Rosa would have your head," said Michael.

"You'd be begging for my medical help. Now get out and let me take a look."

"Kim, just do it," Brandon said.

"If it shuts you guys up, fine."

Marco had just finished torturing, or rather helping, me when my dad came over to where we sat inside the ambulance. He looked at me then turned toward Marco.

"Well?"

"Bleeding has stopped and she shouldn't need any more stitches. She claims she already got a tetanus shot."

My dad looked at me and waited. "I did, I swear."

"Fine, thanks, Marco."

"No problem, Uncle Sean."

My dad reached up and helped me out of the ambulance, but not before Marco could give me a quick lecture about signs of infections and a hug. The latter was appreciated, though I could have done without the lecture. Before the night, or morning as the sun was starting to rise, was through I was sure to receive plenty more of both.

"Kimberly, I've decided to let Detective Tompkins lead the investigation. He'll be here any moment."

"Oh goody," I muttered.

I followed behind him, grateful when instead of going inside the building we went to a makeshift command center in the parking lot of the abandoned factory next door. I'd have walked naked and barefoot over hot coals before I let my family know I was too much of a coward to go back inside there again.

While I had been busy being poked and prodded, Officer Clarkson had given his side of the story. Now it was my turn. We stood in a circle, and since no one had tried to stop them, Brandon and Michael stood on either side of me. Before I could begin, Grant joined our cozy little group, making it a party of six.

"Listen up, there will be no interruptions. Just let her get through this before we start bombarding her," my dad warned. "Go on, Kimberly."

So I started with Officer Duncan finding me in Lindsay's apartment and didn't stop talking until I'd told them about Officer Clarkson shooting Kevin. I was careful to omit my little breaking, entering, and destruction escapade. It wasn't really evidence since it had absolutely nothing to do with this case. I was already in enough trouble. The last thing I needed to do was confess to another crime.

They had all followed my dad's order and not interrupted, but the moment I stopped talking, they all began talking over each other. Officer Clarkson chose that moment to walk over to us.

"What were you thinking?" Michael demanded.

"You could have gotten her killed," shouted Brandon.

"I was undercover and I had a job to do. I did save her life, or doesn't that count?" he snapped.

Michael lunged for him. Brandon and Grant grabbed him before he reached Officer Clarkson.

"Michael," my dad shouted.

"You got him?" Grant asked.

"Yeah."

"Good." Grant let go of Michael, turned, and punched Officer Clarkson in the face. There was a second of complete silence before all hell broke loose. My brothers were yelling at Grant, Grant was yelling at Officer Clarkson, and my father looked at us like we'd all lost our minds. Several officers rushed over from the crime scene next door to see if we needed assistance.

"Stop," my father shouted, and everyone froze.

"You had all better get a grip or I will lock up each and every one of you." He looked around before continuing. "Anyone not working this case, go home."

My brothers started to protest but he cut them off. "Now!" They left without another word.

"Now, Officer Clarkson, do you wish to press charges against Detective Tompkins?"

"No, sir."

"Are you sure? You have every right to do so."

"Nothing happened."

My dad looked pointedly at Officer Clarkson's face.

"I did this myself."

"Officer…"

"That's what my report will say…sir."

"The ambulance is still here. Go get something for that eye."

"Yes, sir." He took off without another word.

"Now, detective, if you ever assault a fellow officer again, I'll have your badge. Is that understood?"

"Yes, sir. It won't happen again."

"It better not. Now if you'll take my daughter back to the station, I'll meet you both there."

"Of course."

"Kimberly, not a word until we get back to the station."

"Fine."

As promised, I didn't speak to Grant on the drive to the station. He parked in the back lot and ran around the car. He opened the passenger door and helped me out of the car. "Thanks."

Instead of talking he just nodded his head.

"Nice right hook. Remind me not to get you mad."

"Too late," he muttered.

Several hours and cups of coffee later my dad and I were on our way to my parents' house. Once

311

there, my mom hugged and fed me before sending me off to take a shower. In the guest room I crawled under the covers and cried myself to sleep.

EPILOGUE

A Week Later

It had felt great and a bit odd to wake up in my own bed for the first time since the night of many kidnappings. A lot had happened since that night. Officer Clarkson, along with some fellow Lakeview police officers, tracked down and arrested Mr. Suit, whose real name turned out to be George Bollinger. George and Kevin were in business together. George owned the home health care company that Sara worked for. Kevin's job was to convince, or rather blackmail, several of the nurses to steal drugs from their patients. They also took advantage of Adam's pot growing facility in his home and were making money off him. Things went bad for them when Brian discovered what Kevin was forcing Sara to do. He turned the tables and blackmailed Kevin. Unfortunately, when Brian refused to tell where he had hidden George's things they had killed him, in front of his sister. It turned out I'd been right about where George's stolen items were.

Grant found them taped behind Lindsay's oven before turning the apartment back over to her, though it wouldn't be hers for much longer. She was planning her wedding to Mr. Hardin, who had hired a private investigator of his own who managed to get plenty of pictures of Mrs. Hardin with Kevin.

As for Sara, she came out of hiding once she found out about George and Kevin. She'd been arrested for her part and was awaiting trial. The other day I got a thank you card in the mail from her mom. It took me a day and a half before I could open it. It must have been devastating to have your son killed and to find out your daughter was indirectly responsible.

Despite everyone's very vocal objections I insisted on going to Angie's funeral. If not for me, she may have still been alive. Brandon had been the only one who seemed to understand why I had to go. It was no surprise when he arrived early and picked me up to go with me. Angie's family had held a viewing at the new funeral home on Leo Street. It was located in the old hardware store right next to the fire station. The sirens went off twice during the time Brandon and I were there. Angie probably would have gotten a kick out of that.

I turned the memory card over to the police. Brian had managed to get several shots of George and Kevin exchanging money and what appeared to be drugs. Too bad his efforts to help his sister had caused his death.

I picked up the card I'd purchased at Wal-Mart along with necessities like pop, potato chips, and chocolate. I opened it and laughed. It was perfect. I only regretted I wouldn't get to see George's face when he opened the envelope and saw a card congratulating him on his new home. That prison cell was certainly his new home and would be for the next twenty years, thanks to his plea agreement with the district attorney.

The doorbell rang and I was reluctant to go downstairs. After all hell had broken loose it had seemed every reporter in Ohio had tried to get an interview. Eventually even the most persistent had given up, but I wasn't taking any chances. I was still screening my calls and watching for lurking reporters when I ventured out of my cozy apartment. When the doorbell rang again I decided to at least see who was there. After all, it could be my mom with more of her homemade lasagna or her eggplant parmesan. Not wanting to miss out on a possible free meal, I rushed down the stairs. I looked through the peephole and sighed.

Grant stepped inside and closed the door behind him. "We need to talk."

"Damn it! I knew it."

"What?"

"You're married or engaged."

"Why do you think that?" he asked.

"Because you want to talk and someone at the station said women keep hitting on you but you turn them down. So, I figure you're married, engaged, or gay, but after the other night I think I can safely say you aren't gay."

"No, I'm not gay. I'm also not engaged or married. There's this one woman I can't get out of

315

my head."

"Oh."

"Yeah, she's obstinate and really needs to stop getting herself into trouble."

"Maybe you should handcuff her and lock her away."

Grant smiled, revealing those adorable dimples. "If you want handcuffed, I'm your man." He grabbed me and pulled me against his lean, hard in all the right places, body.

"Kim," he whispered, his lips kissing a trail down my neck, his hands locking onto my ass. "Christ, I need you. Now."

"Oh, God, yes."

"Now about those handcuffs…"

The End

ABOUT THE AUTHOR

Growing up Violet Ingram spent Saturday mornings in the library. Her first literary loves were Hardy Boys, Nancy Drew, and Encyclopedia Brown. She always imagined herself helping solve the mysteries.

Violet dreamed of being a singer, a world famous movie star, a veterinarian, and a marine biologist. Turns out she can't sing, is a homebody, squeamish at the sight of blood, and can't swim.

After becoming a stay-at-home mom, she dreamed of turning her hobby of writing stories into a career. With the support of her family and friends, this dream became a reality.

Violet lives in the Midwest where she is busy keeping up with her hubby, their 5 kids, and glued to her computer putting the scenes in her head onto the screen.

Facebook:
https://www.facebook.com/violet.ingram.39?ref=bo
okmarks

Twitter:
https://twitter.com/violetingram

Blog:
http://violetingram.blogspot.com/